Praise for **Felix Ever Af**

P9-DYY-395

Stonewall Honor Book
Indie Bestseller
Indie Next pick
ALA *Booklist* Editor's Choice
Vanity Fair Best Book
Forbes Best YA Book
Chicago Public Library Best Teen Fiction
New York Public Library Best Books for Teens
Goodreads Finalist for Best Teen Book of the Year
YALSA Best Fiction for Young Adults selection
YALSA Quick Picks for Reluctant Young Adult Readers selection
Rainbow Book List selection

"Felix is like the story itself—boldly empathic, hopeful,
and full of love."—*Publishers Weekly* (starred review)

"An unforgettable story of friendship, heartbreak, forgiveness, and
self-discovery."—ALA *Booklist* (starred review)

"A powerful #OwnVoices story of identity and self-worth . . .
Full of warmth, love, and support, this is an important story
and an essential purchase."—*SLJ* (starred review)

"Felix does ultimately find love in this sweet and tender trans
romance, but his hardest-won victory is in the fight to validate his
self-worth."—*The Horn Book*

"Full of nuanced looks at how relationships can be both toxic
and supportive, loving and confusing, and exciting but brief, this is
definitely not a book to be missed."—**Buzzfeed**

"An intricate love story for the ages."—**CNN Underscored**

"Felix's fumbling attempts to figure out what love means and what
it's supposed to feel like—while learning he's worthy of it—make
for the novel's most anxious and heartwarming bits."—**NPR**

"Felix is an open, warm, engaging character who extends far off the page."—**them.**

"A firecracker of a book from an author with a powerful point of view, *Felix Ever After* is refreshingly real—full of queer kids who live and breathe and swear and love and make messy mistakes. Teens need this one."—**Casey McQuiston**, bestselling author of *Red, White & Royal Blue*

"*Felix Ever After* never shies away from the beautiful, messy complexity of love in all its forms. This book is a gift, from start to finish."—**Becky Albertalli**, bestselling author of *Simon vs. the Homo Sapiens Agenda*

"This is a story about friendships, finding first loves, and continuing to discover yourself even after you thought you had all the answers. I can't talk about my love for this book enough—it's going to change lives."—**Mason Deaver**, bestselling author of *I Wish You All the Best*

"From effervescent characters that I still can't get out of my head to the sizzling backdrop of a New York City summer, Callender brings vibrance to a story that desperately needed to be told."—**Jackson Bird**, author of *Sorted: Growing Up, Coming Out, and Finding My Place*

"There are stories that are vital and there are stories that are brilliantly crafted. Callender delivers both in this beautiful exploration of friendship, new love, and self."—**Justin A. Reynolds**, author of *Opposite of Always*

"I've never read a book that more perfectly balances hardship, hope and happiness. This story shines a spotlight on the one thing that transcends all differences: a desire to be loved and to love in return."—**Nic Stone**, bestselling author of *Dear Martin*

FELIX
EVER AFTER

KACEN CALLENDER

BALZER + BRAY
An Imprint of HarperCollins*Publishers*

Balzer + Bray is an imprint of HarperCollins Publishers.

Library of Congress Cataloging-in-Publication Data

Names: Callender, Kacen, author.
Title: Felix ever after / Kacen Callender.
Description: First edition. | New York : Balzer + Bray, [2020] | Summary:
    Felix Love, a transgender seventeen-year-old, attempts to get revenge by
    catfishing his anonymous bully, but lands in a quasi-love triangle with his
    former enemy and his best friend.
Identifiers: LCCN 2020003451 | ISBN 978-0-06-282026-6
Subjects: CYAC: Transgender people—Fiction. | Bullying—Fiction. |
    Revenge—Fiction. | Best friends—Fiction. | Friendship—Fiction.
Classification: LCC PZ7.1.C317 Fel 2020 | DDC [Fic]—dc23
LC record available at https://lccn.loc.gov/2020003451

Typography by Michelle Cunningham
21 22 23 24 25   PC/LSCH   10 9 8 7 6 5 4 3 2 1
❖
First paperback edition, 2021

For trans and nonbinary youth:
You're beautiful. You're important. You're valid.
You're perfect.

ONE

WE PUSH OPEN THE APARTMENT BUILDING'S GLASS DOOR, out into the yellow sunshine that's a little too cheerful and bright. It's hot as hell—the kind of heat that sticks to your skin, your hair, your freaking eyeballs.

"Christ, why did we sign up for this again?" Ezra says, his voice hoarse. "It's so early. I could still be asleep."

"I mean, eleven isn't technically *early*. It's—you know—about halfway through the day."

Ezra lights a blunt he pulls out of I-don't-know-where and offers it to me, and we suck on the last of it as we walk. Reggaeton blasts from a nearby park's cookout. The smell of smoke and burning meat wafts over, along with the laughter and screams of kids. We cross the street, pausing when a man on a bike zooms by with a boom box blasting Biggie, and we walk down the mold-slick stairs of the Bedford-Nostrand G stop, sliding our cards through the turnstile just as a train rumbles up to the platform.

The train doors slide shut behind us. It's one of the older trains, with splotches of black gum plastered to the floor and messages written in Sharpie on the windows. R + J = 4EVA.

My first instinct is to roll my eyes, but if I'm honest with myself, I can feel jealousy sprouting in my chest. What does it feel like, to love someone so much that you're willing to publicly bare your heart and soul with a black Sharpie? What is it like to even love someone at all? My name is Felix Love, but I've never actually been *in* love. I don't know. The irony actually kind of fucks with my head sometimes.

We grab a couple of orange seats. Ezra wipes a hand over his face as he yawns, leaning against my shoulder. It was my birthday last week, and we got into the habit of staying up until three in the morning and lying around all day. I'm seventeen now, and I can confirm that there isn't much of a difference between sixteen and seventeen. Seventeen is just one of those in-between years, easily forgotten, like a Tuesday—stuck in between sweet sixteen and legal eighteen.

An older man dozes across from us. A woman stands with her baby stroller that's filled with grocery bags. A hipster with a huge red beard holds his bicycle steady. The AC is blasting. Ezra sees me clutching myself against the ice-cold air, so he puts an arm over my shoulders. He's my best friend—only friend, since I started at St. Catherine's three years ago. We're not together like that, not in any way, shape, or form, but everyone else always gets the wrong idea. The older man suddenly wakes up like he could smell the gay, and he doesn't stop staring at us, even after I stare right back at him. The hipster gives us a reassuring smile. Two gay guys cuddling in the heart of Brooklyn shouldn't feel this revolutionary, but suddenly, it does.

Maybe it's the weed, or maybe it's the fact that I'm that much closer to being an adult, but I suddenly feel a little reckless. I whisper to Ez, "Wanna give this guy a show?"

I nod in the direction of the older man who has straight-up refused to look away. Ezra smirks and rubs his hand up and down my arm, and I snuggle closer to him, resting my head on his shoulder—and then Ez goes from zero to one hundred as he buries his face into my neck, which—okay—I've never actually gotten a whole lot of action before (i.e.: I've never even been kissed), and just feeling his mouth there kind of drives me crazy. I let out an embarrassing squeak-gasp, and Ezra puffs out a muffled laugh against the *same damn spot*.

I look up to see our audience staring, wide-eyed, totally scandalized. I wiggle my fingers at the man in a sarcastic half wave, but he must take that as an invitation to speak. "You know," he goes, with a slight accent, "I have a grandson who's gay."

Ezra and I glance at each other with raised eyebrows.

"Um. Okay," I say.

The man nods. "Yes, yes—I never knew, and then one

day he sat me down, and my wife, Betsy, before she passed, and then he was crying, and he told us: I'm gay. He'd already known for years, but he didn't say anything because he was so afraid of what we would think. I can't blame him for being afraid. The stories you hear. And his own father . . . Heartbreaking. You'd think a parent would always love their child, no matter what." He pauses in his monologue, looking around as the train begins to slow down. "Anyway. This is my stop."

He stands as the doors open. "You would like my grandson, I think. You two seem like very nice, gay boys."

And with that, the man is lost to the platform as the woman with the baby stroller follows him out.

Ezra and I look at each other, and I burst out laughing. He shakes his head. "New York, man," he says. "Seriously. Only in New York."

We get off at Lorimer/Metropolitan and walk down and then back up a bunch of stairs to get to the L train. It's June 1—the first day of Pride month in the city—so there are No Bigotry Allowed rainbow-colored signs plastered on the tiled walls. The platform is filled with pink-skinned Williamsburg hipsters, and the train takes forever to come.

"Shit. We're going to be late," Ezra says.

"Yeah. Well."

"Declan's going to be pissed."

I don't really care, to be honest. Declan's a dick. "Not like we can do anything about it, right?"

4

By the time the train arrives, everyone's fighting to get on, and we're all packed together, me crushed against Ezra, the smell of beer and BO slicking the air. The subway rattles and shakes, almost throwing us off our feet—until, finally, we make it to Union Square.

It's a typical crowded afternoon in the city. The sheer amount of people—that's what I hate most about Lower Manhattan. At least in Brooklyn, you can walk down the street without being bumped into by twenty different shoulders and handbags. At least in Brooklyn, you don't have to worry if you're literally invisible because of your brown skin. Sometimes I try to find a white person to walk behind, just so that when everyone jumps out of that person's way, they won't knock into me.

Ezra and I inch our way through the crowd and past the farmers' market, the smell of fish following us. We're dressed pretty much the way we always are: even though it's summer, Ezra wears a black T-shirt, sleeves rolled up to his shoulders to show off his Klimt tattoo of *Judith I and the Head of Holofernes*. He has on tight black jeans that're cut off a few inches too high above his ankles, stained white Converses, and long socks with portraits of Andy Warhol. He has a gold septum piercing, and his thick, curly black hair is tied up in a bun, sides shaved.

Whenever I'm around Ezra, eyes usually skip right over me to stare at him. I have curly hair, a loose gray tank that shows my dark scars on my chest, darker than the rest of my golden-brown skin, a pair of denim shorts, smaller random tattoos that I'd gotten for twenty dollars down at Astor Place—my dad flipped out the first time, but he's gotten used to them now—and worn-out sneakers that I've written and drawn all over with a Sharpie. Ezra thinks I've ruined them. He has a thing for keeping the *purity of the designer's intent.*

We walk through the crowds of people who idle in front of the farmers' market stalls selling jars of jam and freshly baked bread and flowers with bursts of color, men in business suits shoving past, dogs on leashes and toddlers on three-wheeled scooters threatening to trip us. We make it out of the farmers' market and up the path that cuts through the green lawn where a few couples laid out on blankets. Some kids show off on their skateboards. Girls in summer dresses and shades lounge on benches with books that they aren't really reading.

"Why'd we decide to do this summer program again?" Ezra says.

"For our college applications."

"I already told you. I'm not going to college."

"Oh. Then, yeah, I have no idea why you're doing this."

He smirks at me. We both know he's probably just going to live off his trust fund when he graduates. Ezra is part Black, part Bengali, and his parents are filthy rich. So rich that they bought Ezra an apartment just so that he can live in Bed-Stuy for the summer while he's in the arts program. (And these days, apartments like Ezra's are just about a million dollars.) The Patels are the stereotypical Manhattan elite: endless champagne, fund-raisers, gala balls, and zero time for their own son, who was raised by three different nannies. It's fucked-up, but I have to admit that I'm jealous. Ezra's got his entire life laid out for him on a golden platter, while I'm going to have to claw and scrape and battle for what I want.

My dream has always been to go to Brown University, but my grades aren't exactly stellar, my test scores are less than average, and their acceptance rate is 9 percent. It isn't that I haven't tried. I studied my ass off for the tests, and I write down every word my teachers say in class to stop my mind from wandering. Like my dad's said, my brain is just wired differently.

The fact that I almost certainly won't get into Brown sometimes makes me feel like there's no point in even trying. But people have gotten in despite shitty test scores before, and even if my grades suck, my art doesn't. I'm talented. I know that I am. The portfolio counts even more for students applying to focus on art, and since the St. Catherine's summer program offers extra credit, there's a chance I could raise my grades up from Cs and Bs. I might still have a shot of getting in.

Leah, Marisol, and Declan are already on the Union Square steps for the fashion shoot. St. Cat's is on a different schedule from most NYC schools, and the summer program officially began a few days ago. St. Catherine's likes to kick off the summer program with projects so that we can get to know the students from other classes. Ezra and I signed up for a fashion shoot, using some of his designs. Leah, with her bushy red hair and super-pale skin and curves and tank top and slightly revealing booty shorts, has her camera, ready to take photos. And, of course, Marisol is the model. She's just as tall as Ezra, olive skin and thick brown hair and Cara Delevingne eyebrows. Just seeing her makes my nerves pump through my chest. Her hair's a giant nest, and she has green feathers glued to her eyelashes to match her lipstick. She wears the fourth dress in the lineup we'd planned: a sequin-portrait of Rihanna.

Declan Keane is running this whole thing as the director, which really just annoys the crap out of me. He doesn't have any experience as a director whatsoever, but somehow, he always manages to weasel his way into everything. It doesn't help that Declan acts like it's his only mission in life to treat me and Ezra like shit. He talks crap about us every chance that he gets. He hates us, and he's on a crusade to make everyone else hate us, too.

Declan's busy talking to Marisol when he sees us coming. His eyes flash. He clenches his jaw.

"So nice to see you," he calls out to us as we walk over, loud enough that a few people lounging on the steps turn their heads. "Ezra, thanks so much for coming."

Ezra mutters beside me, "Told you he'd be pissed."

Declan gives a slow clap. "It's an honor—no, really, it

is—to have you come to your own fucking fashion show."

Ezra holds up a fist, pretends to crank it, and slowly lifts his middle finger. Declan narrows his eyes at Ez when we get closer.

"Are you *high*?" he demands, and Ezra turns his face away. "Are you fucking kidding me? We've all been waiting here for over an hour, and you've been getting *high*?"

I try to step in. "Jesus, relax."

He doesn't even bother looking at me. "Fuck off, Felix, seriously."

There's no point in even trying to explain that our train was late.

"You're right," Ezra says. He nods at Leah and Marisol, who're watching us from the stairs. "Sorry. We lost track of time."

Declan rolls his eyes and mutters, "Fucking ridiculous" under his breath—like he's never been late for anything in his life. There was a point, before he decided he was too good for me and Ez, when all three of us would walk into class thirty minutes late together, high as fuck—and now, suddenly he's the Second Coming? God, I can't stand him.

"We're already halfway done anyway," Declan says, smoothing a hand through his curls, as if he doesn't actually give a shit whether we're here or not. Declan's mixed—his mom is Black and Puerto Rican, his dad a white guy from Ireland—so he's got brown skin, lighter than mine, and loose brown curls with glints of red that fall around his ears, dark brown eyes. He's a little stockier, with broad shoulders—a jock in Old Navy clothes: pink graphic T-shirt, baggier faded jeans, flip-flops.

He turns his back on us. "Let's hurry up and finish. I don't want to be here all day. Felix, go hold that reflector."

I don't move. I can't willingly make myself do whatever Declan Keane tells me to do. Not with that dismissive tone.

Ezra whispers, "Come on, Felix. Let's just get this done."

I roll my eyes and walk up the stairs, snatching up the reflector from the stack of supplies. Declan still hasn't even bothered to grace me with a single glance.

"All right," he says, "let's get back to it. Marisol, I don't think you should smile for this one—the juxtaposition of the Rihanna portrait with a serious expression . . ."

I zone the fuck out. About 99.9 percent of the time, Declan's speaking to hear the sound of his own voice. The shoot continues, Leah circling Mari with her camera as Marisol twists and turns, staring off at the sky (which is good, because it's easier to avoid eye contact with her), until it's time for the next outfit. I have to hold up a sheet around Marisol, staring hard at the ground, as Ezra helps her get changed into another dress he made, this one covered in manga panels from *Attack on Titan*. When she's ready, Declan barks his orders.

"Leah, position yourself a little more to the right. Felix, hold the reflector still."

Marisol shields her face. "And can you get the light out of my eyes, please?"

Mari and I used to go out. For, like, two weeks, so it really isn't that big of a deal, but still—I can't help but feel a little riled up around her, I guess, even after all these months. Marisol just acts like absolutely nothing happened between us, sprinkling a dash of salt onto the wound. The way she broke things off doesn't help, either.

Declan snaps his fingers at me. Literally, hand to God, *snaps his fucking fingers at me.* "I said to hold the reflector still. Christ, pay attention."

I hold the reflector up higher. "Fucking bullshit," I mutter to myself.

"Sorry, what was that?"

I must've spoken a little louder than I thought—because when I look up, everyone's staring at me. Leah bites her lip. Marisol raises an eyebrow. Ezra shakes his head from across the set, mouthing, *No, no, please, Felix, no.* That kind of pisses me off, too. Why does Declan get to treat us like crap, and we're just expected to take it, no complaints? I ignore Ezra and look right at Declan. "I said: Fucking. Bullshit."

Declan tilts his head to the side, crossing his arms with the smallest smile. "What's bullshit?"

I shrug. "This." I wave the reflector at him. "You."

His smile becomes a laugh of disbelief. "*I'm* bullshit?"

"You don't know anything about directing a fashion

shoot," I tell him. "You're just here because you're rich and your dad donates a shit ton of money to the school. It's not like you earned this."

I can see Ezra's eyes flicker to the ground, and I feel a pinch of guilt.

Declan hasn't noticed. He grins at me, like he knows it'll piss me off more. "You're just mad because you're not the director," he says, "and you don't get to add it to your Brown application. *Reflector boy* isn't exactly as impressive, is it?"

I hate that he's right—I *am* mad that I can't describe being the director on my application while Declan gets to use this, along with his perfect grades and almost-perfect test scores and family pedigree . . . I know he's applying to Brown, too. I know it's his first choice, because back when we used to hang out, we'd both planned on going to Brown and getting our dual degree with RISD. Ezra would chime in and say he'd move to Rhode Island with us, and it'd be the three of us, like always. That plan didn't exactly last long.

On top of that, Brown University has had a tradition of giving one St. Catherine's student a full scholarship. I can't afford college. My dad won't be able to pay the tuition. I'll have to take out a shit ton of loans and probably be in debt for the rest of my life, just to pursue illustration—while I can't think of anyone who would need, or deserve, that scholarship less than Declan fucking Keane. Just the thought of him getting that scholarship makes me want to stab pencils into my eyeballs.

Declan smirks at me. "What? Nothing else to say?"

"Leave it alone," Ezra tells me.

But I can't leave it alone. People like Declan are so used to getting their way. Acting like he's so much better and more important than everyone else. That's what he does to me—to Ezra. Ez acts like it doesn't bother him, but I get pissed off all over again every time I see Declan and remember the way he's treated us—the way he betrayed us.

"You know what?" I tell him. "Fuck you. You act like you're better than everyone else, but you're nothing but a fucking fraud."

Ezra's shaking his head, like he's annoyed with *me*, as if he thinks I'm overreacting even though he knows that Declan is being an asshole. Leah and Marisol awkwardly stand to the side, glancing at Declan to see what he'll do or say next.

Declan clenches his jaw. "*I'm* the fraud? Really?"

Ezra points at Declan. "No. Don't go there."

Declan rolls his eyes. "Christ. That's not even what I meant."

But the insinuation is there—implication made. It sours the air. Declan lets out this heavy sigh, not bothering to look at me, and out of the countless fights I've had with Declan Keane, I know I've won this particular battle. Even if his last words are still twisting through my gut. I've won, and in any other circumstance, I'd be happy to stay here and bask in the glory—but Marisol and Leah are staring anywhere but at me, and Ezra has these worried-filled eyes, and I know he'll whisper, "Are you okay?" every five minutes if I stay.

I drop the reflector. "Forget it."

I'm halfway down the stairs when Declan says that he isn't surprised. That's the kind of crap I always pull. I just flip him off and keep going.

TWO

THE TRIP FROM UNION SQUARE ISN'T AS BAD AS FROM BED-Stuy, but it's still about an hour before I get off at the 145th stop in Harlem. I've only been living here half a year. My dad and I used to live pretty close to where Ezra is now, on Tompkins. I miss the hell out of Brooklyn, but our landlord raised the rent, and my dad just couldn't afford it. He works most weeknights as a doorman for a luxury condominium in Lower Manhattan, and some days he'll try to take up extra jobs, like making deliveries and walking dogs. I'm on a talent-based scholarship, and even then, all his money goes into me and St. Catherine's—just so that I can pursue my passion for art. The pressure to get better grades, to pull off an amazing portfolio and college application, to make all the sacrifices worth it and actually get into Brown . . . it can fill me up sometimes, to the point where it's hard to even breathe.

Dad tells me not to worry. "Besides," he said, "I've always wanted to live in Harlem." I don't know if he's just lying to cheer me up, but there's definitely something exciting about this neighborhood. Langston Hughes and Claude McKay and all the other Black queer poets of the Renaissance made their art way up here. Maybe being in Harlem will snap me out of whatever the hell this creative block is and inspire me to put together an amazing Brown University application and portfolio—strong enough not only to get in but to get that full-ride scholarship, too. God, how incredible would that be? Getting into Brown would be like giving a giant middle finger to the Declan Keanes of the world—the people who take one look at me and decide I'm just not good enough.

I put in my earbuds and pop Fleetwood Mac into my Spotify station as I head down the steep hill, passing the park I avoid at all costs, ever since a rat tried to climb up my leg as I cut through the grass one night. I pass the Starbucks—the ultimate sign of gentrification in any neighborhood—and the Dollar Tree, the gym, and the fruit stand on the sidewalk. There are lemons, grapes, strawberries, and the brightest mangoes I've ever seen. They look like miniature suns. I pull out my phone and snap a photo for Instagram, even though I wouldn't really classify myself as a #foodporn kind of guy.

The seller glares at me. "You buying anything?"

I shrug. "No?"

"Then get the fuck out of here."

I walk up the block, by the Chinese restaurant and the KFC, kids on bikes popping up onto their back wheel and whooping down the street, fire truck sirens blaring a few blocks off, a shirtless man walking his Shih Tzu without a leash. The building my dad managed to get us into is all red brick with a courtyard where a few guys are sitting around on the ramp's railings. I pass by into the lobby with brown tiles and potted plants in the corners, a girl chatting on her cell phone by the stairs. The elevator takes me up to the fifth floor, and after walking down the hallway that reminds me of *The Shining*, I unlock the door and let myself in.

"I'm home!" I call out, not sure if my dad's even here. Captain, who must've heard me coming down the hall, is waiting by the door. She immediately rubs against my leg, back arching and purring, tail flicking back and forth. I'd found her as a kitten in Brooklyn one winter day when I was walking to my Bed-Stuy apartment with Ezra, and I was afraid that she'd die if I didn't help her, so I brought her home. My dad was pissed, but he let me warm her up and feed her milk, and one day turned into a few days, which turned into a few weeks, and after a few months, my dad had to admit that he liked her, too. I bend over to pick Captain up, but she's gone in a flash, bolting away from me and toward the kitchen.

The apartment is smaller than what we had in Bed-Stuy. The walls are beige, the light brown hardwood floors scuffed and worn down, an AC unit stuck into the living room's only window. This is a one-bedroom apartment, technically, but there's a tiny, windowless den that's supposed to be an office space and has now become my room. It's just big enough for my twin-sized mattress, one side table, and a dresser pressed up against the wall. I told my dad that I felt like Harry Potter, sleeping in the cupboard under the staircase. I was just joking, but I felt bad the second I said it. My dad's really effing trying, I know that he is—and complaining about my new room, when he's been working his ass off for me and my school, wasn't exactly my shining moment.

The wooden floor squeaks on my way into the kitchen, where I see a container from Jacob's, the cheapest and most delicious takeout around: beef stew, peas and rice, plantains, and baked macaroni and cheese. Dad's home, then—not surprising, since he'll have to leave for work in a few hours. My dad's always been the kind of person to have odd jobs. He told me once that his passion isn't work—it's his family. He would've been totally happy as a stay-at-home dad. Mom worked as a nurse at the hospital, bringing home the bacon, I guess—but when she left, everything fell apart. Now my dad's fighting to send me to a private school filled with rich kids, just so that I can live my dream and have a chance to go to an Ivy League school, all while pretending we aren't struggling to stay afloat. Declan Keane's voice echoes in my head. I'm the real fraud. What sucks is that he's kind of right.

I get comfortable in the living room, toeing off my sneakers and grabbing my laptop from the coffee table, sprawling out on the comfy couch. I end up where I always do: my email drafts folder.

I've got 472 emails drafted. All of them are to the same person: Lorraine Anders. Her last name, after she went and divorced my dad and changed it from *Love*.

I click on *compose* to write a new message and type *hi again* into the subject line.

Hey Mom,

This is the 473rd email I have drafted to you.

That's . . . a lot.

Is this kind of weird? Would you think I'm a freak, writing you all these unsent messages for years and hoarding them in my drafts folder?

I'm not going to send this one to you either. I already know that I won't. But maybe, one day, I can get the courage to actually write you an email that I hope you'll read and wait by my laptop, constantly refreshing my Gmail to see If you'll respond. I don't even know what that email would say. *How're you? How's Florida? How's my stepsister and my stepdad? Do you ever think about me? Do you still love me?*

Anyway, you know I just started the summer program and I had a group project. Long story short, Declan Keane was there. I've told you about him before. He pissed me off, like he always does. But—get this—*Ezra* was angry at *me* for fighting with Declan. I mean, what the hell? Marisol was also there. I'm so awkward whenever she's around, and I wish I could figure out a way to . . . I don't know, make her see that she was wrong about me. I know that I can't *make* anyone do anything, but it still really sucks whenever she just ignores me or acts like she doesn't give a shit about me and my existence. It makes me feel . . . well, I guess a little like how you make me feel. Except you're 10,000x worse. Because you're, well, my mom.

Okay, enough self-pity for the day. Maybe one day I'll actually go through and click send on every single one of these messages just to flood your inbox. But until then . . .

Your son,

Felix

The bedroom door opens, and my dad walks out, bleary-eyed. I snap my laptop shut. I realize this makes me look like I was watching porn or something, but my dad doesn't notice. He's got on his white collared shirt and tie, jacket hung over his arm. His gray hair is balding, and his frame seems to get thinner every year.

"Hey, kid," he says, since he still has a hard time saying my name.

My dad and I haven't seen each other in three days. The program is basically an away summer camp, but set in the city instead of in the woods. Most of the other students stay on campus in the dorms "for an immersive creative experience," as St. Catherine's likes to say, and since classes are right down the street from Ezra's apartment, I try to stay with him as much as possible. My dad, however, said that he wants me here, with him. I argued that it's important for me to gain life skills before college and get used to the idea of living on my own, which was only half bullshit, so we agreed on a compromise: I'd spend some days with Ezra, and some days at home. Basically, I've been living the dream. Not many teens get a chance to actually live without adults *before* college.

"You grabbed any food yet?" my dad asks me as he walks over to the plastic takeout container.

"Nope," I say, opening my laptop again and jumping onto Instagram to see how many likes my #foodporn post of the mangoes got. Two so far: one from Ezra, the other from Ezra's fake account.

"How're things?" my dad asks, mouth full of macaroni and cheese. "How's Ezra? You've been eating well and going to bed at a reasonable time and doing your work and everything?" I hesitate. I don't think he'd want to know that we've been staying up until three every morning, smoking weed, or that I'm still struggling to get my shit together. He keeps going. "I'm trusting you to be responsible. You know that, right?" Then—"Ah, shit—God damnit, the cat pissed everywhere again."

I help him grab paper towels to sop up the mess while he mutters something about needing to take Captain to the vet, and I say Captain's probably just anxious. She's never liked this new space—we can't open the only window, and there's no balcony, no fire escape, nowhere to sit outside. I understand. I feel pretty trapped in this apartment, too.

My dad points at the roll of paper towels in my hands and says my name to get my attention—but not my real name. He says my old name. The one I was born with, the one he and my mom gave me. The name itself I don't mind that much, I guess—but hearing it said out loud, directed at me, always sends a stabbing pain through my chest, this sinking feeling in my gut. I pretend I didn't hear him, until my dad realizes his mistake. There's an awkward silence for a few seconds, before he mumbles a quick apology.

We never talk about it. How he doesn't like saying the name Felix out loud. How he'll always slip up and use the wrong pronouns, and not bother to correct himself. How some nights, when he's had a little too much whiskey or beer, he'll tell me that I'll always be his daughter, his little girl.

I put the paper towel down and take the ten steps into my bedroom, closing the door behind me with a soft *click*.

"Kid," I hear my dad call, but I ignore him as I lie down on my bed, staring up at the flickering lightbulb. Captain appears out of nowhere, hopping into my lap and brushing her head against my hand, and I try not to cry, because no matter how pissed I am at him, I don't want my dad to hear me.

I wait outside of Ezra's gray, steel, and glass apartment building, sunglasses on to save my eyes from the bright summer light. It's seven, and the air still has that early-morning chill. Ez comes bounding down the stairs and out the front door, shades also on. I kind of hate how predictable we are right now.

"What's wrong with *you*?" Ezra immediately says. His hair is down, but it doesn't look like he bothered putting a comb through it, so tangled curls flop into his eyes. Ezra can always tell when I'm pissed or upset. He says that he's an empath. I think he's full of shit.

"Nothing." He keeps staring at me as we walk, waiting, so I say, "It's just my dad. He deadnamed me again."

"Shit," Ez mutters. "I'm sorry."

I shrug, because while I want to say *it's okay*, it really isn't. Some trans folks have always known exactly who they are, declaring their correct gender and pronouns as toddlers and insisting that they be given different clothes and toys. But it took me a while to figure out my identity. I'd always hated being forced into dresses and being given dolls. The dresses and dolls weren't even the real issue. The real issue was me realizing that these were things society had assigned to girls, and while I didn't even know what *trans* was, something about being forced into the role of *girl* has always upset the hell out of me. I'd always tried to line up with the other boys whenever teachers split us up. I followed those boys around the playgrounds, upset that they'd ignore me and push me away. I had dreams, sometimes—dreams where I'd be in a different body, the kind of body society says belongs to men. I'd be so effing happy, but then I would wake up and see that nothing had changed. I remember thinking to myself,

Hopefully, if I'm reincarnated, I'll be born a boy.

It wasn't until I was twelve, almost five years ago now, that I read this book that had a trans character in it: *I Am J* by Cris Beam. Reading about J, it was like . . . I don't know, not only did a lightbulb go off in me, but the sun itself came out from behind these eternal clouds, and everything inside me blazed with the realization: I'm a guy.

I'm a freaking guy.

It took me a few months of flipping out and going back and forth over whether I was really trans or not. Another few months to figure out how to tell my parents. I sat my dad down in the living room of our old Bed-Stuy apartment. I felt like I was going to throw up the entire time, and I was so nervous that the only words I could get out were, "Dad, I have something to tell you," and, "I'm trans." He was quiet. He had this expression, like he was confused. And then he said, "Okay." But I could tell it wasn't okay, not to him—could tell the whole *coming out* thing wasn't going so well. He said he was tired and went to bed, and that was the end of the conversation. I emailed my mom the next day, since she's lived in Florida with my stepdad and my stepsister since I've been ten years old. She never responded. It was the first and last time I actually hit *send* on an email I wrote her.

It was almost an entire year of begging before my dad agreed to let me see a doctor for hormones. It isn't always easy to start hormones, so I'm lucky that I could. That was around the time I started to show I was really talented in art and he decided to send me to St. Catherine's, which was great, because I didn't have to be around people who knew the old me. I didn't have any friends at my former school anyway, so it wasn't a big deal. It took a lot of convincing, and my doctor's help, but almost a year ago now, my dad even helped me get top surgery. I know how lucky I am for that. Not everyone who wants surgery can afford it. My dad had to do a lot of paperwork with letters and providers and everything, and he had to figure out my health insurance to make it happen. Even then, he still had to pay some money out of pocket. No matter how much he pisses me off sometimes, I wouldn't have been able to start my physical transition without my dad. Maybe that's what's most confusing of all: Why would he pay for my hormones, my surgery, my doctor's visits, everything—but refuse to say my real name?

Ezra met me right at the beginning of my transition. We sat next to each other in class and gravitated to each other's sarcastic comments, until we found ourselves spending practically every second of every day together. Ezra has only ever known me as Felix. I haven't told him, or anyone else, my old name. I've tried to wipe out all evidence of my past life: photos or videos where I have long hair, or where I'm wearing dresses, or anything society's prescribed to *girls*. It just isn't who I am anymore—who I ever was. It's funny. In a way, I guess I did experience reincarnation. I've started a new life, in a new physical form. I got exactly what I'd wished for.

My dad asked me to keep a few of my old pictures—*for*

the memories, you never know if you'll want to remember who you used to be one of these days. It wasn't really for me. I could tell he wanted those pictures for himself, one last anchor to who he thinks I was, or who he thinks I still am, which is enough of a reason for me to want to delete each and every single one of them. I have the pictures stored on Instagram, and I've come pretty close to deleting the photos a few times. I get a lurch of nausea whenever I see the old me pop up in my gallery. But I still keep the pictures. It's weird. He pisses me off, but he's still my dad, and I shouldn't feel like I owe him anything for helping me with my transition, but I do. I guess I figured it doesn't really matter. I've hidden the photos from the public. Only I can access them anyway. It doesn't really hurt to keep them around until my dad can finally accept me for who I am.

But . . . Even after coming out, even after starting my transition, sometimes I get this feeling. The feeling that something still isn't right. Questions float to the surface. Those questions begin to pull on this thread of anxiety, and I'm afraid if I pull too hard, I'll unweave and become completely undone. Maybe that's why I hate my dad deadnaming me, more than anything else. It makes me wonder if I really am *Felix*, no matter how loud I shout that name.

THREE

THE WALK TO ST. CATHERINE'S FROM EZRA'S PLACE IS pretty short. We step over cracks and dog shit on the sidewalk as we pass the basketball and tennis courts and the park, guys doing pull-ups on the monkey bars and little kids chasing each other and squealing as their moms sit and watch. There's a new wood-paneled coffee shop on the corner—not quite a Starbucks, but all signs point to gentrification. I glance at Ezra. He might not be white, but he still has a million-dollar apartment down the street. And what about me? Even if we're poor as fuck, my dad and I are basically doing the same thing by moving to Harlem, aren't we?

Eventually, the apartments become smaller until there's a series of bodegas and bars with rainbow Pride flags hanging on their doors, and the fenced-off campus with its hedges and trees appears. St. Catherine's is affiliated with an arts college that takes up four blocks on its own, but we get a private building in the corner of the campus near the parking lot. We've got about one hundred students, all enrolled on talent, wealth, or both. Most people in my grade do the summer program to work on their portfolios for their college applications, and I need as much help on my portfolio as I can get. I don't even know what my portfolio's theme is going to be yet, while everyone else is almost halfway finished. Brown has one of the lowest acceptance rates in the country, and I have to get in— *need* to get that scholarship if I want to attend. Sure, there're other good art colleges, and I'm applying to a bunch of them, too, but I don't know . . . I want to prove, I guess, that I'm good enough for a school like Brown.

The St. Catherine's building is old-school red brick with giant modern black-glass windows. Ezra and I get to the parking lot where a bunch of other students are hanging out in the shade of the trees. We automatically walk up to Marisol, who's leaning up against the building's brick wall as she talks to Leah, smoking next to the No Smoking within 25 Feet sign. I hate that I still can't meet Marisol's eye. She always has a steely gaze, hair and makeup and nails perfect, haughty smirk tugging on the edge of her lips. There're some people who're careful to only show the part of themselves they want others to see. I know that there are other sides to Marisol. She just never shows them to me.

"God, I need about another five hours of sleep," Marisol

says, offering her cigarette to Ezra. "Why the hell is this program so early?"

Ezra taps ash off the end of the cigarette. "That's what I want to know."

"I saw a study," Leah says, "that says it's really unhealthy to force teenagers to wake up at, like, seven in the morning. Something about our biological internal clocks."

"Think we should make an official complaint to the dean?" Ezra says. "We could start a protest."

"A sit-in," Leah offers, "until classes begin at noon."

Marisol snorts, playing with the ends of her thick, curled hair. "Tell me how it goes."

They keep talking, but I can feel myself getting too wrapped up in my head to pay attention. When I first met Marisol in class, I'd been impressed by her—and intimidated. There was something . . . I don't know, intoxicating about her confidence. Marisol *knows* that she's beautiful and talented and intelligent. She doesn't question if she's worthy of respect and love. When I asked her out last summer, just a couple of months after my top surgery, I was still getting used to my new body, feeling a little insecure with all the stares I would get, people clearly confused about my gender . . . and I guess I hoped some of Marisol's confidence would rub off on me.

Marisol had shrugged. "Sure," she said, like it was no big deal—and maybe it wasn't to her. She'd gone on dates before, but this was my first time. The three dates we attempted were awkward as fuck. We just couldn't figure out what to talk about without Ezra there as a middleman, and I could tell Marisol was bored with me, staring off into space as I talked to her about my acrylic techniques. I can't blame her for being bored—I was nervous, babbling, desperate to fill the silence. Finally, on the third date as we sat at Starbucks, Marisol suddenly said, "You know, I haven't been able to put my finger on why I'm not interested in you, but I think I understand now. In the end, I just don't think I can date a misogynist."

I'd startled, fear clutching my heart. I was worried I'd done or said something sexist without realizing it. "I'm sorry," I said automatically. Then, "Why am I a misogynist?"

"Well," she said, "you deciding to be a guy instead of a girl feels inherently misogynistic." She told me, "You can't be a feminist and decide you don't want to be a woman anymore."

Fear turned to shock, then anger, then shame. "Okay," I said, because I didn't know what else to say. We told each other goodbye, and we haven't spoken about that day since. I kept what she said to myself. I was too embarrassed to tell anyone else. And a part of me—a splinter in my chest—was, and still is, worried that she might be right. It's ironic, I guess. I wanted to date her so that I could prove I'm worthy of love. Instead, she managed to solidify this slowly growing theory that I'm not.

"I'll be in the classroom," I say, but Ezra doesn't hear me, still wrapped up in the conversation with Marisol, which has now rapidly switched to whether Hazel and James are hooking up in the supply closet (Leah is positive that they are). Ezra can never pass up a good piece of drama, and since he doesn't know what Marisol said to me, the two still hang out all the time.

I walk in through the sliding glass doors and into the blast of AC (seriously, why is the AC always on level infinity in the summer?) and make it about three steps across the white tile before I look up.

There's a gallery on the lobby walls. There are always student art installations in the lobby during the school year, so I'm not really surprised. What does surprise me are the images. Photos blown up to about 16 x 16.

Photos from my Instagram.

Photos of who I used to be.

Long hair. Dresses. Pictures of me with these forced smiles. Expressions showing just how uncomfortable I always felt. The physical pain is strained across my face in those photos.

That discomfort is nothing compared to now.

I can't fucking breathe.

I walk up to one slowly, blinking to clear my eyesight, like I'm not sure if this is even real. A placard underneath has a title with my deadname and the photo's year. What the fuck? What the actual, holy fuck? These were pictures that I'd hidden on my Instagram. Who the hell did this? How the fuck did they get into my account?

I reach up, trying to unhook the framed photo in front of

me. I can't even look at it without my stomach twisting, and it's embarrassing, but I can feel hot tears coming—I'm too short, can't reach it, and there are seven others that need to be taken down, too—

The door opens, and over my shoulder I can see a few students walking in, stopping for a second to stare, confused, before—thank God—they keep moving—

"Felix?"

I turn, and Ezra comes in after me. He mouths the words *what the hell* as he stares around. "Is—is that you?" he asks.

"No, it's not fucking me," I say, louder than I mean to.

He locks eyes with me, realizing his mistake. "Shit—sorry, no, I know it's not you."

Without another word he marches over and reaches above me, grabbing the frame and pulling it off the hook to take it down. He hurries to the next one, and I sink to the floor, sitting with my back against the wall, watching him. A few students—I think they're in sculpture—walk in, glancing at the photos and then at me.

"Keep it fucking moving," Ezra barks, and they jump before hurrying down the hall. He moves faster and faster so that he's flat-out running from one frame to the next, until all the images are down. He picks the frames up together at once, looking around for a place to trash them, then hides the photos behind the empty security desk. The guard doesn't come during the summertime. Whoever put up the gallery must've been waiting for this moment.

I shut my eyes and pull my knees up to my chest. I can feel Ezra sitting down beside me, the rustle of his T-shirt against my arm—his hand, unsure, on my shoulder.

"You okay?" he asks, his voice low.

I shake my head. "I think I'm going to be sick."

"You need me to take you to the bathroom?"

I shake my head again. "No. Just—don't talk for a second. Let me . . ."

We sit there. I don't know for how long. More sounds of sliding glass doors, voices and footsteps. Someone calls out, asking Ezra if I'm all right, and he doesn't say anything, but from his body shifting beside me, I think he might be waving them on.

"I don't think too many people saw," he whispers to me, hand rubbing my shoulder. Instead of throwing up, a wave of pain hits me, and I hunch forward. The urge to scream is deep in my chest. He rubs my back. The bell rings, and we stay exactly where we are.

I open my eyes with a breath and let the back of my head rest against the wall. Ezra watches me, worry and concern all over his face, eyebrows pinched together. He swallows, hard.

When I feel like I can talk again, I tell him, "I just want to know who the hell it was."

He shakes his head. "I mean—who would've even known?"

A lot of people, I think. I'm not exactly stealth. I don't hide my scars from my top surgery, and it's come up in conversation enough times that I'm pretty sure everyone is fully aware. . . . But that's also never been a problem before. I thought no one gave a shit.

"I think everyone knows I'm trans," I tell Ezra.

"No, I mean—" He hesitates. "Who would've known your . . . old name?" he asks. "Or even where to get these photos?"

I have no idea. Not even Ezra knew my birthname. The realization that he does now sends another stab of pain through me. I start hunching forward again, but he turns to face me, both hands on my shoulders.

"Hey," he said. "Look at me. I've got you, all right? We'll figure out who this piece of shit is and get them kicked the fuck out of St. Catherine's. All right?"

I'm nodding, trying not to cry. Ezra pulls me into a hug, bone-crushingly tight, and he doesn't let go, not for a solid ten seconds. When he pulls away, I'm wiping my eyes.

"What do you want to do?" he asks. "Should we tell a teacher or something?"

I roll my eyes. "They won't do shit."

"Do you want to go back to my place?"

I shake my head. "No. I don't want whoever did this to know they got to me." They're probably in class right now, sitting on the edge of their seat, waiting to hear that I ran out of the building sobbing.

Ezra nods. He stands and pulls me to my feet. We stop off at the bathroom so that I can splash water on my face and wait until my eyes aren't so red.

"It could've been literally anyone," I tell him as we walk out the doors and down the hall to our first class in acrylics.

"God, how did they even—I don't know, get that gallery approved?"

"I don't think it was. No security guard. No teachers around. They must've snuck the picture frames up early this morning when no one was here."

"Who the fuck would go through all of that trouble?"

"I don't fucking know, Ezra."

"Sorry," he says. "It's just—it's hard to believe anyone would go out of their way to hurt you like that. Why? Why the hell would they do that?"

"Anyone could be secretly transphobic—or maybe they just straight up don't like me."

I try to say it flippantly, like I couldn't care less either way, but my voice cracks, and I'm on the edge of tears all over again. I know I haven't been alive long, and that for these seventeen years, I've had a pretty privileged life. I get pissed at my dad for his shitty mistakes, sure, and I still feel pretty fucked-up over the fact that my mom left me and my dad to start a new family—but I have a place to live and food to eat. I attend a private arts school, and I might be able to go to college. I've never known a pain like this before.

I'm definitely feeling it now.

I feel like I've been physically attacked. Like someone took control of who I am. Took that control away from me.

Maybe Ezra's right. Maybe I should just go back to his apartment.

We walk into the acrylics class. It's a maze of corkboard walls that lets us spread out to work, but first there's always our daily check-in. The professor—she tells us all call her by her first name, Jill, to prove she's cool and down-with-the-kids—spreads herself out on a pink, paint-splattered corduroy couch, while everyone else sits on their stools at the high metal tables that're cramped together. Marisol sits in the back with Hazel and Leah, where Ezra and I always sit with them. Declan and his dumbass friends sit at the next table over.

Ezra and I walk in while Jill's in midsentence.

"It's about pushing yourself creatively, but knowing the craft, and using that craft as a tool," she says, glancing at us, waving us inside. "Thanks for joining us."

"You're welcome," Ezra says, holding my hand as we walk through the room. A few heads turn, and there're some whispers. Three guesses about what. We sit at our usual table. Leah leans over.

"I heard what happened," she says. "In the lobby."

"Stop," Ezra says.

"I just wanted to say I'm so, so sorry," she tells me.

"I said *stop*, Leah."

She sits back in her seat, staring forward.

Jill gives us a brilliant smile. She's a talented artist, but she's kind of small and mousy and young for a teacher, maybe only twenty-five or something—I'm pretty sure this is her first job—and she always feels the need to prove her dominance as the professor. "Would you like to offer an explanation for your tardiness?" she asks.

Declan, of course, decides to insert himself into the conversation. "Oh," he says, leaning back in his stool, hands folded behind his head, "those two never have an explanation. You're lucky they decided to show up at all."

I'm not in the mood. Really, *really* not in the mood. Ezra squeezes my hand.

Declan clearly isn't over what happened yesterday. He sits a little taller in his seat. "You know, Ms. Brody—"

"*Jill.*"

"Yes. Right. I think it's unfair. They get to waltz in whenever they want, and there are no repercussions? What about everyone else who makes a point to get into class on time? To hand in their work on time?" You'd think that he would decide he made his point and finally shut up, but no—he keeps going. "It's especially unfair if we're applying to the same schools and scholarships."

"Yeah," Ezra says sarcastically, "and what about the assholes who should mind their own fucking business? It's not fair that we have to deal with their bullshit, either!"

This gets a few scattered laughs. Jill clearly doesn't know what to do, so she just lets us off with a warning, which leaves Declan glaring at me and Ezra as she continues her morning lecture.

I pull out my phone, under the table, and open my

Instagram. I click on each and every single one of the photos that'd been in the gallery, and I delete all the pictures. I was hoping that, with each press of the trash can, I'd feel a little less sick, but it doesn't help. If anything, I'm pissed at myself for not doing this sooner—before someone somehow got into my account and stole them.

I zone out. Acrylic is my favorite medium, but there's no way I can concentrate, not right now. I stare around the classroom at all the students. Nasira pops bubble gum and stares forward with glazed-over eyes beside Austin, who texts beneath the table. Tyler flat-out sleeps with his head in his arms, and across the room, Elliott and Harper whisper to each other, Harper sneaking a look at me over her shoulder before turning to face forward again. There're dozens of others who could've put up the gallery, but I can't help but start to wonder if the asshole is in this room. My gaze lands on Declan. He catches me looking and rolls his eyes. His friend James leans closer to me.

"Hey," he says, "so your name's really—?"

He deadnames me. He might as well have punched me in the gut. Ezra tries to stand up, and I think he might actually walk over and hit James, so I grab his arm and shake my head at him. Not worth it. Ezra would get kicked out of St. Catherine's for the school's zero-tolerance policy on violence.

James snorts and turns back to the front. Declan just keeps staring at me. That sneer still on his face.

Declan. Declan fucking Keane.

Is it just a coincidence? The day after he calls me a *fraud*, there's a gallery with my old photos, my old name? Would it really be that surprising, if he and his shitty friends figured out how to hack my social media accounts, printed out my pictures, and hung my photos up in the lobby?

Jill lets us get started on our projects for the day. Ezra and I choose spots next to each other at a wall, canvas already stretched and prepped.

"It was Declan," I whisper to him.

His eyes snap to mine. "What? How do you know?"

"The way he was looking at me just now. And yesterday— he called me a *fraud*, remember?"

"Yeah, but—" Ezra pauses. He turns back to the canvas and starts—unsurprisingly—squeezing black out of a tube. I start squirting red, orange, and yellow blobs.

Ez lifts his brush. "I mean, it's not like I'm defending him or anything, but that's not really proof, is it? What if it isn't him?"

I know Ezra's right—but I can't explain this feeling I've got deep in my chest, wedged in there right next to the pain, which has become a dull ache—an ache I'm not sure will ever leave, not even twenty years from now, maybe not ever. Declan Keane did this. It's the only thing that makes sense.

"It's him," I say firmly. "I know it is. Who else would do something like that?"

He shakes his head. "I don't know, but—"

I can already sense what he's going to say. Maybe I'm

just fixating on Declan because I need a place to put all this anger building in me. I know that's what he's thinking, so I cut him off.

"It was him," I say again.

"Okay," Ezra says. It pisses me off, that he sounds like he's trying to soothe a kid throwing a tantrum. "Okay. Say it *was* him. What do you want to do?" He glances around. "Tell Jill? Go to the dean?"

"No," I tell him. "Fuck that. Declan Keane? They'd call his dad, let him off with a warning maybe, but they wouldn't do shit to him. No, I'm not going to tell the dean."

Jill comes around the corner. She strolls behind us serenely as she looks over our shoulders to observe our work, which is nonexistent.

"Less chatting, more painting," she says with a smile.

When she moves on, Ezra glances at me.

"So what're you going to do?" he asks.

Isn't it obvious? "I'm going to fucking destroy him. That's what I'm going to do."

Ezra shrugs, smirk twitching on his face. "Well, whether it was Declan or not, I wouldn't mind seeing that." He starts a sketch with the black paint, brushstrokes loose. "What's the plan?"

40

FOUR

Even though I had absolutely no desire to go to Dean Fletcher and tell her what'd happened with the gallery, word must've spread enough that the teachers overheard, because right as acrylics ends, a student pops his head into the classroom and says I have to go to the office. Dean Fletcher, with her Afro and single silver streak, is a no-nonsense, terrifying badass in a business suit and six-inch heels. Her office—all rich, deep mahogany panels except for the single glass wall—is surprisingly bare and minimalist. Not exactly what you'd expect of an arts school. She waves me inside, asks me to sit on the hard chair in front of her heavy wood desk, and wastes no time asking about the gallery.

"Do you know who might've been behind it?"

"No."

"Has there been anyone bullying you, or making remarks about your identity?"

"No." God, I just want to leave.

Dean Fletcher folds her hands together. "It was unacceptable, and installed without the permission of this administration," she says, and I get the hollow feeling that this was really why I was called into her office—to cover their asses. She's afraid I'll sue St. Catherine's or something. "I'm sorry that this happened to you, Felix. Do you want to speak with the summer counselor?"

"No," I say, a little too quickly. The counselor would just ask a whole bunch of questions, and eventually those questions would veer into abandoned-by-mother territory, and that's definitely something I don't want to talk about. "No," I say again, "thank you."

Dean Fletcher pauses and looks like she might want to pressure me into some counseling sessions, but she finally gives me a single nod. "We'll begin an investigation." I stop myself from rolling my eyes. The most they'll do is ask a few students if they saw anything, and when those students say no, the gallery will be declared a cold case. "If you hear anything, please tell me right away," Dean Fletcher says. "We have a zero-tolerance policy for this sort of hateful behavior."

And even if I'm annoyed, and the school won't do shit to find who it was, it still feels good to hear her say that.

* * *

It's after the fourth *I'm so sorry, Felix* and the third question about my deadname that I take Ezra up on his offer to peace the fuck out of classes and head to his apartment early. We stop at the Chinese place that's on the corner one block down for two cartons of what are the best chicken wings and French fries in the entire city, and then hop into the wine shop that's right next door, using Ezra's fake ID to grab two bottles of cheap chardonnay because, as he says, it's time to get fancy. At the counter, the owner looks from the ID to Ezra's face and back to the ID, like she knows it's total bullshit. She takes Ezra's credit card and tells us this story about when she was sixteen and sneaking off into her neighborhood bar in Paris. We take that as permission to escape with our illegal bottles, taking the wine and chicken back up the block to Ezra's apartment.

There're men with bulging muscles and white tanks across the street, shouting in Bajan accents and standing around cars that have their rumbling engines on, blasting an old Dixie Chicks song. Ezra unlocks the front glass door and lets us into the asphalt-gray-tiled and scuffed-white-walls hallway. We stomp up the three floors, Ezra muttering a prayer that his neighbors aren't home—"I don't know what the fuck they're doing—no one has sex like that at three in the morning, they were rolling around and slamming shit on the ground, seriously"—before he unlocks his apartment.

The apartment has a single brick wall, dark wood floors,

and a pretty nice kitchen area with granite countertops, along with a stainless-steel refrigerator and gas stove—but other than that, the place is basically empty. Ezra's been here for almost an entire month now, but he hasn't bothered buying any furniture with the exorbitant amounts of money his parents gave him to spend. So far, all he has is a mattress out in the living room, facing a tiny-ass TV stand with a 12-inch flat screen. He doesn't even have any lightbulbs. At night, we'll just turn on Netflix and use the orange of the streetlights outside to see. The bright sunlight shines into the apartment now. There are some plotted plants over by the window—one mint, one basil, one cannabis. Two of those are more for aesthetics.

Ezra drops the wine and food next to the mattress and flops onto it, kicking off his shoes. "Think we'll get in trouble for ditching half the day?"

I sit down next to him, pulling the chicken to me. "Uh, no, probably not." Literally the only teacher who's ever cared about schedules and tardiness has been Jill.

"Okay, look, I hate the guy," Ezra says, "but do you think Declan had a point?"

"About being late?" I say, mouth full of fries. "Fuck no."

"What if we get in trouble? Or we end up—I don't know, getting kicked out or something?"

"Everyone's always late to everything, Ez. Declan's just singling us out because he's a dick." I try to ignore the tingle of fear in the back of my mind—not that we'd get kicked out, but that Declan was right about one thing, at least: I'm fucking around, procrastinating on my portfolio because I'm too afraid to actually get started—too afraid to try, only to fail. Terrified that I won't get into Brown. I've worked hard these past three years so that all my dad's sacrifices wouldn't go to waste . . . but what if none of that matters in the end?

Ezra grabs the wine and twists off the screw cap. "Cups or no cups?"

"No cups."

I'm a little annoyed at Ezra for even saying Declan's name. After all, he's the one I can thank for that fucking gallery. The pain isn't as sharp as it was earlier, but it's still there, echoing through me.

Ezra snuggles his head into my lap, like a dog trying to get comfortable. As if he's read my mind—I don't know, maybe he really is an empath or something—he says, "Sorry. I shouldn't have brought him up."

"S'okay."

"Should we not say his name anymore?" he says. "I wouldn't argue with calling him something else. Asshole Motherfucker. Shitty McShitterson." He sits up to take a gulp from the wine, then lies back down. "Commander Dickwad."

I lean my back against the wall. "No, I don't mind saying his name," I say. "As long as I get to fuck up his world."

"Fucking ruin him."

"Destroy his life as he knows it."

"He won't see it coming."

"No, he fucking won't." What might've started as a joke

feels a little more serious to me now. "He won't even recognize himself when I'm done with him."

"You're such a Slytherin."

"I know," I say, grabbing the second bottle of chardonnay, "but you love it."

"I *do* love it," Ezra says, sitting up to grab a piece of chicken, then hisses and pulls his hand back, saying it's too hot. "Thought more about what you're going to do yet?" he asks.

"What did Jill say earlier?" I ask. "That thing about craft."

"Use craft as a tool," he says, "to find your creativity."

"I guess the craft is Instagram. Declan figured out how to hack into my account and find my pictures. He must've looked at the photo's tags, figured out my old name." The photos were taken and uploaded before I'd even begun to think about transitioning, back when I still had to lie about my age to join any sort of social media.

"Okay," Ezra says slowly. "So what're you suggesting?"

I shake my head. "Not sure. If there was a way to—I don't know, do the same thing that Declan did to me . . ."

It wouldn't be the same as posting my photos and deadnaming me. Not even close. But if I could learn a secret of Declan's and use that against him—post his secret, and hurt him like he hurt me . . . That'd definitely be a start.

"Maybe I can find a way to talk to him. Get a secret out of him, something he doesn't want anyone else to know." I begin to think of the possibilities. What dark shit might

Declan Keane be hiding? Maybe there's even something I can use against him. Something so bad, he'll have to give up on his Brown application. Without Declan in the running, I'd pretty much be guaranteed the spot. My grades and my test scores aren't the best, but I'm pretty fucking talented, and there isn't anyone else on our level that's applying for that scholarship.

I hear Ezra's earlier question—*What if it isn't him?*—but I push that shit to the side. I'm pretty positive that it's Declan . . . and if it isn't, Declan Keane still 100 percent deserves whatever's coming to him.

"Get a secret out of him," Ezra repeats. "Like—what? Catfish him?"

I snap my fingers. "Yes. I can make a fake account on Instagram. Declan's always posting stupid shit. I'll start commenting and messaging him. Try to start up a friendship. Get him to trust me."

Ezra squints at me. "Uh—I mean, it *sounds* like a good idea. In *theory*. But I can't think of anyone who's less trusting than Declan Keane." He bites his lip. "He didn't mind—you know, the physical stuff. Making out and all that. But whenever I tried to get him to talk about his life, his feelings? You remember. He's like a brick wall."

I always try to forget that Ezra and Declan used to go out. For an entire seven months during our first year at St. Catherine's, it was the Ezra Patel and Declan Keane show. It took exactly one day of hardcore flirtation on Ezra's part before they were all over each other. Inseparable. Hand-holding, cheek-kissing, the works. I accepted my role as the third wheel—and to be honest, I didn't even mind. Not really. I'd considered Declan my friend, too. All three of us would hang out. Talk about our future, our plans. They were the first two people at St. Catherine's I came out to as trans. That pretty much says it all, when it comes to how much I trusted Declan Keane.

Then, suddenly—seriously, out of fucking nowhere—Declan broke up with Ezra and became the mightiest of all assholes. One day, he was hanging out with us, like he always did—and the next, he broke up with Ez via text. Ezra didn't cry or anything, but I could practically feel the confusion and hurt coming off him in waves. To this day, he has no idea why Declan suddenly ended things like that. But, I mean, we're mature enough to hang out with our exes, right? That's what Ezra and I thought when we walked up to Declan the next morning. He was sitting with James and Marc, who were already the two most popular bro-jocks at the school . . . and when we tried to say hello, Declan just stared at us blankly, as if he didn't even know who we were.

Ezra had wanted to ask if he'd done something wrong—to see if they still had a chance to make things work. "Can we talk?" he'd asked.

I still remember the disgust on Declan's face. "I'd rather not."

James and Marc were sneering at us. I could feel Ezra's embarrassment, but he only nodded. "Okay. I guess I'll just . . . leave you alone, then."

You'd think Ezra leaving Declan alone would be enough, but no. Declan would roll his eyes whenever Ezra and I had something to say in class, would complain to the teacher whenever we were late, would talk shit about me and Ez to anyone who would listen. He made it clear that he thought he was better than us—that he wanted nothing to do with us. He never said why. No explanation. Nothing.

Ezra shrugged it off and acted like he wasn't really hurt. He decided to move on. But I'll admit it: Declan really made me feel like shit. I know he made Ezra feel like shit, too. I've never forgiven him for that. I probably never will.

Ezra tests the chicken out again, breaking a wing in half. "I'd ask him, you know, about his family, or what it was like growing up in upstate New York, but he'd just sidestep all of those questions. Trying to get a secret out of him is a good idea," he says again, "but I don't think Declan would tell anything to a stranger he met online."

Crap. I know Ezra's right. "But I don't know what else to do," I tell him. "I'll just have to try."

He shrugs. "All right," he says with a *Good luck* tone.

I pull out my phone. "What should my username be?"

"Shit, this chicken's so fucking good," he says, mouth full.

"That might be a little long."

He takes a second to think. "Felix is a thing in Harry Potter, right?"

"Yeah," I say, racking my brain, trying to remember—it's

been a while since I read the series. "It was that thing Ron thought he drank for luck in that Quidditch match." *Felix* means "lucky" in Latin. Its meaning is why I chose it to be my new name in the first place. When I figured out that I'm not a girl, and I started making all the necessary changes, I knew I'd lucked out.

Ezra nods at me. "How about Lucky?"

"Oh—what about Lucky?"

"That's what I just fucking said."

I type on my phone, trying a bunch of different iterations of *Lucky*, until I finally have a username that hasn't been taken: luckyliquid95.

"Sounds dirty," Ezra says with a smirk.

"Whatever." I enter the username. I hate that I remember Declan's username, but I do—I type it in the search bar: thekeanester123. (Honestly, that name should've been a red flag for me and Ezra from the start.) I swipe through Declan's images. A bunch are pretentious black-and-white photos of himself, set up with severe lighting from antique lamps and gauzy curtains. A couple are of food, cityscapes with the sun shining in between buildings, some of him and James standing in front of graffiti, him and Marc at Yankee Stadium.

But most of the posts are of his illustrations.

I hate Declan Keane. Like, really freaking hate him. But even I have to admit that the guy's got talent. Real talent. The kind that can't be taught. The kind that can't be imitated.

I've always leaned more toward acrylic portraits, and I

know that I'm good. But Declan's artwork is . . . indescribable. There's no label to put on it. Collage, maybe? He uses so many different mediums. Charcoal sometimes, pastel others, simple pencil or ink. But it's really his use of negative space that's so stark. It seems simple, at first glance—but it's the kind of negative space that reminds me of looking up, through the branches of trees, to see the sky shining behind it, or the space that's between something as fine and intricate as lace. The subjects of his pieces are always interesting—a bird with a broken wing, a woman with traditional neck rings and modern hoop earrings, a simple hand. But it's always—always—the negative space that he builds around the subjects with his designs and pieces of newspaper, leaves or crumpled-up tissue, what seems like literally anything he'll find on the ground—that puts his artwork above everyone else's.

What makes him a better artist than even me, really.

It pisses me off to admit it. I hate that it's true. But it is. Declan's a better artist than me.

With his artwork, and his Ivy League pedigree, and his impeccable grades, Declan is definitely going to get a spot at Brown. He'll probably get that scholarship, too, even though he doesn't need it. Even though he's an asshole and he doesn't deserve it.

I scroll through his artwork and start liking a bunch of the posts at random. I comment on one piece. **Great use of negative space!** I comment on another. **What materials did you use for this?**

Ezra's decimated an entire carton of chicken and fries and begins to start in on mine, so I grab a wing. "I don't know if I want to look at my dad for at least another twelve hours," I tell him. Especially now, after the gallery—if my dad calls me by my birthname, I might just flip out on him. "Okay if I stay over tonight?"

"You ask that literally every time," Ezra says, "and literally every time, I say yes."

"I don't want to be presumptuous," I say. "What if you—I don't know, have a special friend coming over or something?"

He lets out a barking laugh. "*Special friend?* Felix, you're with me twenty-four seven. When am I supposed to meet this special friend?"

I shrug. "Or what if you get tired of me, but don't know how to say it?"

Ezra rolls his eyes, grabs my phone, and turns it to Spotify. The Fleetwood Mac station is still on, so "Spirit in the Sky" by Norman Greenbaum begins to play. Ezra gets up and starts pirouetting around and around—he's been classically trained since the age of five. I pick off a couple leaves of the weed, grab some of the paper that's waiting beside the TV, and roll while Ezra kicks his leg all the way up to the beat, toes pointed and all. The lighter is at the edge of the counter in the kitchen—I click, click, until the paper sizzles and smoke wisps into the air. Ezra slides to my side, and I pop the bud in his mouth. I yank open the window that faces an empty alleyway, and we crawl out onto the fire escape, legs dangling. The sun is starting to make its way down. The sky's darker, purple hues off on the horizon.

"You ever wonder," he says, squinting up at the sky, "why we're here?"

Oh, God. High philosophical Ezra is the literal *worst*. "There's no reason why we're here. We just exist. That's all. That's it."

"No. Not like *that*." He screws up his face in frustration. "Why here, in Brooklyn? Why this program? Why art?"

"Uh—"

"Why any of this?" he asks a little too aggressively. "Seriously, Felix. Why not science, or business, or—literally anything else?"

"I think you're a little young to be having a midlife crisis, Ez."

"What if this *is* my midlife crisis?" he demands. "What if I'm going to die in exactly seventeen years and I've wasted my life on this, on art and painting and fashion and all this creative bullshit, because I *thought* it was my passion, when really, I'm meant to be doing something else?"

There's a spark of frustration in my chest. Ezra gets to have a midlife crisis at the age of seventeen because of his privilege and his family's wealth. Me? I have to figure out what I want to do and work my ass off for it if I want to have a chance of any sort of future. I'm never going to have anything handed to me, the way that things are just handed to Ezra. But I try to push those feelings aside—and maybe it's the weed, but Ezra's paranoia sinks into me, too. I mean, who's to say that I shouldn't be an astrophysicist? Or that I'm not actually the next Bach?

"You know those people who get into car accidents?" I ask Ezra. "Or who get hit by lightning? And then they're in a coma or something, but when they wake up, they've become this genius in something they'd never even tried before?"

Ezra stares at the sky. "No."

I frown at him. "Really? Well—I mean, I guess I'm just saying the same thing as you."

"Okay." He turns his head to me. "Want me to run you over with a car?"

"Fuck off, Ezra."

"No, really, I can do that. I mean, if you want me to."

I try not to laugh. "You don't even have a car."

"I will absolutely steal a car so that I can run you over with it."

I shove his arm, and he flashes a grin at me. "Maybe you should. Then I could have a chance at being talented at something."

He groans and leans on me. "What the hell are you talking about? You're talented."

"I'm—I don't know, someone with a smidgen of talent, who decided that this is what I wanted to do when I was a kid, and then decided to practice my ass off for ten years, just to get to where I am now. Which is nowhere in comparison to some people."

"To *what* people?"

"To you," I say—and I mean it. Ezra's artwork is always great. He's instantly a genius in anything he decides to try. First, it was watercolor; the next year, sculpture. Right now, he's focusing on fashion and taught himself how to stitch and make patterns in a *single summer*. Ezra's so good that he didn't even bother to sign up for the summer sewing workshop; he decided to just follow me into acrylics so that we could hang out during class.

"*Moi?*" Ezra says, pretending to be flattered.

I hesitate. "And people like Declan Keane."

He lets out a heavy sigh. "Are we really going to talk about him right now?"

"No," I say. "But I mean—both of you have this natural talent, and it's like . . . I don't know, sometimes I wonder if talent comes from experience, you know?"

"I really, really don't," Ezra says, passing me the weed. "You need to relax, Felix. You're always second-guessing yourself. Your shit is *good*."

"You have to say that because you're my friend."

"No, not really. As your friend, it's my job to be honest. For example, that particular Beatles tank top," he says, waving a hand at my shirt, which has portraits of the four members. "Do you even *like* the Beatles?"

I elbow him. "Sometimes."

He takes the weed back, sucking in one long draw, staring down at the street below.

"I haven't—" I hesitate, because it's a little embarrassing to say, but I say it anyway. "I've never been in love. Which is ironic, because, you know—my last name and everything."

Ezra snorts, but doesn't say anything.

"I *want* to be in love. I've never, you know—felt the kind of *passion* great artists talk about. I want that. I want to feel that level of intensity. Not everyone wants love. I get that, you know? But me—I want to fall in love and be broken up with and get pissed and grieve and fall in love all over again. I've never felt any of that. I've just been doing the same shit. Nothing new. Nothing exciting."

Ezra doesn't say anything for a long time, until he nudges me with his head and looks at me with puppy-dog eyes. "I'm not exciting?"

"Shut the fuck up."

"I'm too boring for you? Really?"

"Shit, Ez, I'm trying to be serious."

"Yeah. I am, too." He sits up, stares straight ahead. "You'll get to do all of that at some point," he says, "but in the meantime, you're forgetting that you're right here, with me—and that I'm pretty fucking awesome."

I roll my eyes. "Come Together" starts playing on the Spotify station. "See? I listen to the Beatles."

"Congratulations."

"Thanks."

He grins at me for a split second, then leans his head on my shoulder. I'm a lot shorter than him, so it must strain his neck, but he doesn't seem to care. "Did the Keanester respond?"

I check my phone and scroll through my notifications. "Nope."

"Told you."

I shrug. I'm patient when it comes to destroying my enemies. I'll just have to keep trying.

It's only as we're cleaning up and getting ready for bed that my phone buzzes. I grab it and swipe open Instagram, holding my breath, thinking that it might actually be Declan—but the notification is for my real account. I frown and click on the Message Requests link. An anonymous account, grande-queen69, sent a single line:

Did you like the gallery?

FIVE

Hey Mom,

Here's something I haven't told you yet: even though I came out to you as a trans guy in an email—yeah, exactly, that one you never responded to—I'm not sure if I'm actually a guy. It's a hard feeling to describe. It's like . . . just this sense, this feeling, in my gut that something isn't totally right. I know that I'm definitely not a girl. But that's all I know.

I've been doing research. Trying to look up different definitions and labels and terms. Some people say we shouldn't need labels. That we're trying to box ourselves in too much. But I don't know. It feels good to me, to know I'm not alone. That someone else has felt the same way I've felt, experienced the same things I've experienced. It's validating.

But it's embarrassing, too. I made this big deal about

being a guy. And now I'm, what, changing my mind? Or is it that my identity is evolving? I don't know. Something pretty bad happened to me. There was a gallery at school of my old pictures, telling everyone my deadname—and right after, I got this Instagram message taunting me. I'm hurt that anyone would go out of their way to attack me, but at this point, the hurt is very quickly turning into anger. Rage. I'm pissed off. Like, to the point where I kind of want to beat the crap out of the person who's doing this to me. And I'm pretty sure it's all Declan Keane.

I didn't even tell Ezra about the Instagram message. I didn't want him to freak out about it. And if Declan's the one behind all of this, then it doesn't matter—I'm taking him down pretty soon anyway.

It's kind of ironic, I guess, that I'm writing to you about all of this, when you're the one who's hurt me most of all—yes, even more than the gallery and even more than that Instagram message and even more than the daily bullshit I have to see in the news, about trans people like me fighting for the right to live. Kind of hard to believe at this point, but it's true. It's like I'm constantly trying to prove that I deserve love—but how can I, when even my own mom doesn't love me?

Your son . . . ?

Felix

This is the sort of revenge plot that will require biding my time, so I don't continue commenting on Declan's posts. Two unanswered comments are enough for now—I don't want to creep him out . . . but I do start building my profile more. Over the next couple of days, I snap a close-up shot of Ezra's brick wall for my first image, and another photo of the weed, basil, and mint side by side. I start liking and commenting on other posts, so that it doesn't look like I'm fixated on Declan. Ezra makes me like every single one of his posts, and I hop onto Marisol's Instagram also, trying to ignore the photos of her making out with different people from St. Cat's. I probably should've told Marisol to go fuck herself the second she told me I was a misogynist for being trans, but she's always hung around the same crowds as me and Ezra, and it was kind of impossible to just rip her out of my life. There's that . . . and this urge to convince her that she is wrong.

When it's been a full weekend of nothing but Instagram, chicken wings, and chardonnay, I get a text message from my dad while I'm in class on Monday: **U OK?**

I text him back: **Yeah, I've just been busy with Ezra.**

He responds: **K. See U 2nite.**

I figure this is a sign that he's not happy I haven't been staying in touch, even though we agreed that I'd split my time between home and Ezra's apartment. My dad's always been pretty easygoing, in comparison to my mom, before she abandoned us for her newer and better family. I have memories of her being strict. I had to wear everything she told me to: those stupid lace dresses and shiny shoes and pearl earrings, bows and barrettes in my hair. My dad was always the one that left the discipline to her, and even after she left us, he's never been great at setting rules or curfews or anything.

I jump back into my project. Our thesis class takes up the second half of the day, after lunch, before classes let out at two o'clock. The thesis class is our chance to work on whatever we want to, and for most rising seniors like me and Declan, we're focusing on the portfolio we'll end up using for our college applications. Declan's taken up a corner of the room with his collage work spread across *two tables* (the narcissism is impressive, truly), but I end up in front of a prepped and stretched canvas, acrylic paints waiting in a neat stack beside me.

I'm sitting at one long white table with Ezra, Marisol, Leah, Austin, Hazel, and Tyler. Well, it's more like I'm sitting with Ezra, and everyone else is sitting with him. Leah's focused on her laptop, editing photos for her portfolio—I've heard her say that she wants to work in photojournalism, so she takes her photography super seriously. She was really pissed when she was told she had too many photography credits for the summer program, forcing her into acrylics instead. She's the only one in the room who's completely silent. Everyone else is whispering while they work.

"Astrology isn't real," Hazel says. Hazel has dark skin and hair that's dyed purple, piercings and tattoos. "It's like Hogwarts houses."

"Excuse me," Ezra says. "Hogwarts houses are real."

"I still haven't read the books," Marisol says, leaning back in her chair.

"What? Really?" Austin doesn't glance up from his landscape. Austin has blond hair, blue eyes, a dimpled smile, and gives the vibes of someone who might wear a sweater tied around his shoulders unironically. "They're, like—a cultural phenomenon."

"I kind of hate reading," Marisol says.

"That explains a lot," Hazel mumbles. Marisol gives her an icy look. I guess the breakup isn't going very well.

"Astrology is real," Tyler insists. "Listen. The moon controls the tides, right? The human body is mostly water. It'd make sense if the moon controls us, too."

"Tyler," Hazel says, "no one knows what the fuck you're talking about."

Marisol snorts. Tyler looks frustrated. His cheeks go pink.

"I kind of think astrology is real, too," Austin says, earning a smile from Tyler. "I mean, it can't be a coincidence that so many people relate to their signs, right? And the way signs interact with each other. I'm a Libra, and I'm always attracted to Leos, without fail."

Ezra perks up at that. "I'm a Leo."

Austin blushes a little. Leah says, without looking up, "He knows."

I blink and glance at Ezra, who gives a small, surprised smile. Okay. Weird moment.

Hazel's bored with whatever micro-flirtation is happening. "You probably believe in destiny and soul mates and all that crap."

Austin hesitates. "Well," he says, "yeah, I do."

"I definitely do," Tyler tells us.

"Oh, come on," Hazel says. "How can you live in the twenty-first century and believe in bullshit like that?"

"Okay, all right," Ezra says. "Calm down. It's just a conversation."

"Yeah," Marisol says. "Why're you getting so riled up?" She says this, clearly for the sole purpose of riling Hazel up. From the expression on Hazel's face, it's working.

"I don't know," Austin says. "It just feels like so much is connected, you know? Don't you ever feel like you were put on this planet for a purpose? Like you're meant to do something important? I think about that all the time. What's my destiny? What if I'm missing out on what I'm supposed to be doing?"

"What if it's your destiny to miss out on your destiny?" Marisol says.

"That's . . . slightly terrifying," he says.

I can't blame Austin. It's something I've thought about before—the question of if I'm doing what I'm meant to be doing in this lifetime. The thought sends a spike of fear through me. I was having a hard time concentrating before, but I'm having an even harder time focusing now. I stare at the blank canvas in front of me. Portraits have always been my specialty, but the portfolio can't be a random collection of paintings. Should I choose one subject? Should there be a running color theme? What am I trying to say with these portraits? What's the story I'm trying to portray?

What the hell am I supposed to make, to convince Brown that I'm good enough?

The questions make me freeze. I could do anything, but it somehow feels like I don't have any options. I can already feel the years of hard work, resulting in nothing but my average grades and less-than-average test scores, going down the drain. My dad's going to be disappointed. He'll smile and say that he's proud of me, but how could he not be disappointed? He's given up everything for me, for this education, so that I could do something great with my life—and instead, I'm sitting here with nothing but a blank, white canvas.

I start gathering the acrylics to put them away in the supply closet.

"Where're you going?" Ezra whispers, barely glancing up from his sketches of dresses sprawled out in front of him. A few of the others glance up, too.

"Home. Nothing's coming to me."

"Home? You mean my place?"

"No," I tell him, "my dad wants me back tonight."

"Oh, good," he says. "Now I can finally invite my special friend over."

"See you later, Ez."

"All right," he says, and actually looks a little sad to say goodbye. "See you later."

I walk to the door, ignoring Declan, who rolls his eyes and shakes his head, muttering something across his two tables to

James as I leave. Things have calmed down at school. I don't know if Ezra made it a personal mission or what, but somehow, everyone figured out that I did *not* want to talk about the gallery. I just want to pretend it never happened. And so that's what everyone's doing. This has made being back in class bearable, even though my throat still closes up every time I walk through the lobby, or whenever I open my Instagram app, afraid that there'll be another message waiting for me. To be honest, the only thing that makes any of this better is thinking about how I'm going to destroy Declan Keane's life. I can't help it. I'm a little obsessed.

The trains are running pretty smoothly for once, and I'm back up to my dad's apartment in less than two hours. He's in the kitchen, cooking stir fry from the smell of it. Smoke fills the tiny apartment and instantly burns my eyes. The TV is on, playing *The Real Housewives of New York*. My dad's love of reality TV is immeasurable.

I cross over into the living room and make myself comfortable on the plush chair. Captain sits in front of the screen on the TV stand, staring right at me, purring deeply. "The prodigal son returns," my dad says, only slightly passive-aggressively.

I stop myself from rolling my eyes. I don't know why he's suddenly annoyed that I'm staying at Ezra's. I get that I'm the kid in this situation, but this is still supposed to be a chance for me to break free and get used to the idea that in a year, I'll be living on my own as an almost-adult. We agreed that I'd split my time between home and Ezra's, so it's pretty frustrating that he's acting like this.

I tell him that I need to grab clean clothes. I bring my backpack into my bedroom to pull out my dirty laundry, tossing them into my basket. I'm a little bit of a neat freak, and there isn't much space to be messy anyway, so the floor is spotless, bed made, *Akira* on my nightstand. I pull open my drawer and grab a few tanks and T-shirts, jean cutoffs, and boxers, before I stuff them into my backpack and head into the living room again, switching off the light. My dad puts plates on the dining table that's pushed up against the wall.

"Hey, kid," my dad says as I sit down with my food, "maybe you should give Ezra's apartment a break."

"What do you mean?"

"I mean it'd be nice if you stayed home a little longer than one night every few days."

I frown as I pick out the green beans, pushing them to the side. "I thought you said it was okay to stay with Ezra."

"Yeah," he says, "every once in a while. I was thinking every few weeks."

"The program is over in two months. It wouldn't make any sense for me to just stay down there once every few weeks."

"So it makes sense for you to not live here, at home, with your father?"

"It's not a big deal," I say. "It's not like I've never stayed over at Ezra's before."

"I'm not sure how I feel about you spending all that time with a boy."

I freeze. It's the sort of thing my dad would say before he knew I was a guy. The sort of *father must protect daughter* stereotype that pissed me off before, and sure as hell pisses me off even more now. "Is that what it is?" I ask. "You don't like me staying over at Ezra's because he's a guy?"

My dad hesitates. "His parents aren't with him—"

"I'm a guy too, though," I say, and I'm met with silence. "If I'd been born with a penis, would it be as much of a problem?"

"You're putting words in my mouth," my dad tells me. "The issue would be the same. You two are in that apartment without any adult supervision."

"We're seventeen," I say. "We're going off to college next year. We're not little kids."

My dad's shaking his head. "Never said you were."

Neither of us says anything for a while. There's a scraping of knives against plates, clatter of glasses against the table.

"Besides," my dad says, "just because you're both boys, doesn't mean you can't be . . . *inappropriate* with each other."

"Ezra and I are friends. Best friends. Nothing else going on there." My dad won't meet my eye, and I know I should stop, but there's so much about this conversation that pisses me off. "I like staying down by Ezra's, because at least with him, I never have to feel like he doesn't respect me."

My dad frowns at me. "And what does that mean?"

"I mean he knows that I'm a guy," I say, ignoring the flinch of shame deep inside me—these days, I don't even know if I'm a guy myself. "I don't ever feel like I have to convince him of that. I mean that he calls me by my name: Felix."

"Listen," he says, "it isn't easy to just suddenly switch my idea of who you are in my head. For twelve years, you were my baby g—"

I cut him off before he can say it. "That's never who I was. That's who you assumed I was."

He's quiet. A woman on the TV screen is crying, tears leaving streaks on her fake orange tan. My dad breaks the silence. "I'm trying," he says. "I've shown you that. I've proven that. I don't always get it right, but I'm trying to understand."

Sometimes, I don't know if that's enough. I feel like a shitty son, getting angry at my dad when he's the one who paid for my hormones, my doctors' visits, my surgery, everything—but every time I'm around him, I feel like I have to work hard to prove that I am who I say I am. It pisses me off that he doesn't just accept it. That there's something he has to *understand* in the first place.

"I need you to be a little more patient," my dad tells me. "I've had a certain idea of who you are in my head for twelve years. That's a long time." He hesitates, and I can tell he almost called me by my old name.

My dad won't look at me. I don't know if he even knows how to look at me. He can't see me for who I really am—only who he wants me to be. Maybe this is fucked-up, I don't know. . . but somehow, it's his approval I need most, even more than anyone else's. I need his validation. His understanding, not just acceptance, that he has a son.

I'm not sure that's something he'll ever give me.

I stand up, scratching my chair against the floor, grab my backpack, and head for the door.

"Where're you going?" my dad calls, but I ignore him as I slam it shut behind me.

SIX

EZRA'S EITHER ASLEEP OR NOT HOME WHEN I BUZZ HIS apartment number, and when he doesn't answer his phone, I sit down on the concrete stoop steps, knees curled up to my chest, cheek resting on top of them. It might've been a little overdramatic, storming out of my dad's apartment like that, and guilt is building in my chest. It's going to be awkward as fuck the next time I try to go home.

I must fall asleep like that, leaning against the rusting railing, because when I open my eyes, there's a hand on my shoulder. I blink away the bleariness to see Ezra leaning over me, illuminated by the orange streetlight.

"Hey," he says, voice low. "What're you doing here?"

"Fight with my dad," I murmur, still half-asleep.

He sits down beside me and lets me lean against him

instead of the railing. "You okay?"

I shrug. "Where were you? Special friend's place?"

He nudges into me. "No. Couldn't sleep, so I took a walk."

"Insomnia again?"

"Guess I got used to staying up all night with you."

Ezra helps me to my feet, and we stomp up the steps and to his apartment. He unlocks the door, and I let myself in first. The time on Ezra's stove blinks 11:03. I head straight for the mattress, ready to crash. The two of us can stay up until three in the morning on a good night sometimes, but right now—after that fight with my dad—I'm exhausted.

But before I can drift back to sleep, Ezra sits on the edge of the mattress, kicking off his scuffed Converses. "I know something that'll cheer you up," he says, twisting to look over his shoulder at me.

"Yeah?" I mumble. "What's that?"

He flashes a grin. "A party."

I stare at him. "What?"

"A party," he says again. "Let's have a party. I'll invite some people over."

"You're kidding, right?"

"No," he says. "Why would I be kidding?"

"Because it's eleven o'clock on a Monday night."

"Christ, you're an old fuck," he says. "Real St. Cat's summer parties don't actually start until midnight anyway." I wouldn't know. I'm not usually the partying type. "The dorms are close. People should be able to get here pretty fast.

I'll tell them to bring booze for entry."

He already has his phone out, scrolling through contacts. I reach out a hand to stop him, but he yanks his phone away.

"Look, if you don't want to come to my party, that's fine," he says, standing up, fingers flying over the screen as he—I'm assuming—texts out an invite. "But this is my apartment, so you'll have to wait outside until the party's over."

I groan and roll over, hunching myself into the fetal position. "You're not inviting Declan and his dumbass friends, are you?"

"Who the hell do you think I am?" Ezra says. He starts marching around the apartment, tossing crap into the one trash can he has in the corner of the kitchen. It feels like three minutes barely pass before his intercom starts to buzz. He grins at me as he hits a button, and after listening to echoing footsteps on the staircase outside, there's an impatient knock on Ezra's door.

He throws it open, and Marisol comes sauntering in, makeup smeared across her face, tight dress and combat boots on. She'd clearly already been out. She ignores me as she holds up a six-pack of beer and stares around.

"Where the fuck is everyone?" she says.

"You're the first person here."

"Balls," she says, walking in and dropping the beer on the kitchen counter. "Suckiest party ever, Ezra."

"Relax," he says, grabbing a beer bottle and using his

T-shirt to twist the cap off. "Some serious shit's about to go down."

And he's right. Within the next few minutes, over a dozen people show up. Most are St. Cat's students. Some are people I've never seen before in my life. Ezra asked Leah to bring her speakers, and an iPhone is hooked up, blasting Hayley Kiyoko and BTS. Ezra still hasn't gotten lightbulbs, so the only way to see is from the dim glow of the TV screen, the orange streetlights outside, and the phones people wave around. No one seems to care. A few take advantage of the dark, from the sounds of smacking lips and a little too much moaning. There's dancing, laughing, shouting as a guy yells to pass the weed. Someone brings a string of blinking white Christmas lights, I have no idea why, and half the crowd spends a good few drunken minutes decorating Ezra's apartment with them.

Marisol dances with Hazel, kissing, hands beneath shirts. Austin is there, leaning into Ezra, whispering in his ear, hand on Ezra's leg. Leah and Tyler are screaming the words to an old Lizzo song in each other's faces, jumping up and down. Everyone's shorts and skirts and sneakers and platform heels surround me while I sit on the mattress, back against the wall, watching.

Watching, watching, watching. It feels like that's all I ever do sometimes. Watch other people dance, watch other people kiss. Marisol was the first—and last—person I worked up the nerve to ask out. We never kissed. We barely touched. What do you call someone who's never been kissed? A lip virgin? I guess I'm a lip virgin.

Why am I always the person who just sits to the side and watches? What is it about me that no one likes, that no one wants? It's like it's too much for other people—me having brown skin, and being queer, and being trans on top of that . . . or, maybe that's just what I tell myself because I'm too afraid to put myself out there again, too afraid of being rejected and getting hurt. Maybe it's a little bit of both.

I pull out my phone and place it on long-exposure mode, snapping a photo. When enough time has passed, I look at it. The photo is a smear of cell phone and Christmas lights, streaks of white across the screen, blurs of legs and shoes.

I go to Instagram to post the image, but I hesitate. The piece of shit who'd messaged me—I'm positive it was Declan with a stupid fake account—hasn't said anything else, but I don't know if posting this would make him want to message me again. I shouldn't be afraid to post photos on my own Instagram account, but I am. Besides . . . I don't want anyone to see this picture. It feels too vulnerable. Too lonely. People right here at this party could check their phones and see it. It'd be weird.

But something like this—I want, no, *need* to put the photo out into the world, into the universe, as if the second that picture exists somewhere besides my phone is the moment I'll start to exist, too. I log into the luckyliquid95 account and post it. The caption reads "the watcher." Perfect.

There's a furious pounding on the door. When Ezra

cracks it open, his upstairs neighbor yells that it's one in the morning, some people have to wake up for work tomorrow, turn the fucking music down or he's going to call the cops, etc. Ezra is nowhere near as petty as me—Ezra's neighbor is a jerk, so I 100 percent would've kept the party going—but Ez says things are winding down anyway and turns off the music. People eventually trickle out the door, yelling that they'll see each other in class tomorrow, laughter and loud voices and footsteps echoing on the staircase, until finally it's just me, Ezra, Marisol, Leah, and Austin.

Ezra and Austin are sitting by the open window as they smoke weed, whispering, eyes shining as they lean forward and laugh, making intense eye contact. I feel like I'm witnessing something private, like I shouldn't even be looking at them. Leah and Marisol are lying down flat on their backs on the hardwood floor, arms and legs spread out like they're about to make snow angels. After Marisol and I attempted our three dates, she declared to everyone one morning before class that she's only interested in dating other girls. I try not to be too self-involved, but it almost felt like she was saying that just to make a dig at me—to say that while I'm misogynistic, she is clearly not (how can she be, when she loves girls so much that she'll only date them?); to suggest, somehow, that she only dates girls, which is why she was willing to go on a date with me. I don't know if she's purposefully trying to hurt me—if she even realizes she's doing it, or if I'm just being oversensitive. It can be hard to get a feel for what Marisol's thinking, and I'm pretty sure she likes it that way. What's worse is that I can't even talk to Ezra about it—not without admitting what Marisol had said.

Marisol is in the middle of a monologue about Hazel. "She's so confusing. I mean, what was that tonight? Is she just fucking with me? She'll do this thing where she won't answer a text for, like, five hours, and I don't know if she's just playing it cool, or if she actually just doesn't look at her phone."

"Probably just not looking at her phone," Leah tells her. "Anyone would jump for a chance to make out with you." I have a feeling that Leah is only half joking.

"I know, right?" Marisol says, then adds with a laugh, "Sorry you never got a chance, Felix."

I'm on my stomach, head on my folded arms. There's a pinch of shame in my chest. "Thanks, I guess?"

Ezra's heard us from the window. He groans with a grin. "Totally forgot you two dated." He pauses. "Is it weird that you went out for, like, approximately three seconds?"

"First of all, fuck you, it was two weeks," Marisol says. "And second of all . . ." In the dim light of the muted TV and the blinking Christmas lights, she sits up to face me. "Well, it isn't weird for me. It just didn't work out. It happens. Is it weird for you, Felix?"

She smiles a little, like she's taunting me. She knows that things are weird as fuck. I hesitate. I never told Ezra about what Marisol said. It's embarrassing, on the edge of humiliating, and I don't want to deal with the awkwardness. Ezra would be pissed, he and Marisol would fight, and there'd be unnecessary drama at St. Cat's. Marisol's stupid-ass comment isn't worth fucking up my last school year over. Unlike Declan Keane's gallery.

"Uh," I say, suddenly aware that everyone's staring at me. "No. Not weird."

Leah scratches the back of her neck, and Austin bites his lip. Ezra gives a Chrissy Teigen grimace-smile. "So, really fucking awkward, then?"

Marisol shrugs. "I had no idea you felt awkward," she tells me. "We can talk about it, I guess, if you want to."

No, I definitely don't want to talk about it—especially when Marisol somehow has a way of making things out to be my problem. As if she has nothing to do with why I'm uncomfortable with her. As if she has no memory of telling me that I'm a misogynist.

Ezra walks over, plopping down beside me on the mattress. Austin puts out the bud and follows, sitting cross-legged next to Leah on the floor. "We can make a Dr. Phil episode out of it," Ezra suggests.

"Dr. Phil?" Marisol echoes. "What are you, fifty?"

Ezra ignores her. "Group therapy. It could be good for us."

I can't think of anything more awful. "Thanks," I say, "but no thanks."

Leah grins up at me. Her face becomes extraordinarily red when she's intoxicated. "Felix, can I ask you a question?" She goes on without waiting for my response. "You dated

Marisol," she says, "but are you also into guys? Since you went out with Ezra, I mean."

Marisol begins cackling. Ezra chokes on air, and I screw my face up in confusion. "What?"

Leah's surprised. "You two went out, didn't you?"

"No, we really didn't."

Marisol's laughter gets louder.

"Oh," Leah says, looking at Marisol and Austin in confusion. "I thought you went out. I'm not the only one who thought that, right?"

"Everyone always thinks that we did," Ezra says, giving a small, embarrassed smile without looking at Austin. Austin takes a sip from Leah's beer bottle. Awkward.

"Yeah," I say, "I'm also into guys. Why?"

Leah recovers quickly. "I was just wondering if you consider yourself bisexual or pansexual or anything. I thought I was bisexual," Leah tells us, "but I think it was only because it was like I had to be. It was almost like a habit, until finally one day, I was like—wait, why do I say I'm attracted to guys when literally the last guy I thought was cute was Simba?"

There's silence. Marisol blinks at Leah. "You know that Simba was a lion, right?"

Austin adds, "And a cartoon."

"Simba was fucking hot, okay?" Leah says. "That jungle scene with Nala? Come on now." She pauses. "Though now that I think about it, maybe I was actually more attracted to Nala . . ."

"I thought Kovu was pretty hot," Ezra tells us, leaning against the wall.

"I was all about Lilo's sister," Marisol says. "Those curves. Seriously."

"Zuko, too," Ezra adds.

"Oh," Leah says, sitting up. "What about Mulan? And those fucking Li Shang bisexual vibes?"

I'd been super into *Mulan*, I suddenly remember, until she started dressing like a girl again. I was disappointed when she was forced to leave the army, forced to say that she was a woman. It's funny—I hadn't really thought about it until now, but it's yet another clue. My memories are peppered with little pieces of evidence that I'd always been trans, even before I knew what *trans* was. Sometimes, I'm a little frustrated with myself. What if I'd been one of the folks who knew, without a doubt, that they were trans since the time they were toddlers? How many years have I wasted living this lie, and all because I hadn't even known that I could've been living my truth all along? But I'm also grateful. Happy that I'd figured it out at all.

"Wait," Ezra says, "is everyone here queer?"

"Yeah, of course," Marisol says. "I only hang out with gay people."

Leah twists a curl around her finger. "Straight people are so exhausting."

"Did you all see that article on whether women have any value if they don't get married and have children?" Austin asks.

"I see at least one thing a day that makes me wonder if the straight people are all right."

"And then there was that article saying that queer TV shows are making more people gay."

"I never saw a single TV show with a gay person until, like, last year," Leah says, "and I didn't turn out to be straight. So."

"The shows aren't making people gay," Austin says. "They're just making people realize it's even . . . I don't know, a possibility. It's like we're all brainwashed from the time we're babies to think that we have to be straight."

"The straights say that we've got an agenda to turn people gay," Marisol says, "but then will try to force toddlers on each other and say it's *so cute* and they're *destined to get married*. Seriously."

I understand what Austin means. Kind of like reading *I Am J* for the first time, and everything just *clicking*. I'd already gone through the whole *questioning sexuality* thing a few years before that. I'd had crushes on girls and guys before, but I never had a crush on both a girl and a guy at the same time. It was almost like a cycle. I'd be attracted to girls for a few months, then to guys for a few months, then back to girls again. And whenever I was into a guy, looking back on it now, it's difficult to figure out if I was actually into him, if I just wanted to *be* him—or both. It was one of the most confusing times of my life. I thought, for some reason, that I had to figure out which I was more attracted to—either I was gay or I was straight. One day, a few weeks after meeting Ezra—right around when he started dating Declan—I told him that I felt like I was going crazy.

"I don't get it," he said, eyebrows pinched together. "Why do you have to choose?"

And it really was as easy as that. It took a second to get out of the habit, but I eventually stopped worrying about the question and just went with the cycles—and as I stopped worrying about it, I started to notice different things about the people I'm attracted to, and the sorts of things that connect them. Confidence. A flame inside of them almost, like they know exactly who they are, and no one's ever going to be able to tell them otherwise.

"Ezra," Leah says, "are you bisexual, too?"

Ezra's a lazy drunk. He shrugs with a slow smile. "I honestly don't care that much about labels. I mean, I know they're important to a lot of people, and I can see why—I'm not knocking them. It's just . . . I kind of wish we could exist without having to worry about putting ourselves into categories. If there were no straight people, no violence or abuse or homophobia or anything, would we even need labels, or would we just be? Sometimes I wonder if labels can get in the way. Like, if I was adamant that I'm straight, does that force me into only liking girls? What if that'd stopped me from falling in love with a guy? I don't know," he says again. "I get that labels can be important."

"They connect us. They help create community," Leah says. "I can see what you're saying. If the world was perfect, maybe we wouldn't need labels. But the world isn't perfect, and labels can really be a source of pride—especially when we've got to deal with so much crap. I'm really freaking proud to be a lesbian."

"Yeah, and that's cool," Ezra says, nodding. "I like that a lot. I just don't really want to use labels for myself. I feel better without them."

"Okay," Leah says. "That's your choice. I respect that."

We all fall quiet, and it's late. I can tell everyone's tired, and my eyes are starting to close. My pocket buzzes, jerking me awake. Marisol's texting on her phone from the floor. Fear spikes through me. What if it's another fucked-up message on Instagram? I grab my phone and swipe the screen open. The notification *is* from Instagram—but this time, it's not for my real account. It's for luckyliquid95.

"You all right?" Ezra asks, nudging me with his knee. I give a distracted nod as I tap my phone's screen. My image from the party, the streak of lights and blur of legs, got a like—and a comment. I sit up, excitement beating through me.

thekeanester123: Nice image. Really draws the viewer in. Also interesting that the subject is the watcher, but in a way, viewers are the watchers as well.

Jesus Christ. The rush of excitement is instantly gone. Of course Declan Keane would be a pretentious dick, even on Instagram.

"Felix," Ezra says, "what's going on?"

I hand him the phone.

"Oh, holy shit," he says.

"What is it?" Marisol asks, leaning forward to see—but I shake my head quickly at Ezra. There're two types of gossips: Ezra, the kind who's all ears and happily listens to any and every sort of secret; and Marisol, the kind who spills all the secrets in the first place. If she finds out about my plan with Declan, he'll know about it before dawn.

Mari notices me shaking my head. A shadow of hurt crosses her face. "Seriously?"

Ezra winces. "Sorry. This is a little too personal."

She rolls her eyes and gets to her feet. "Fine. Whatever. I know when I'm not wanted."

Ezra gives a halfhearted wave. "See you tomorrow."

She blows a kiss at him. "Goodbye, my love."

"I should go home, too," Austin says.

"Same," Leah says, jumping to her feet.

Austin hesitates, meeting Ezra's eye. Ezra should probably get up and walk Austin out, after having his tongue down the guy's throat for approximately an hour, but he stays beside me, blinking up at Austin. "Ah—I'll text you, okay?"

Austin gives a half smile. "Okay."

The three head out, and the door slams shut behind them. Ezra holds out the phone.

"Austin, huh?" I say as I take it back.

Ezra bites his lip, rubbing his neck. "Yeah, I didn't really see it coming."

"Is he a candidate for your new special friend?"

Ezra shrugs, and it's clear he doesn't want to talk about it. I don't know why, but I drop it and turn my attention back to Declan's comment, nerves starting to course through me as I read and reread the message. How do I respond? If I don't answer his comment in exactly the right way, I might mess this up. This could be my one and only chance to get him to actually talk to me. Figure out a secret of his that I can use to fuck up his world.

"What're you going to do?" Ezra asks in a hushed voice.

"I have no idea."

He glances up at me. "I mean—you're going to answer, right?"

"Yeah, of course. I just don't know what I'm going to say."

The two of us stare at the phone.

"Well," Ezra says, lying down, "I'm going to bed."

"Wait, what? Aren't you going to help me figure this out?"

"Sorry." His back faces me. "I can't in good conscience help your evil Slytherin tendencies."

This is news to me. "You were all for ruining Declan's life a few days ago."

"Yeah, but that was before I realized this is literally the sort of thing we could get arrested for," he says, looking over his shoulder at me. "I don't know, Felix. Maybe you shouldn't do this."

"Are you serious?" I say, anger rising. I almost feel like he's betrayed me. "It's easy for you to forget what Declan did to me, I guess—you weren't the one he humiliated."

"No, I wasn't," Ezra agrees, "but that's where the *school* should come in. We should go to the dean or something. Not—I don't know, this way-too-complicated revenge plan. It just doesn't seem like it's worth it."

The anger snaps. "I'm the one he fucked with, Ezra, not you. I'm the one he deadnamed. The one whose old pictures he put up in a fucking gallery. The one he's been sending fucked-up Instagram messages to. *I'm* the one who gets to say if this way-too-complicated revenge plan is worth it. Spoiler alert: it fucking is."

"Okay," Ezra whispers. "You're right. I'm sorry."

Neither of us says anything for a while. I can feel the anger swelling in my chest, my eyes stinging, and it's suddenly a little hard to breathe. I know it's not Ezra I'm really angry at. I shouldn't have taken it out on him. The upstairs neighbor, probably still pissed about the party, starts stomping around and throwing shit on the ground. The apartment walls vibrate and echo. A car blasting the newest Drake song rushes by. I can hear Ezra swallow.

"What did you mean," he says, "by fucked-up Instagram messages?"

I didn't want to tell him, but I guess it's out in the open now anyway. "I don't know. There was this anonymous account, grandequeen69. They told me—I don't even want to say what they told me. But I'm pretty sure it's Declan."

"Shit, Felix. Why didn't you say anything?"

I shake my head. "I don't know. It doesn't matter. As long

as I can take Declan down—it doesn't matter."

Ezra frowns, not meeting my eye. It's obvious he's back to thinking the same thing he had that first day: there's no real proof that any of this is Declan, not really.

"It's just," he tells me, "I don't want you to . . . I don't know. Obsess over this?"

"Obsess?"

"Obsess over this, when you could be putting your energy into other things." He twists to me, leaning on an elbow. "Like your portfolio."

"I'm fine," I lie. "I don't need you to worry about me. I just need you to be supportive. All right?"

Ezra turns onto his back, staring up at his ceiling as there's a particularly loud crash. "Okay. All right."

I take a deep breath, swiping on my phone again, squinting at Declan's comment in the dim light. Ezra and I don't argue often, but when we do, I try to move on and pretend it didn't happen, and he's usually on the same page. "Christ. What the hell am I supposed to say?"

Ez doesn't look at me. Maybe he's still a little mad. "I guess one way to get him to talk would be to ask a question, right? Declan loves talking about himself."

"Yeah—you're right," I say. I immediately know what to ask. My fingers fly across the screen.

luckyliquid95: Thanks! Do you like long exposure photography?
I stare at the phone, waiting to see if he'll respond.

"Felix," Ezra says, "you're obsessing."

"I'm not obsessing."

"You're one hundred percent obsessing."

I turn my back to him and hold the phone screen up, staring, waiting for a response—until, yes, I get a notification.

thekeanester123: Not usually. Overexposure can be a little overdone.

I roll my eyes.

thekeanester123: But you used it well.

I bite my lip, thumbs hesitating—I can't take too long to respond, he might get bored of waiting and stop talking to me altogether, but I still have to be careful of what I say. . . .

luckyliquid95: What's your favorite medium?

thekeanester123: It depends. There's a lot that can inspire me. I don't like to box myself in.

Still pretentious, but I can kind of understand what he means.

luckyliquid95: What're some things that inspire you?

He doesn't respond. "Shit," I mutter, biting my lip, waiting, waiting. Maybe it got too late—it's almost two in the morning now—and he decided to go to bed. Maybe he just got bored, and I asked too many questions. I can't give up here. I try again.

luckyliquid95: I'm still trying to figure out what inspires me.

Ezra's breathing softens beside me, and I know he's fallen asleep.

luckyliquid95: I guess I just . . . haven't experienced enough to make the kind of art I want to make. How am I supposed to make

people feel things, if I've never felt anything myself?

A few seconds pass, and then:

thekeanester123: Yeah. I know what you mean.

My eyebrows raise at that one. Declan's always acting like he's the Second Coming. This is the first time I've seen even a hint of vulnerability from him in the past two years.

luckyliquid95: What sort of things do you want to experience?

I can't help it—I hold my breath. This is the kind of question where Declan's answer could tell me something he wouldn't want anyone knowing—a secret I could use against him. But this is also the sort of question that might just take this conversation a little too far. Why would he tell something like that to a stranger?

But a second later, he responds:

thekeanester123: I don't really know, to be honest. I guess not knowing is a part of it all. Not even knowing what experiences I need to live to be inspired.

Shit. He's still a dick, but that's a pretty good answer.

thekeanester123: What about you?

I swallow, hesitating—I know what I want to say to that question, but would this be taking the conversation over the edge?

I take a risk:

luckyliquid95: I want to fall in love.

I stare, unblinking, refreshing my Instagram every few seconds—but he doesn't say anything else.

That's it.

Plan ruined.

I can try again, but there's little to no chance he'd respond if he was freaked out by my oversharing.

Fucking hell.

I toss my phone and lie down on my back with a groan. Ezra mumbles in his sleep and rolls over to slide an arm around my waist, nestling his head against my shoulder. His hair smells like IPA, and it's too effing hot to cuddle tonight.

"Ezra," I mutter, pushing him off.

He peeks open an eye at me, glowing in the blinking Christmas lights. "Felix. Jesus Christ. Why're you still awake? Go to sleep."

I close my eyes. "I can't. I think I fucked up. He stopped responding."

"Who stopped responding?"

Ezra is basically useless when he's half-asleep. "Declan."

"Oh," he says. He doesn't say anything for a long time, and I think he's fallen asleep again—until he says, "Declan Keane doesn't deserve you."

"What?" I look at him. "What the fuck are you talking about?"

"I would know," he says. "I dated him for, like, almost a year, and I can tell you that he doesn't deserve any of your attention. You're too good for him."

I roll my eyes. I can't tell if he's drunk, high, asleep, or all of the above.

"Can we cuddle?" he asks.

"It's too hot, Ez."

He doesn't say anything. I think he's sulking, but it's too dark to tell.

I sigh. "Fine. But don't lie down on top of me. You're too heavy."

He's immediately at my side again, arm around my waist, IPA-smelling hair falling onto my cheek. He's back asleep within seconds, but I have too many thoughts swirling through my head, too many dreams of Declan Keane and Instagram and that fucking gallery in the lobby of St. Cat's. I sleep on and off, waking up every hour or so, sweating—it really is too hot, and Ezra's managed to roll half of his body onto me, long legs tangled with my own.

When I open my eyes again, sunlight is pouring in through the window. My mouth feels like sandpaper. I grab my phone: 8:24. Fuck. We've got five minutes to make it to class on time.

I roll Ezra off me, jumping to my feet—but before I take another step, I see a notification from Instagram. My heart stops for a split second. I swipe, and my conversation with Declan pops open.

thekeanester123: I wish I could fall in love, too.

SEVEN

DECLAN KEANE WANTS TO FALL IN LOVE.

That's the only thing I can think about on the walk to St. Cat's. Ezra is still half-asleep, dragging his feet and moaning that he just wants to skip today. I'd usually be up for it, after staying up until three in the morning—but I can't help but want to see Declan. Look at him, after the conversation we'd had.

Declan Keane wants to fall in love.

Is that a big enough secret I can ruin his life with?

No, probably not. But it's still interesting.

"Hey, Ezra," I say as we walk.

He grunts. "What?"

"Were you and Declan in love?"

He furrows his brow at me, and even behind his sunglasses,

I can tell he's glaring at me. "What the fuck sort of question is that?"

"I really want to know," I say, defensive.

"Why would you want to know?"

I shrug. "After that message Declan sent . . ."

I'd told Ezra about the conversation, of course, but he's been less than enthused. He sighs loudly. He's never been much of a morning person.

"Love's a strong word," he says. "I don't know. We liked each other fine enough, I guess. But he never said the words *I love you.*"

"Did you love him?"

"You're being so effing nosy today."

"Sorry," I say in a tone that's pretty obvious I'm not sorry at all.

He doesn't answer, not right away—but then he says, "I mean, at one point, I thought, maybe . . ."

I clench my jaw. "Really?"

"Yeah, really," he says. "I mean, the guy's a jerk, but that was my first serious relationship. I don't know. I guess I got all wrapped up in the feels."

He flashes a smile at me for a split second, but even if he tries to hide it, I can still see the pain in the way he hunches his shoulders a little, the way the corners of his lips twitch. I nudge him with my elbow. "Well, you know—his loss and everything."

"Right," Ezra says.

Declan Keane wants to be in love—and he may or may not have loved Ezra. It's a strange thing to suddenly know about him. It was easier not knowing. Easier not to see him as a person with feelings, when he's been such a piece of shit, putting my old photos up in a gallery and deadnaming me and sending me a fucking awful, taunting message on Instagram. Even when I'd thought we were friends—before he suddenly turned his back on me and Ezra—he never really talked about himself this way.

I glance up at Declan. He's sitting at the table beside mine, as usual, and as fate would have it, the only stool open was just a few feet away from his. Jill's giving us her usual morning check-in speech—today's topic: love the craft, not the artist.

"It's important to focus on the craft without knowing the creator," she says. "Does it matter who the creator is? Should the artist's identity matter when it comes to reviewing and connecting with a piece they created?"

"Yes," I whisper to Ezra, "especially if the artist is an asshole."

Jill's head spins to me. It's like she has supersonic hearing or something, I swear to God. "What was that?" she says with her over-friendly smile, excited that someone in her class actually has an opinion for once.

I sigh. Jill loves these early-morning debates a little too much. "I said it does matter if the artist is an asshole."

"Why's that?"

I shrug. "I don't know. I mean, isn't all art a piece of the creator's soul? If the creator is an evil piece of shit, doesn't that mean we're being influenced by evil in their work?"

She seems to consider, shine in her eyes—seriously, it's too early for anyone to be this excited. "But isn't the craft all about expressing the creator's point to the best of their ability? Does morality have anything to do with the craft of the piece itself?"

Declan is leaning back on his stool, at danger of falling off, but somehow managing to balance himself and look relaxed at the same time. "Besides," he says, "who gets to be the judge of what's *evil* and what isn't?"

"Great point!" Jill says, nodding. "Yes, great point. Should the question of morality be kept out of art?"

Declan throws a fake smile my way. I roll my eyes. "Morality, at its essence, defines what is human," I say. "Keeping questions of morality out of art suggests keeping humanity out of art itself."

Jill nods slowly. "Yes, that's an interesting point as well."

"So you would restrict artwork?" Declan asks me. "Censor it?" He nods his head at Ezra's *Judith I and the Head of Holofernes* Klimt tattoo—Ezra blinks at Declan with a blank face, still half-asleep. "It isn't exactly moral to cut someone's head off. Should that piece never have been created?"

I shake my head. "No, but there's a line."

"What line is that?"

"A line that could hurt people."

"Hurt people?"

"Yes. Propaganda against different races, illustrations depicting groups of humans as lesser than others. Art for the sake of art, without any regard to other people—"

I pause. There's too much emotion in my voice, and everyone's staring at me now, people turned in their seats to watch me over their shoulders. Ezra's waking up, glancing between me and Declan. I sit straighter in my seat. "There needs to be moral judgment in creation."

It could've ended there. Should've ended there. But Declan Keane—he never knows when to just fucking stop. "I guess this is in reference to that gallery of you," he says.

The room goes still. Silent.

Ezra gets tense beside me. "Shut up, Declan."

Declan shrugs. "If that's what you're talking about, you should just say it."

"I said shut *up*, Declan."

"It's hard to say who the artist is, or what their motive was, but—"

My foot swings out before my brain even registers what I've done. I kick Declan's stool, and he falls backward, crashing to the ground. There's a scream from our table—Leah—and Jill rushes forward as Declan sits himself up, hand to the back of his head. He checks his palm. There's no blood, but that doesn't stop him from looking up at me with full-on rage.

"Are you fucking kidding me?" he shouts.

"Okay, all right." Jill tries to help him up, but he pushes her hands away, jumping to his feet.

Shit. Shit, shit, shit. "Accident."

"Bullshit!" Declan tries to get in my face, but Ezra's between the two of us in a heartbeat, hands out.

"It was an accident!"

Jill's shaking her head. Fuck.

Declan points at me, still trying to get around Ezra. "You kicked my stool. I could've gotten hurt. I could've died."

"Don't be so melodramatic."

"Fuck you, Felix—"

"Enough!"

Jill's voice echoes across the classroom, all hints of her earlier enthusiasm gone. Everyone's eyes are wide. Austin's hand is to his mouth, and Hazel has her phone out, filming the whole thing from across the room. My heart drops. St. Cat's has a zero-tolerance policy for violence, and Declan is just about the worst person I could've fucked with. His dad could have me kicked out in about three seconds flat—especially if me getting kicked out means Declan won't have any more competition for a spot at Brown. I can kiss both Brown and that scholarship goodbye.

"I'm sorry," I say, my voice hoarse—a whisper in the otherwise silent room. "I swear, it was an accident."

Declan's jaw and fists clench, unclench, clench.

"Dean's office," Jill says. "Both of you. Now."

"I said I was sorry—"

"Why *me*? He's the one who—"

"*Now*," she says again.

Ezra looks the way I feel—terrified—as I grab my back-pack and walk out of the room, Declan trailing behind. *Fuck.* I wasn't thinking when I kicked. I didn't mean to do it—it'd barely been a thought. He just wouldn't shut up about the gallery, and he was talking about it so smugly, like he was rubbing it in my face, the fact that he'd been the one to post my photos and my birthname in the first place, had sent me that message on Instagram—

The halls have brick walls, dark wood floors. There aren't any elevators, so we have to stomp down about three airless staircases, my shirt sticking to my back in the heat. Declan follows, but not closely behind, as if he can't trust himself not to shove me down the steps if he gets too close. We make it to the first floor where there are a bunch of offices, including the dean's. The secretary listens to our oversimplified story—"we were sent by Jill"—and she tells us to wait on the metal bench outside the dean's office.

She leaves us there. I close my eyes and take in a deep breath. I need to have a level head when I walk into the office. I need to get my story straight. It was an accident. I kicked out without meaning to. My foot slipped. Anything.

Declan sits at the edge of the bench, knee bouncing up and down. He checks the back of his head again, as if he thinks he'll have magically produced blood this time around. He won't look at me. I'm having a hard time looking at him myself.

"You're such a prick," Declan mutters, arms crossed.

"Kettle. Black. Et cetera."

"I'm a prick because I disagreed with you about the place of morality in art?"

He watches me, and I hesitate. It's weird, but—right here, right now, I remember the conversation we'd had last night. Remember that the guy in front of me had been the one typing those messages into his phone. I bite my lip, look away.

"No," I say, "you're a prick because you always treat me like shit."

"How's that?"

The gallery. That Instagram message. I almost say the words. He waits, staring at me, and I could say it—could reveal that I *know* it was him—but then I'd also be giving up on my payback plan. If I tell him, he'd probably figure out that I'm the one he's been talking with online. I could go to the dean as a last resort, but the most he'd get is a slap on the wrist. He wouldn't get any of the shit he deserves, not until I manage to find out his darkest secret, something I can use to destroy him. I can't tell him that I know it was him—not yet.

"How, exactly, have I treated you like shit?" Declan demands again.

"Seriously?" I say. "You've treated me and Ezra like shit for the past two years for no fucking reason."

He rolls his eyes. "I may treat Ezra like shit," he says, "but I don't treat *you* like shit. And it's not for no fucking reason, either."

"You're kidding, right?" He takes in an impatient breath,

turning away, but I keep going. "You've been a condescending asshole to me any chance you get. You talk shit about me and Ez, you're always trying to get us into trouble—"

"You're just pissed because we're both applying to Brown, and you know you're not going to get in."

"Oh, Jesus Christ, fuck off."

"What?" he says, looking at me again. "It's the truth, right? You know I'm going to get in. Might get the scholarship, too. And you can't get your shit together. You're never on time, never working on your portfolio, and you're pissed about it, so you're taking your shit out on me."

I shake my head, staring at the closed dean's door. "I have my shit together."

He snorts. "Okay. Whatever you say."

We're quiet for a long time.

"You don't even need the scholarship," I tell him.

"It's not exactly your place to say whether I need the scholarship or not."

"From what I know of you, you don't need the scholarship. Not in comparison to me."

His voice is quiet. "You don't know shit about me."

Before I can say anything else, the dean's office door opens, and Dean Fletcher, with her silver-streaked Afro, waves us into her office of wooden panels. We take our seats in front of the heavy desk.

She holds her hands together as she watches us. "What happened? Ms. Brody called me to say there'd been a fight."

I stare at my marked-up sneakers, waiting for Declan to jump in, but he's quiet also.

"Come on," she says, "let's hear it."

"We had an argument," Declan says slowly.

"And?" she prompts. "I heard you fell?"

Declan takes in a deep breath, not looking at me. "It was a freak accident, I guess. His foot slipped, I was leaning back . . ."

I glance up at him. The dean raises an eyebrow, looking between the two of us. "An accident?"

Declan doesn't say anything else. I nod slowly. "Uh—yeah," I say. "An accident."

The dean looks from me to Declan and back to me again. "All right," she finally says, clearly not believing either of us, but there's nothing she can do unless there's an official complaint. "I urge you both to work through your problems so that you won't be disruptive to your future classes. In the meantime, can I see a handshake and a truce?"

She's taken things too far. Declan's roll of eyes shows he agrees with me.

"Let's go," she says. "A handshake and an apology, from both of you."

Jesus Christ, let's just get it over with. I swivel in my seat to Declan, hand stuck out. His arms are crossed, but he uncrosses one and plants his hand in mine. It's larger, an artist's hands with dried paint in the creases of his skin. Declan meets my eye.

"I'm sorry," he says, squeezing my hand a little as he shakes.

"I'm sorry, too," I tell him.

We let go immediately.

The dean stands, scratching her chair back. "That's a start."

Declan is out the door first, several paces ahead of me, not bothering to look over his shoulder. I don't know why I do it, why I even bother, but I struggle to keep up, striding down the hall beside him.

"Why'd you say that?"

He doesn't look at me. "Say what?"

"That it was an accident."

"So it *wasn't* an accident?" he says. "Shocker."

I don't speak—just keep walking down the wood-paneled hall, until he throws open the door at the end, letting us out into the lobby. My heart tightens and my stomach twists. Declan finally stops walking. He turns to look at me.

"Listen," he says, "I didn't mean anything by bringing up the gallery. I was just making a point—"

"You don't get to use my pain to make your point."

He lets out a sharp breath. He stands there for a second, moving his jaw back and forth, and I stare at him, waiting, all too aware of the fact that I'm facing Declan right here, right now, in the very space he used to hurt me.

"I said it was an accident because it wouldn't be worth going through four months of disciplinary hearings just to get you expelled."

"Okay," I say slowly.

He takes a step forward. "And I also want you to know that, when I get into Brown over you, it isn't because I got you kicked out of school," he tells me. "It'll be because I deserve it more than you."

I stare at him blankly. "I'm always amazed by the depths of your bullshit."

A smile twitches on his face, and for a flash, he looks as surprised as I am. Declan Keane, laughing at something I said?

He recovers quickly, looking at the white tile. "Sorry, I guess," he says, "for mentioning the gallery."

He turns on his heel, leaving me in the lobby with nothing but an echoing sensation of *What in the holy fuck just happened?*

EIGHT

DECLAN KEANE HAS NEVER APOLOGIZED. NOT ONCE, NOT ever, not for anything he pulled with me and Ezra.

"Maybe he's just not as much of an asshole as we like to think he is," Ezra says, eyes closed. He sounds bored, like he's already over talking about Declan for the day—and, I mean, if I'm going to be honest, I think Ezra's been tired of talking about Declan since the minute they broke up. It's kind of impressive, actually: when Ezra's feelings were hurt, he said he would move on, and that's exactly what he did. Unlike me. When someone hurts me, I either obsess over how to convince them I'm worthy of their love or obsess over how to destroy them.

We're lying down in the park grass with warm cans of Pabst hidden in our backpacks. Classes are over, and it's a quiet Tuesday—no cookouts, no barking dogs or screaming children. Just the breeze and some faraway chatter from an older couple sitting on a park bench. Ezra's phone is playing Solange and SZA and Mila J singing about how she's in airplane mode and don't need no drama, and it's so calming, so relaxing, the heat from the sun beating down on my face and my shoulders and my arms.

"I mean," Ezra continues, "no one likes to admit it, but we can all be assholes. We all fuck up sometimes. As long as we learn and grow and do better next time. Right?"

"It almost sounds like you're trying to make excuses for Declan."

He frowns a little, eyes still closed. "No. I'm just saying—I don't know, maybe we don't know the full story. Maybe he's not as bad as we like to think he is. It's easy to assign roles to people. Easier to just think that Declan Keane is an asshole, and that's that."

I squint at him. "Are you high?"

He opens one eye. "No. Why?"

"You just sound a little high."

"I'll take that as a compliment."

"Wasn't a compliment, but okay."

He reaches up and hooks an arm around my neck so that in about three seconds flat we're wrestling in the grass. Ezra wins, of course, pinning me down, grinning at me—until he just collapses, cackling as I struggle to push him off. He rolls over onto the grass again. The elderly couple is watching us with a smile.

"I guess I kind of understand what you were saying, though," I tell Ezra. "With locking in an idea of someone in your head."

"Yeah?"

The words are coming out faster than I can keep up with them. "Yeah. And, like, I think we do that for ourselves, too."

"How so?"

I'm not sure I'm even ready to talk about this. It's hard, maybe even impossible, to articulate the feelings I've got swarming through me—all of these questions about my identity. But I've already started, and Ezra's watching me expectantly, and—I don't know, maybe speaking about all of this will help me understand.

"With me, for example," I tell him. "I locked in this idea of who I was. I told myself I'm a guy, and that's that, nothing else to really think about."

Ezra goes quiet. He props his head up as he watches me, waiting.

"And I mean, for a long time, that's what I thought, no questions asked, since I did the whole coming-out thing, and I put my dad through so much."

"Okay, sorry, just—let me interrupt you real quick," Ezra says. "You didn't *put your dad through anything*. But okay. Yes. Continue."

"Well, whatever," I say. "I mean I made this big deal about being a guy, and now . . ."

"And now?"

I shrug a little, embarrassed to actually say it. I feel guilty—ashamed, that I've been questioning my identity all over again. "Sometimes I feel like I'm definitely a guy, no doubt about it. But then other times . . ." I take a deep breath and let the words out. "There's just this niggling."

"Niggling?"

"Yeah. A niggling. Like something isn't quite right, you know? I've been doing research online, trying to figure it out, and . . ."

Ezra's nodding slowly, but I don't think he really gets it, and now I feel embarrassed and ashamed and stupid on top of that.

"Never mind," I say quickly, hiding my head in my folded arms, lying down on my stomach.

"No, hey," Ezra said. "Okay, I don't really know what you mean, because I've never really questioned my gender identity before—but that doesn't mean I'm not listening. It's okay to keep questioning, isn't it?"

"Yeah," I say, a little hesitation creeping into my voice. "I guess it's just kind of like—I don't know, when Declan called me a *fraud* . . ."

"Oh, come on. No, really. You're going to let something that asshole said get in your head?"

"I thought he wasn't an asshole."

"I said he might not be as much of an asshole as we think, not that he isn't one." Ezra grins at me, but even as it fades, he keeps watching me carefully. "Seriously. Forget him or what anyone else thinks. Do what you need for yourself."

"I guess you're right."

"You *guess* I'm right?"

"You're definitely right."

Ezra smirks at me and plops a big hand on top of my curls. "I love you, Felix. Okay?"

I glance up at him, and Ezra's watching me without looking away, just staring at me, waiting for me to say something—for any sort of reaction—but what the hell do I say to that? Ezra's never said *I love you* like that before. I know it's supposed to be something friends who love one another can say, in theory, but . . . it makes me feel a little too vulnerable right now.

"Thanks," I say, a little uncertain.

He pinches my cheek and lets go when I swat his hand. "Just let me know if I should use different pronouns for you."

I nod. "Yeah. Okay."

We drink enough cans of Pabst until we're a fair amount of drunk. The sprinklers on the kids' side of the park are on, and we go running through them, shouting and chasing each other until we're soaked through. We dry off on the swings, going back and forth, the metal chains creaking.

"God, I'm so excited for Pride," Ezra says. "All the parties . . . and the march, too, obviously."

"Obviously."

"Are you going to come to the march with me this year?"

"Hard pass."

Ezra loves anything and everything to do with Pride month. He goes to the Manhattan parade every. Single. Year. He even stays from beginning to end, which I don't think is actually possible, since the parade is, what, ten-hours-plus long? But he somehow manages it, live-texting me and posting pictures and videos on Instagram the entire time. The parade is just a little too . . . emotional, I guess? Everyone screaming, people crying, those freaking floats where people are *literally getting married and having their first freaking dance*—I mean, I don't know. It's just all a little much for me, but Ezra *loves* that shit. He says that the Pride March is a place of pure joy. Whatever the hell that means.

"Fine," Ezra says, not looking at me. "I might have someone else to go with this year anyway."

I frown at him. "Yeah? Who—your special friend?"

Ezra doesn't laugh this time.

"No, shit—really?" I pause. "Is it Austin?"

He shrugs. "I don't know, we've been texting."

I don't know why I suddenly feel so self-conscious, or why Ezra won't even look at me. "How's it been going?"

Ezra shrugs again. "I don't know if it'll actually go anywhere. He asked me to meet up with him sometime this week. I guess I figured, why not?"

I'm still frowning as I turn to look up at the sky. The day's suddenly not as relaxing anymore. Austin is in our classes, but we've never really hung out a lot before. He's just always been there, following Leah and Marisol around. And now, suddenly, he might be Ezra's new *special friend*? I'm happy for Ezra—at least, I should be. This is his first maybe-boyfriend since Declan, and that was a couple years ago now. But I can't help the twinge of jealousy, either. It seems like everyone around me is always falling in love.

"Don't worry," Ezra says. "You're still my number one."

"Who's worried? I'm not worried."

He snorts. We sit in silence for a while, but it isn't the calm silence that I'm used to having with Ezra. It's the sort where we've clearly both got a lot on our minds, words on the tips of our tongues, but neither of us is saying anything. It's a little awkward.

I start to feel sick from the rocking motion on the swings and all that beer in my otherwise empty stomach, so we lie back down again. The sun gets hot enough and the grass feels soft enough that when I close my eyes, I can feel myself drifting in and out of sleep. I have random dreams where I don't know if I'm awake, dreams of an Instagram gallery and Declan Keane buying my paintings and Ezra saying that he loves me. By the time I wake up, the sun's almost down, the sky purple with streaks of red clouds. Ezra's on his back, scrolling through his phone.

"You're awake," Ezra says, his voice low and grumbly enough that I know he probably just woke up from a nap himself.

"Yeah," I mumble, stretching and rolling onto my back.

"I got a text from my mom," Ezra says, and I glance his way, catching the pinch in his eyebrows. "She and my dad are back in the city for the night and want me home for some dinner party."

"Oh," I say, sitting up.

Ezra shakes his head. "I should be more excited to see my own parents, right?"

I'm not about to tell Ezra how he should and shouldn't feel. "I don't know."

Ezra sighs and stands up. "I have to go. They're expecting me in an hour."

"All right." Ezra offers a hand and helps me stand up, too. The streaks of red are gone from the sky, and a darker blue is setting in. The orange streetlights flicker on. The park will close, and officers will be through any second now to kick us out.

As we head onto the sidewalk, Ezra says, "Do you want to—I don't know, come?"

I think he's joking for a solid ten seconds, but his grim expression doesn't change.

"To your parents' dinner party?"

"It's supposed to be a fund-raiser." His voice sounds pained. He's even wincing.

I hesitate and look down at my tank and my shorts. "I'm

not exactly dressed for a gala." Not to mention I've never even met Ezra's parents before. From all the stories he's told me, they sound horrifying.

"I've got some button-downs and ties that might fit you," he tells me.

In all the three years that I've known Ezra, I've never been to his childhood home on Park Avenue. Any brief mention about the penthouse apartment was always described like a tower in a fairy tale, where Ezra was the princess, locked away and desperate to escape. He'd spend every second he could away from that place, even before his parents bought him his Brooklyn apartment. It isn't exactly the average teenager's experience growing up, I guess—but then again, Ezra Patel isn't an average teenager.

"It could be fun," he says. "We eat, we drink, we dance, we piss off the Manhattan elite . . ."

Though he flashes a small smile, I can see the desperation in his eyes, too. He doesn't want to go back—not alone. I start to wonder if there's a place Ezra ever feels . . . I don't know—safe, maybe, somewhere he can go and know that he'll be loved, no matter what. Even if my dad messes up, I know that he loves me. Does Ezra have that, too?

Ezra looks like he's on the edge of begging me to come, and even if I'm nervous about it, I want to be there for him. "Okay. I mean—yeah, let's go."

He rewards me with a grin as he throws an arm over my shoulder. "Thanks, Felix."

As we walk to the station, I tug on the end of Ezra's T-shirt. "Hey," I tell him, "about what you said earlier—with Austin being your new special friend. I'm happy for you. Really."

He watches me closely before giving me the twitch of a smile. "Thanks."

NINE

WE TAKE THE EMPTY G TRAIN TOGETHER BEFORE WE TRANS-
fer to the 7 at Court Square. The icy train is filled with drunk
businessmen swaying on their feet and tourists staring at the
map on the train's wall, arguing in Italian. We get off at Forty-
Second Street and walk through the massive crowds that push
through the hot, sticky streets that smell like piss and garbage,
flashing lights of Times Square cloaking the night sky in a
sheen of white. I follow Ezra down streets and avenues, away
from the crowds and closer to Park Avenue, to a building of
classic stone and intricate architecture. A doorman tips his hat
at us as an older woman with a snippy little dog on a leash
walks past.

The lobby is all marble—floors, walls, *and* ceiling. There's
a huge golden chandelier above the lobby's receptionist, who

says good evening with a smile. "Welcome back, Mr. Patel."

"*Mr. Patel?* I feel like I'm in *Downton Abbey*," I whisper to him as we get on the elevators, all glass walls and glimmering lights. I try not to look visibly uncomfortable, to not fidget or smooth down the creases in my tank. It's even more unsettling to notice how relaxed Ezra seems with all of this. Seeing him stand tall, eyes glazed with boredom, really brings home the fact that he grew up in this sort of wealth—and that he still is incredibly fucking rich. There's a pinch of jealousy in my chest, alongside the guilt. I shouldn't be jealous of Ezra, especially when I know how hard of a time he's had with his parents, but I can't help it. What would my dad and I do with even a tenth of this kind of money? We'd probably still be in Brooklyn in our apartment, for starters; I wouldn't feel so guilty about attending St. Catherine's, and maybe all that stress and pressure wouldn't get to my head. Maybe I'd be a better student.

The elevator lets us off on the top floor with a *ding*, the doors sliding to show the entryway of the actual apartment. My mouth gapes open, and I don't even bother to close it. The marble floors shine, and the walls—it looks like they're thirty feet high—are all glass, looking out over the New York City skyline of skyscrapers and blinking lights. The space itself is *huge*. I could fit ten of my apartments in this living room alone. There're some servers getting ready for the party with bottles of champagne in buckets of ice. A man with broad shoulders, a straight back, and a neatly trimmed goatee stands by the door in a three-piece suit, arms crossed as he watches the workers bustle around. He glances at Ezra, unfolds his arms and extends one large, meaty palm. Ezra shakes the man's hand.

He eyes Ezra, like he's critiquing a piece of art. "You look well," the man says with a gruff voice. "Despite the outfit."

"Thank you," Ezra says with a surprising amount of formality, ignoring the jab. "This is Felix Love."

The man nods to me, extending a hand also so that I can shake it. I'm a little confused by who he is—until I actually take a second to look at him. He and Ezra have the same noses, the same brows.

"Your mother is around here somewhere," Mr. Patel says. He sounds both bored and exhausted. "Get changed, before she sees you like this."

Ezra nods and gestures at me to follow him. I glance over my shoulder at Mr. Patel. Isn't this the first time they're seeing each other in months? I get annoyed at my dad, but I couldn't imagine him practically ignoring me, not being excited or happy to see me after that much time. But Ezra doesn't seem bothered. He acts like this is completely normal. For him, I guess it is.

Ezra leads me through the living room and down a hall, into another open space where it's clear the gala will be taking place. Small circular tables are set up, and there's even a small stage at the far end of the room. There're more workers here, arranging a giant ice sculpture and lighting candles on each of the tables and hurrying back and forth with empty champagne glasses on trays. I see a woman with dark skin and curled hair in a gold dress and high heels standing in the center of it all.

"Shit, that's my mom," Ezra whispers.

We try to sneak past, but we barely take three steps before she calls Ezra's name. Ezra mutters, "Fuck," under his breath as he turns around. I stand to the side, slightly mesmerized. She's really freaking beautiful. Like, the most beautiful woman I've ever seen. She has Ezra's dark eyes and long lashes, his mouth, and even his smile. She clips over to us, arms spread wide, and pulls Ezra into a hug, kisses both of his cheeks and brushes his curls away from his face.

"Ezra, Ezra, my beautiful Ezra," she says with a slight British accent. Her eyes are sparkling, her smile infectious. I can't help but grin, seeing the way she looks at him. I feel a flinch of pain, knowing that my mother has never looked at me this way, and probably never will. "I've missed you so much, my darling boy."

Ezra's smile is strained. I'm confused, watching the two of them. Ez has always told me that his parents treat him like a lapdog: cute when it's time to take photos, but other than that, they don't really care about him—and yeah, I guess I could see his dad treating Ezra like that, now that I've met him . . . but his mother seems to be overflowing with love for Ez.

He steps out of her hug. "Mom, this is my friend Felix. He's going to stay for dinner."

She glances at me, and my heart almost stops under her

gaze. I say with a trembly voice, "It's nice to meet you, Mrs. Patel."

Though her smile is still plastered on her face, I can feel her taking in my tank, my shorts, the sneakers that I'd scribbled on with a Sharpie. Before she says anything, she notices something behind us—servers, carrying in trays of hors d'oeuvres.

"That belongs in the kitchen," she says to the staff. She gives Ezra another smile, barely glancing at me. "Excuse me. The party begins in an hour. You should start to get ready. Your father wouldn't want you to be late," she tells Ezra. With that, it's clear we've been dismissed. She clips away toward the server, giving her instructions rapidly.

Ezra's forced smile is gone. I see an echo of what might've once been hurt, years ago, and disappointment—but now, his blank expression suggests that this is exactly what he expected from her. "Come on," he whispers to me. "Let's hide in my room."

Ezra's bedroom has two floors. The first floor has a miniature living room: couches, a flat-screen on the opposite wall, three different gaming consoles, doors to a private bathroom and walk-in closet. The second floor is a loft that holds his gigantic bed. That's where we sprawl out, maybe because we're so used to hanging out on his mattress in his Brooklyn apartment. We even keep the lights off. The only glow comes from the miniature world of New York City below, blinking at us from his glass walls. I think I can understand how Ezra might've felt like he was a princess locked away in a tower, once upon a time. I feel like I'm in a cage, or in a fish tank with all of these glass walls and windows. Still, even then, jealousy snakes through me.

"Your mom didn't seem that bad," I tell him.

"Yeah?" He's on his back, staring up at the ceiling. "Wait until the party begins. It's like she thinks she's the star in a show, and everyone else around is in the audience. She'll make sure to hug me again when there're enough people watching."

"What about your dad?"

"He thinks he's the scriptwriter," Ezra says, "sitting by the sidelines and watching his fantasy play out on the stage. He had a special part for me once: loyal son, following in his father's footsteps to become CEO, entrepreneur, philanthropist . . . What's funny is that he didn't even really care that much when I told him I wanted to study art, and that I didn't want to go to Harvard or Yale for business school. He just revised me out of his play." He huffs out a short laugh. "I don't know. Maybe that's why I'm having such a hard time figuring out what I even want to do with my life. I broke free from what my dad expected of me—but now there're so many options, so many different paths. Which one am I supposed to choose?"

The jealousy mixes with frustration to create an unsavory flavor of bitterness. Ezra's taking so much for granted. To say, so flippantly, that he decided he didn't want to go to Harvard or Yale, knowing that his father would've paid for everything—knowing that his life is made, no matter what path he takes, and that he's still complaining . . .

"That seems like a pretty great problem to have."

He frowns at the ceiling. "What does that mean?"

"I mean—look around you. You're literally rolling in privilege and wealth. You could do anything." I shrug. "What do you have to complain about?"

He sits up, blinking at the white sheets beneath us, still not looking at me. "That's kind of harsh."

I bite my lip. Something in the back of my head tells me I should shut the hell up, but once the words have risen, it's difficult to push them back down again. "It—you know, it kind of pisses me off to hear you complain when you could have anything in the world, if you actually had the—I don't know, the motivation to do something about it."

"That's unfair."

"Your mom—she loves you, I can tell, even if she doesn't show it the way that you want her to."

He's shaking his head.

"And you could go to any college, any university, just based on your family name and wealth alone—not to mention how talented you are at everything you try. So it pisses me off, you know, it really does, to watch you just waste it all away because—because why? You're too privileged, and you don't know what you want to do with your life?"

When he looks at me, the words die in my throat. Ezra's eyes are narrowed, anger burning, expression smoldering. I don't think Ezra's ever looked at me this way before. This is how I honestly feel—have felt for a while now—but I've taken it too far. I know I have.

Even if he's pissed, Ezra's voice is calm. "I think that you're projecting," he tells me.

"What?"

"You're angry at me for not having the motivation," he says, "but what about you? You haven't even started your portfolio yet."

Anger bites through me. I roll my eyes. "I'm just . . ."

He sits there, watching me, waiting for me to finish my sentence—and as the silence grows between us, and I find it increasingly difficult to swallow, I know that he's right. Anger retracts to shame. I rub the back of my neck. "I'm sorry," I tell him. "Maybe I'm projecting a little."

"You're right," he says. "I am privileged. And I can forget that sometimes. I'm sorry if I seemed ungrateful. I know that I'm really fortunate to have this life. But not knowing what I want to do, not wanting to be forced to follow my father's footsteps and freaking out about it—that's all real and valid, too."

Shit. "I'm sorry," I say again. "I don't know why I said any of that. I was being a dick."

"We all fuck up sometimes, I guess."

"As long as we learn and grow, right?" I roll my eyes at myself. "Maybe it's the stress. Brown. Fuck, you're right. I can't figure out my portfolio, and if I don't get started soon there's no way I'm going to have it done in time."

Ezra's watching me carefully. "Can I ask you a question?"

"Yeah."

"I don't want to offend you."

"Just ask it, Ez."

"Why do you want to go to Brown?" he asks.

The question surprises me. I blink at him. "I mean—it's an Ivy League school. It has a dual-degree program with RISD. It's where I've always wanted to go."

From the look on his face, I can tell Ezra knows there's more, and that he's willing to sit there and wait until I'm ready to tell him the whole truth.

"And," I add, hesitating, "I don't know. I just want to prove, I guess, that I can get into Brown. That I'm worth an Ivy League school."

Ezra frowns at that one. "Worth an Ivy League school?" he repeats.

"Yeah. I mean, people can look at someone like you, and there's no question about it—you're good enough for an Ivy League. And people like Declan, and Marisol—no one would question whether any of you are worth getting into a place like Brown. But me?" I'm embarrassed now, can feel the heat building in my throat. "I just want to prove that I'm good enough, too. That I deserve it. It's kind of like proving that—I don't know, proves I deserve respect and love, too, even if no one else agrees with me. Even if no one else believes it." I stop myself, and kind of wish I'd stopped about ten sentences ago. Emotion is burning my neck, building up in my face and starting to reach my eyes.

"Okay," Ezra says. "First of all, I don't know if you need to prove anything to anyone. Places like Brown and the other Ivy Leagues—they boil your worth down to a bunch of bullshit. You're not your grades. You're not your test scores or your college application or even your portfolio."

I open my mouth to argue, but he keeps going.

"Second of all," he says, "it doesn't matter what they think. It only matters what you think. Do you think you're worthy of respect and love?"

My mouth is still open, but now, no sound comes out.

"I think you are," he tells me, still watching me—totally unashamed to be staring. I almost want to ask him how he can manage to keep eye contact like that, because as the seconds grow, heat builds in my chest, my neck, my face, and I have to blink and look away. I don't even know what I'm feeling. Embarrassment? Self-consciousness? Ezra doesn't seem to be feeling any of that. I can still sense him looking at me in the dim light.

I try to think of something stupid to say, to fill the awkward silence, but before I can speak there's a knock on the door down below. "Mr. Ezra?" a voice calls. "Your mother is asking for you."

Ezra collapses into the bed and groans into his arm, then shouts back, "We'll be there in a second!" He sighs, pushing himself to his feet. "Come on. Let's get changed."

He goes down to his walk-in closet, as if we hadn't just had an emotional heart-to-heart, and he pulls out a white, long-sleeved shirt that's way too big on me, tucking it into my shorts. I look like an idiot, but Ezra says he likes the style and changes into a similar pair of shorts and a white-collared shirt.

When we step outside, it looks like over one hundred guests in glittering gowns and three-piece suits have magically appeared. We get a bunch of stares and double takes, and one woman literally raises her nose at us in disgust, but something tells me this is the way Ezra likes it. He grins, laughing in the face of the snobs of New York City. This is his way of fighting back. But I don't like this. It's a whole other world—one where I don't feel comfortable at all. I don't like the way the guests and Ezra's parents stare at me, or the way I feel embarrassed after laughing too loudly into a champagne glass while Ezra and I get drunk in a corner.

My heart breaks for Ezra. I don't know how the hell he survived so many years in this penthouse, with these galas and balls. I feel like even more of a horrible person after the shit I told him earlier, and to make it worse, Ezra really seems like he's already over it—like he's just happy that I'm here with him, distracting him from his privileged and perfectly fucked-up life.

Ezra suggests we hijack the DJ and start playing trap music so that we can dance, but before we make it across the room, my phone buzzes. I think it might be my dad, asking me where I am, but I see that it's a notification from Instagram. I get a bad feeling, and the feeling sinks even lower when I see who the message is from: grandequeen69. I already know that reading the message is a bad fucking idea, but I open my in-box anyway.

Why're you pretending to be a boy?

I stare at the message. There's a *whoosh* that goes through me, and I can feel my emotions become still as numbness prickles. Besides the gallery, I've never really had to experience this kind of hate for who I am before—not directly. I always see it on the news. The ways the government is trying to erase me, the ways politicians try to pretend transgender people don't exist, even though we do exist, and always have, and always will. I see the articles, the stories about transgender people being refused health care, students like me bullied and forced into the wrong bathrooms, teens my own age being kicked out of their homes, adults being fired from their jobs just for being who they are, so many of us attacked and killed just for walking down the street—so many of us deciding to take our own lives because we aren't accepted.

I know that, as a trans person of color, my life expectancy is in my early thirties, just because of the sort of violence people like me face every day. I know all of this—but somehow, everything's always felt so far away. I can exit out of the articles online, switch the channel from the news, laugh with Ezra in the park and eat chicken wings and smoke weed and drink cheap chardonnay and only worry about things like my future and what I'm going to do with my life. I've felt safe, even with the mistakes my dad makes, even with a mom who I'm pretty sure doesn't love me anymore, if she ever did. I'm ashamed of it, but these messages—they're almost surprising. Like I somehow thought that the sort of hate I see every day, happening to other trans people, would never actually touch me.

Ezra notices something's wrong—asks what it is—but I don't want to tell him. A part of me wants to close the app and pretend it never happened. . . but I'm not sure I can actually ignore the message this time. Ezra turns my hand gently with his fingers, taking a look at my phone.

"What the fuck?" His gaze cuts to me. "Felix, what the hell is this?"

I don't answer him. I stare at the message, biting my lip. I begin typing.

Who are you? Why're you trolling me?

And, when grandequeen69 doesn't respond, I keep going.

I'm not pretending to be a boy. Just because you haven't evolved to realize gender identity doesn't equal biology, doesn't mean you get to say who I am and who I'm not. You don't have that power. Only I have the power to say who I am.

I hit *send*, feeling a bit proud of myself for fighting back, even if I shouldn't have had to in the first place—but the victory feels short-lived, tinged with anger and unease. I'm already dreading the moment grandequeen69 sends a message again.

TEN

EZRA WANTS ME TO STAY SO THAT WE CAN RETREAT TO HIS bedroom and talk about the Instagram message, but I can't wait to leave the penthouse. I was already uncomfortable, but the message from grandequeen69 really fucked with my head. Rage and fear and anxiety buzz through me, my stomach tightening until I feel queasy—and suddenly, even pretending to have fun at the Patel gala isn't a whole lot of fun anymore. There's only one thing I want to do: get home, pull out my phone, and fuck with Declan Keane.

"Are you sure you're all right?" Ezra asks, again and again, and even his concern is starting to get to me. No, I'm not all right, but I have to pretend that I am so that he won't worry about me, which takes its own emotional toll. I nod, and he kisses my forehead goodbye so that I can take the A train uptown to 145th Street.

My dad and I never really spoke after our last blow-up fight. I have no idea if he's still pissed at me. After what I just witnessed of Ezra's parents, I'm dealing with a mix of emotions. On the one hand, I have a warm feeling of gratitude for my dad. He makes a lot of mistakes, but at least he cares enough to sit down with me at dinner and ask me how my day was and act like he actually wants me around—to not abandon me in some apartment while he travels the world. But on the other hand, I still can't help but be annoyed with him for all the shit he says and does. He wants me to know he's trying—but I'm not sure if there should be anything for him to *try*. If he loves me, and he knows that I'm his son, then it should be easy for him to say my correct pronouns, even if I'm not always so sure of them myself. It should be easy for him to say my name.

I make it to our apartment building, up the elevator, and down the hallway. The AC is blasting when I unlock the front door. My dad sits on the couch, feet up on the coffee table while Captain precariously balances on the sofa's thin armrest.

My dad looks over his shoulder at me, his expression falling a little. "Hey," he says. "It's after ten. I didn't think you were coming back tonight."

"Is it okay that I'm back?" I close the door behind me.

I'm just joking—sort of—but my dad clearly doesn't think I'm very funny. He frowns at me before turning back to the TV.

I kick off my shoes and drop my backpack, sitting on one

of the plush chairs, putting a pillow in my lap and fiddling with the fringe. Captain leaps onto the pillow and stretches, claws prickling the fabric. I try not to move, so that I don't scare her off. It's enough to simply bask in the blessing the Captain has bestowed upon me.

"How was your day?" my dad asks, eyes glued to some cooking show.

"Fine," I say, staring anywhere but at him. Captain's ears twitch as she gets comfortable.

"How's Ezra?"

I decide to take a risk and reach for Captain's back to pet her, but as soon as I shift my arm, she's gone—onto the floor, tail twitching. She pads away. So, so close. "All right," I say. "With his parents."

My dad nods, and that's the end of our conversation. We never really talk about what I want to talk about. I never ask him what I wish I were brave enough to: Why doesn't he call me by my real name? Why was he willing to help me so much with my transition, but he can't stand the idea that he has a son?

I grab my phone from my pocket and flip open random apps until I make it to Instagram. The app itself makes my heart spike with anxiety now, but I have to stick with my plan if I want to make Declan pay for what he's done—for his stupid anonymous messages as grandequeen69. He would've looked me right in the eye earlier today, knowing that he was going to send me that transphobic post tonight. How fucking evil and vindictive can a person be?

I log into my luckyliquid95 account, scrolling through the feed—Ezra's posted one of his parents' dinner party, looks like it's still going strong, and Marisol has baked a blueberry pie. Declan's uploaded something recently also. Another piece of art. The moon, craters and all, created by crumpled-up pieces of newspaper clippings. Frustration and jealousy pumps through me. It's beautiful. Even I have to admit that the piece is extraordinary. It doesn't seem fair, that such an evil bastard can be so talented.

I double tap to like the image. Ask in the comment section what it means. As I type, I try to imagine Declan—maybe in his father's SoHo apartment, legs crossed as he sits on his bedroom floor, pieces from his collage-themed portfolio spread out all around him. Just an hour or so ago, he would've decided he was bored, or—I don't know—feeling particularly diabolical, and grabbed his phone to send me that message. I try to see it in my head, to remind myself why I'm doing this . . . but the more I try to imagine Declan caring enough to actually take the time and energy to send me a message on Instagram, just so that he can hurt me, the harder it is to picture it.

It's true, I guess, that I don't really have any proof that he was behind the gallery, or that he's actually grandequeen69. I don't know. Maybe Ezra has a point. Maybe this revenge plan isn't really worth it. I can't stop thinking about earlier today—sitting on the bench beside Declan, our argument in the lobby, his weird-ass apology. The overwhelming realization that the guy looking at me was the guy I'm fucking with online, even as fury beat through me.

"This show always makes me hungry," my dad says, staring at the TV.

I get a response from Declan a second later.

thekeanester123: The point isn't really what it means to me. It's what it means to you.

Is that his way of asking what his piece means to me? Christ, why can't he just say that?

luckyliquid95: I guess it means . . . I don't know, this dichotomy. Newspaper clippings, symbolizing the world and humans and all our problems, crumpled up into a ball of the moon, so far away from it all. It makes me feel lonely.

thekeanester123: Lonely? Is the moon lonely to you?

luckyliquid95: Yeah. I mean, that's the feeling I always get, anyway, whenever I look up at it.

thekeanester123: I look at the moon, and I can't help but think of everyone else on the planet who's looking up at it, too, and how alone I am, even though we're all here on the same Earth. I think about the fact that we should all be connected, but we're not. We're too preoccupied trying to hurt each other. It makes me think of how hypocritical I can be, and the mistakes I've made, and the ways I've hurt people, too.

My breath catches in my throat. It almost feels like

Declan's about to confess to everything—to the trolling, to the gallery.

luckyliquid95: What're the mistakes you've made?

thekeanester123: I don't know. The usual, I guess.

There's a pause, and frustration builds as I try to think of what I could say to get him to keep going in a way that wouldn't be too obvious, too desperate—but the phone buzzes in my hand.

thekeanester123: This has become a little too "forgive me father, for I have sinned."

I smirk a little, even as I feel a wave of disappointment. I feel like I was seconds from getting the truth out of him.

luckyliquid95: There're worst things than being a priest, I guess.

thekeanester123: I've kind of got a thing for priests, actually.

I stop, staring at my screen.

luckyliquid95: Um, sorry. What?

thekeanester123: I was raised Catholic, and there was this after-school program with the Sunday school priest, Father Duncan. He had no idea I had a crush on him, but he was always really nice and was never judgmental, and it was the first time I actually heard any sort of religious authority say that it's okay to be gay, that God loves all of His creations. I'm not super religious now, but . . . I don't know, I guess Father Duncan made a lasting impression on me.

luckyliquid95: . . . Priests? Really?

thekeanester123: Lol, yes. Don't judge me.

luckyliquid95: I'm not judging you!

I'm 100 percent judging him.

luckyliquid95: So that, uh—priest uniform really does it for you?

thekeanester123: You just made me spit out my coffee. Priest uniform?

Of course he's drinking coffee at eleven at night. It's probably black, no cream or sugar.

luckyliquid95: I don't know what it's called. That white thing they wear around their necks.

thekeanester123: The . . . clerical collar . . . ?

luckyliquid95: I mean, of course you'd know what they're called. You're into them.

My dad shifts on the couch. "What're you grinning about over there?"

I look up with a frown. "Grinning? I'm not grinning."

He raises his eyebrows. "Uh-huh. Sure."

I roll my eyes and look back at my phone.

thekeanester123: It's not that I'm specifically into priests or their collars. It's more like . . . I don't know, I didn't always have the easiest time being out, and sometimes I still feel a little . . . ashamed. Embarrassed. There's something about priests, or any sort of religious figure, and being accepted by them that makes me . . . attracted to them.

luckyliquid95: Doesn't seem super healthy.

I'd typed and pressed *send* without really thinking, but when he doesn't respond right away, I bite my lip. I thought we were having fun, but maybe I took it too far. What if I say one wrong thing, make one wrong move, and he decides to stop speaking to me? But my phone buzzes in my hand again.

thekeanester123: Yeah. You're probably right.

luckyliquid95: You know, I'm not a priest, but I can still listen. If you want me to, anyway.

This is its own particular brand of evil—telling someone that they can trust me, hoping that they'll tell me something personal, just so that I can betray them.

thekeanester123: I appreciate that. It's . . . easy to talk to you. I've never really spoken with anyone like this before.

The guilt twists in deeper.

luckyliquid95: If it makes you feel any better, I've made mistakes, too. I think we all have, even if no one really wants to admit it.

thekeanester123: I think that's why I like talking to you. That's something you're actually willing to admit.

I can't think of anything to say to that. There's warmth in my chest, which I know I shouldn't be feeling—not for Declan, and not while I'm trying to destroy him. I get another notification.

thekeanester123: Do you go to school in NYC? You don't have a lot of details up in your bio.

It'd be stupid to say I'm not in New York—half of my photos on this account are of random streets, restaurants, skyscrapers. If I say I'm not in New York, Declan will realize I'm lying.

luckyliquid95: Yeah, I do.

thekeanester123: Which school?

I hesitate. I could tell him I'm going to another school, but what if he digs for more details, or he randomly has a friend or cousin or something that goes to that school, and he tries to ask about me, only to realize I don't actually go there? But if I tell him the truth—that I'm a St. Cat's student—he might be able to figure out that I'm luckyliquid95.

luckyliquid95: Why do you want to know?

thekeanester123: I'm just curious. I like the way you think. About art, and life, and everything, I guess.

My dad gets up from the sofa with a groan, muttering that he's getting old, and makes it to the kitchen. I'm not sure how to answer Declan. He could call me out for pretending to be someone I'm not. Maybe he's even known it's been me all along, and he's just playing with me before he fucks me over.

thekeanester123: I know this is weird, but do you think you'd want to exchange numbers?

I stare at the message. Read and reread it a good handful of times.

thekeanester123: Maybe we could text instead?

Another chef is sent home, and the winner cries victorious tears as he thanks his daughter for being his inspiration, his motivation, his very reason for living. My dad sniffs from the kitchen as he clatters pots and pans.

Declan sends his number. **No pressure.**

I hesitate, finger hovering over the screen. We never had each other's numbers, even when we used to hang out. Ezra was always the point person between us, so I would text Ez, and Declan would text Ez, and we'd end up at the same place. But now . . .

134

This is a good thing, right? This means Declan's opening up to me. Starting to trust me.

I press the number and hold before hitting the *send message* button that pops up. My heart's going a little too crazy. I type out a short text:

Hey. It's Lucky, from Instagram.

Declan responds almost immediately.

Thanks for texting. Didn't know if you would. Not that I would blame you. Texting with a stranger is a little weird, right?

I don't know. Maybe?

I wouldn't normally do it, but there's something about your comments, I guess.

What do you mean?

Your comments are open. Vulnerable. Honest. No one's ever like that. Makes me want to be the same way.

You're not normally open?

Nope.

Why not?

I don't know. It isn't easy to make yourself vulnerable like that. Makes it easier for people to hurt you.

I frown at that one. **Do people hurt you a lot?**

Maybe not more than anyone else. Don't you ever get hurt?

I'm not actually very open and vulnerable in real life.

Really? That's surprising. Maybe it's because we're strangers that you open up more. . . .

Yeah. Maybe.

Declan doesn't answer for a while. My father's making

popcorn. It's sizzling and burning in the microwave. When my phone buzzes, my eyes scan the screen.

I have to start getting ready for bed, but is it okay if I text you again in a little while?

I don't know why I'm excited. I really, really shouldn't be this excited.

Yeah. Sure. I'd be okay with that.

I keep texting with Declan. While I'm brushing my teeth, under the sheets in bed with the lights off, I'm glued to the screen that buzzes in my hands every few seconds. At first we only talk about art and his new collage pieces, but the texts eventually spiral. I lie on my back in my bed, Captain curled up at my feet—it's three a.m., and my dad thinks I'm asleep.

Are you kidding me? First best show is Boruto, THEN FMA: Brotherhood, then Death Note.

You're out of your mind, I tell him. **Out of your freaking mind. How can you put BORUTO before FMA?**

Boruto's hilarious.

FMA is funny!

Yeah, but Boruto also made me cry.

And you didn't cry during FMA??? What are you, a monster?

Declan sends some laughing emojis. After a pause, another message comes in.

That's one of the things you're thinking of doing after college, right? Declan asks. **Working in animation?**

I hesitate. It was a random tidbit I'd slipped into our conversation earlier. I'd told him that I liked illustrating other people—could see myself working in comics or animation as a character designer, though I'm not really positive that's what I want to do. I told him that getting into college was the be-all, end-all right now, so it was hard to think about what would come after. I regret telling him any of that now, though. Would it be easier for him to figure out who I am?

Yeah. I like Disney/Pixar. A part of me wants to run away to California and start interning for them.

Not a bad dream. **What's stopping you?**

It's not exactly easy to just pick up and go. I'm only seventeen.

Right. **Sometimes I just want to say fuck it all. Leave school, not go to college, just travel the world or something.**

That's effing news to me. **Why?**

I don't know. All this pressure, I guess.

I have split emotions. One half of me wants to tell him to leave, then. Get the hell out of here. There are people who could use the spot he'll inevitably get when he applies for school. Why go to college if he doesn't even really want to? It pisses me the hell off, thinking that after all this, he doesn't even *want* the spot at Brown, or the scholarship—and he might still get it over me.

The other half, though, completely understands what he means. All this pressure fills me up so much that it's hard to think, hard to move, hard to even breathe. How nice would it be, to not care? To just take a gap year? Travel and dream and learn more about who I am? Maybe all the answers to the questions I have about myself would materialize out of thin air.

Is your name really Lucky? he asks me.

Why do you ask?

I don't know. I'm curious about you, I guess. I like talking to you.

I sit up, my chest getting warm. *This is Declan Keane*, I try to remind myself. *This is Declan fucking Keane*. The guy behind the gallery, who's been sending messages on Instagram. But right here, right now . . . it's hard to believe that it was really him. Maybe I'm just telling myself that, because I've actually been enjoying our conversation, which seems impossible. Wrong, even.

Sorry if that's weird, he says.

It's not weird. I take a deep breath, even though it's absolutely, completely weird. **I like talking to you, too.**

Maybe we can meet up someday. We're both in New York.

Yeah. Maybe.

Declan doesn't respond immediately. Things have escalated so quickly. It isn't too late to stop all of this. Just not reply to any of his messages. Then, finally:

I'm kind of scared you go to my school or something.

I wince. Shit.

Why would you be scared of that?

People kind of hate me at my school.

It's my turn to pause. What the fuck is Declan talking about? Everyone's constantly flocking to him. He's the effing golden boy of St. Cat's. He's literally on the front cover of the school's brochure.

Why do you think that?

Well, not everyone, I guess. I just don't actually feel like I have friends I can talk to. I'm surrounded by acquaintances.

I raise an eyebrow. That's surprising to hear. So his dumbass friends James and Marc aren't even really that close to Declan? I remember Ezra's words—that we might not be getting the full story.

Another text comes in right away. **And, okay. There are at least two people who really fucking hate me.**

My heart seizes. I clutch the phone.

Really? Who?

There are these two guys. I used to go out with one of them, and it didn't end well.

I can't help myself. **What happened?** I know what happened, I know what the hell happened—Declan decided he wasn't interested and brushed us the fuck off—but I want to hear that from Declan himself.

That's a story for another time.

Disappointing. I hesitate—but then, fuck it, I'm already pretty deep in this anyway. **Okay. What about the other guy?**

The other guy. God, I can't figure it out, actually.

What do you mean?

I mean he really can't stand me, and I have no idea why.

I stare at the screen. I want to laugh. I want to chuck the phone against the wall. I want to scream. *What the hell do you mean, you have no idea why?* Is Declan really that oblivious? Does he really have no fucking clue that he's treated me like total and complete shit for the past two years?

I mean, okay, we both want this spot at Brown, and we're both pretty competitive, but he REALLY hates me for it, and I only hate him a little bit.

Haha, that's funny. I'm clutching my phone so tightly my hands are starting to shake.

Yeah. I actually feel kind of bad for him.

I sit up so fast Captain hisses and leaps from the sheets. **Why?**

It's a long story. Basically, the guy is trans, and someone outed him, I guess?

My heart's hammering. I can feel my vein throbbing in my neck.

They put up this gallery of photos of him from a few years back before he transitioned, and had his old name up and everything. I didn't see it, but I heard he had a breakdown.

I wipe my eyes. I don't even know why I'm crying.

And no one knows who did it?

Nope. It's wild, right? I feel like the person has to be straight-up evil to do something like that. What's kind of creepy is that whoever did it is just chilling in any one of the classes I'm in.

I don't know what to say. I sit there, unmoving. Captain starts to tear at the rug on my floor. A minute passes. Five minutes. Declan texts, asking if I fell asleep. Shit. Fucking shit.

So you'd never do something like that? Not even to someone you hate?

Declan doesn't respond right away. I think he might've fallen asleep himself, but then my phone buzzes.

I'd never do something like that, not even to my worst enemy. That's like—I don't know, someone being racist or homophobic or any sort of ignorant shit. That's unforgivable.

I put my phone down on my nightstand. Another buzz, and another, and another, but I ignore the messages.

It wasn't Declan.

It wasn't fucking Declan.

Ezra was right. I knew there was a possibility he was right. I'm not surprised. Even I was starting to question if it was really Declan or not. I'd wanted it to be him—hoped it was him, because it was easier to make sense of it all. Easier to put my anger and hate on a target that I was already angry at, already hated.

Now? It could be anyone. Literally anyone at St. Cat's could've put that gallery up. Could've gone out of their way to hurt me.

Who the hell was it?

Another buzz. I sigh and snatch up the phone, ready to tell Declan to shut the fuck up, I'm going to bed—when I see the messages.

Lucky, I hope this isn't weird . . . but you go to my school, don't you? You go to St. Catherine's.

Okay, sorry, that was weird.

But I really think you do. I feel like I know you.

I hope you tell me who you are.

Because this is what's weirdest of all. Sorry in advance.

But I think I might be falling for you.

ELEVEN

I HAVE TO GET MY T-SHOT BEFORE I GO TO CLASS THE NEXT morning. I get one every two weeks, have been for the last couple of years. There're a few different options to get my hormones, but this is the one that works the best for me. My dad offers to go with me to the clinic, just like he always does, and I don't know . . . I guess that's another weird thing about all of this. The way he's supportive as fuck on paper, in all the right ways, but still won't accept me as his son. I tell him I'm all right and head to the train on my own.

I open up my Instagram once I have a seat. When I'd woken up, I saw that I'd gotten a new Instagram message from grandequeen69, one that I've been too afraid to read. I tap on the message.

Why're you pretending to be a boy?

Who are you? Why're you trolling me?

I'm not pretending to be a boy. Just because you haven't evolved to realize gender identity doesn't equal biology, doesn't mean you get to say who I am and who I'm not. You don't have that power. Only I have the power to say who I am.

And the new message:

I'm not trolling you. I'm just telling you the truth. You were born a girl. You'll always be a girl.

Pain sparks and fury burns through me. It's no one else's right to say who I am, or what I identify as—but not everyone believes that. I know grandequeen69 isn't the only person in the world who would think my identity is based on the gender I was assigned at birth—to force me into a box, to control me for their own comfort, because they're afraid of what they don't understand. Because they're afraid of me.

To know that there are people out there who hate me, want to hurt me, want to erase my identity, without ever even seeing me or knowing me, just like there are people out there who hate me for the color of my skin—it's enraging, infuriating, but it also hurts. The old hollow pain that burrowed its way into my chest the moment I saw that gallery of the old me is still there, and it feels like it's growing every second, like a black hole in the middle of my body. And what's worse is that I know I've been questioning my identity. My guilt and shame swell.

Something tells me that I should just delete the messages and block grandequeen69, but the urge to argue, to make them understand, to make them *see* grows.

I'm not a girl. You don't get to tell me who I am. You don't have that power. What do you get out of messaging me like this?

There's no immediate response. A part of me is relieved, but there's dread there, too, at having to wait for the next time this evil piece of shit messages me again.

I get off at Fourteenth Street. It's a little chilly this morning, gray clouds covering the sky, strong gusts of wind almost blowing me off my feet. Callen-Lorde is in one of the more expensive neighborhoods of Manhattan. The block is lined by brownstones with vines and lace-curtained windows. Queer folk are everywhere. Two women openly hold hands, and another guy zooms by on a skateboard wearing a rainbow Pride shirt.

I get to the tinted glass doors of Callen-Lorde and push into the lobby of stained tile and walls plastered with flyers for Pride month events. I go around to the back to grab my prescription. The waiting room is full, and the line wraps around. There's always a line at Callen-Lorde. It's one of the few clinics and pharmacies specifically for LGBTQIA+ folk in NYC, and there are so many people desperate for good health care that Callen-Lorde even reached capacity and had to close its doors to new patients. I was one of the lucky last few who managed to get an appointment two years back.

As I get into line, I try not to stare at the people around me. There's a man with white hair in a blue business suit, a couple of women speaking in Spanish, a tall college-aged

girl with purple hair—she catches me looking and smiles—
an older man with a cane. I never get tired of seeing the
patients who come here. So many different sorts of people,
all of us connected by this one thing, our one queer identity.
I'm a little bit in awe, I guess. But I'm also a little jealous.
I'm the youngest person here. Everyone else has had years to
figure themselves out already. They probably don't question
anything about themselves anymore. No annoying *niggling*
thoughts about their identity. How did they know, finally, if
they were a gay man, or a trans woman? How did they figure
out their answers?

I grab my prescription and head to the elevator, getting
off at the second floor to sign in with the youth center's receptionist. I'm called into the back, prescription bag crinkling in
my hand, palms a little sweaty. I'm always nervous before my
shot, even though it's been two years now.

My nurse Sophia is waiting for me in the hall. "How're
you today, Felix?" she asks as she leads me into one of the
rooms. She has pale skin, dark brown hair pulled into a loose
bun. I hand her the prescription bag.

"All right," I mumble. I'm also still a little shy to get my
shot, even after all this time. I unbutton, unzip, and pull down
my jean cutoffs before taking a seat, knee jiggling as Sophia
rips open the bag and does her thing, grabbing the needle and
wiping my thigh with a disinfecting cloth.

"So cold today, right?" she says brightly. "Ready?"

I hold my breath and nod.

She jabs the needle into my thigh, so smoothly I barely feel a thing—Sophia's always the best at giving me my shot—and she injects the testosterone. I stare at it as it drains into my leg. It's strange, to feel so grateful to some yellow fluid, but I kind of feel like it's my elixir. I know it's going to give me the changes I want to see—the changes I need others to see, too. Back when my dad was arguing with me over whether or not I should take testosterone or get the surgery, he'd asked me if I would still want to do any of this if I were on a deserted island.

"What if it were just you, with no one else around to say what your gender is?" he'd asked.

"But that's the point," I answered. "I'm *not* on a deserted island. I don't want people to look at me and decide what my gender is, based on how I look now."

The testosterone helps with that. I'm at a low enough dose that I'm basically going through the same changes other guys my age are going through, too. Hair growth. Lower voice. And . . . other things that were insanely embarrassing for Dr. Rodriguez to tell me about with my dad in the room. That day, when I met with my doctor for the first time, I was sent off with the assignment to do more research—to see if this is what I really wanted—and I ended up on a bunch of Tumblr posts, following a shit ton of trans people on Instagram, sifting through Twitter . . .

But no one ever mentioned that, even after my surgery and T-shots—after years of being positive that I'm a guy—I'd still have so many questions.

Sophia pulls out the needle and holds the disinfecting wipe in place as I massage my thigh, working the testosterone into the muscle like I was taught, the ache already starting. She grabs a Band-Aid, sticking it on smoothly.

"You're such a pro," she tells me with a smile.

"Can I ask you a question?" I say as I button and zip and jump to my feet.

"Of course," she says.

"Do you ever," I say, and it's embarrassing to continue—scary, even. What if she tells me that I'm only pretending to be trans, and I'm not allowed to be a patient at Callen-Lorde anymore? But I swallow and force myself to keep going. "Do you ever have any patients who know that they're trans, but are—I don't know, still questioning their identity?"

Sophia doesn't seem surprised by the question, but she's probably trained not to react. "I don't usually speak with patients about their identity," she admits, "but if you have any questions, or want to talk to anyone, I can have someone sign you up for an appointment with our youth counselor. There's also a group that speaks about identity—"

"No," I say, probably a little too quickly. "No, thanks. I'm all right."

She seems concerned. "Are you sure?"

I nod, heading for the door.

"You know, Felix," she says before I can grab the handle, "I think that it's fine to keep questioning your identity. You don't owe anyone any answers. And," she adds, "I'm sure you're not the only person who's ever questioned after they started transitioning. Maybe it's worth doing some research online. See what comes up."

I thank her, tell her to have a good day, and pass through the halls. I've already *done* research—that's what helped me realize that I'm trans in the first place . . . but, I don't know, maybe Sophia is right. Maybe it'd be worth continuing to look around online. There's got to be an answer somewhere, right?

It's a quick ride on the train into Brooklyn. I keep rubbing my thigh, imagining the testosterone sinking into me like a magical drug. It's kind of stupid, I guess, but sometimes I feel like trans folk are superheroes. It's a little like I'm Peter Parker, bitten by the T-shot, magically going through all these changes—or like Captain America, getting that experimental drug. When I first started doing my research, a Tumblr post I saw said that trans people used to be considered gods in a bunch of different cultures and religions. Dionysus was the god of transgender people, and Loki could change genders at will, too. We're still considered spiritual guides in some places around the world. That's pretty cool to think about.

The train rumbles to a stop—doors open, doors close— and it continues on. I see a couple of other kids in my classes. Leah and Tyler stand by the doors as Tyler holds on to his bike, laughing, Leah fiddling with the camera around her neck. Leah catches my eye and waves. Hazel sits a few seats from me with her earbuds in and swipes through images on her phone. Elliott is fast asleep in the corner.

Who is the person behind the gallery and the messages? It could be anyone. Any of the other one hundred students at St. Catherine's.

Somehow, knowing for a fact that it isn't Declan makes all of this so much worse.

I shake my head and bury my face in my hands. It wasn't Declan Keane.

A big part of me knew it wasn't him. I just didn't care. I *wanted* it to be him, so at the time, that's all that mattered. But now, I can't hide from the fact that he didn't put up the photos—that there's a transphobic asshole I go to school with, sending me anonymous messages. All the feelings from the gallery that I'd initially pushed down and suppressed are starting to rise to the surface.

I sit back up, letting out a deep sigh, the back of my head leaning against the subway window.

Leah makes a face at me across the train. "I know, right? It's so freaking early."

I hold out my phone and swipe through my messages.

I hope you tell me who you are.

Because this is what's weirdest of all. Sorry in advance.

But I think I might be falling for you.

I squint at the message. I did the same thing last night. I just squinted and stared at the message for a solid thirty minutes.

I mean, what the fuck?

My heart feels like it's bouncing around in my rib cage. I read and reread the text.

But I think I might be falling for you.

I mean, seriously—what the actual, holy fuck?

Okay, so first question is: How could Declan Keane ever *fall* for someone? After he dumped Ezra, that was it—he chose his popular jock friends and made it clear that the only person he really cares about is himself. So, that Declan would ever say he has a crush on someone is absolutely, 100 percent effing shocking.

My second question: How the hell could Declan fall for someone he's never even *met*? Because one thing's for sure: I'm not Lucky, so Declan doesn't have a crush on me. I mean, yes, I know that Lucky had to come from somewhere, and I did text genuine shit sometimes, but if Declan ever found out that *I'm* Lucky, I'm pretty sure . . .

I have no idea what he would do.

He already hates me—he admitted exactly that last night—so not much would really change. Maybe he'd go back to the dean, say that me kicking his chair wasn't an accident after all, go through those long months of disciplinary hearings to make sure I'm expelled and have no chance at Brown.

I guess how Declan would react doesn't really matter, because I know one thing for sure now: I have no reason to respond to him.

The whole point was to get close to Declan—to figure out a secret of his, to hurt him like he hurt me. But now that I know for a fact that he wasn't behind the gallery, and that he isn't sending those messages, I don't have any purpose to continue this plot for revenge.

No reason to keep messing with him. No reason to keep talking to him.

The problem? I kind of want to.

By the time I get to St. Cat's, there're only a few minutes until the bell is supposed to ring. I drag my feet as I walk, and nod at Leah and Hazel as they pass by. Everyone stands around in their groups, talking and laughing and sharing their phones to look at videos and texts. My heart—I can't help it, I really can't—starts to beat harder the second I see Declan. He's alone under the shade of a tree. I remember what he'd told me: that he doesn't have any friends here, not really, not even James and Marc. He's got dark circles under his eyes—probably from staying up late, like I did—and he keeps glancing at the phone in his hand as if he's waiting for something.

It hits me. He just confessed his feelings to Lucky, and he's waiting for Lucky to say something. Anything.

He must be freaking the fuck out right now. I mean, I

would be, if I told a guy I liked him, and he didn't respond.

Crap. I almost feel bad.

Okay, no—I *do* feel bad.

I walk past Declan, staring hard at my Converses. I'm having a hard time breathing. I half expect Declan to look up, to smile and acknowledge me—but why would he? He doesn't know that I'm the person he spent all night talking to.

I cross the parking lot to the school's entrance. Ezra's leaning against the brick wall near the doors with Leah and Hazel, who've made it here before me, along with James and Marisol. Mari smokes next to the No Smoking within 25 Feet sign, as usual. Austin is there, too. Ezra told me that he and Austin have been texting, but it's still weird to see someone new hanging out with him. There's something a little uglier, too, buried in my chest. Jealousy, I guess, for Ezra and his new maybe-boyfriend.

As I get closer, Ezra waves me over. I feel awkward. I don't want to admit to Ezra that he was right: Declan *didn't* put up the gallery after all. I also know I shouldn't tell him about Declan's text. *I think I might be falling for you.* Ezra would just shrug, say that he doesn't care—and I don't know, maybe he really wouldn't—but I think something like that has to sting. The guy you once loved, telling your best friend he's got a crush on them?

Christ, what a fucking mess.

When I join the group, Austin looks from Ezra, to me,

and back to Ezra. It's not like I've never spoken with Austin before—but, suddenly, I have absolutely no idea what to say to him.

"Felix, true or false," Leah says. "Aliens exist."

"True," I say. Hazel and James roll their eyes.

"Two against five," Leah says with a grin.

"Of course you guys believe in aliens," James says with a tone of *fucking losers* as he checks his phone.

"Come on," Leah says. "How can aliens *not* exist? Do you really think we're the only ones in this entire universe?"

"I'll believe it when there's proof," Hazel says.

"We literally have videos of orbs hanging in the sky and pilots saying they've been chased by nonhuman spacecraft. What more proof do you need?"

"An actual alien."

Austin smiles at me while Leah argues with Hazel. Now that I know he's Ezra's new maybe-special friend, I pay a little more attention to him than I would have before. He kind of reminds me of a golden retriever, with his floppy blond hair and blue eyes. The first time I saw him in acrylics class, I kind of immediately hated the guy. He's the sort of person the world adores, just based on the way he looks, a little like the way people obsess over men like Chris Hemsworth and Chris Evans and Chris Pine and all the other famous Chrises, plus Ryan Gosling, claiming that they're liberal and that they aren't racist and that they're feminists, but not really thinking about why they're so obsessed with white men, and why they don't love any people of color the same way. I love that I have brown skin. I love that I'm queer, and that I'm trans. But sometimes, I can't help but think how much easier my life would be if I was someone like Austin.

"How's your portfolio going?" Austin asks me. "I'm hitting a wall. I have no idea what I want to do. I've just been painting the same landscapes."

"I've been brainstorming," I say, which is technically true.

"Have you guys heard the theory," Leah says, "that aliens are actually just humans from the future, and that we've put ourselves into some sort of simulated world so that our future selves can observe us for an experiment?"

"No," Ezra says slowly, "but now I'll have nightmares about that for the rest of my life. Thanks."

"You're welcome."

James doesn't look up from his phone. "You're such nerds."

Leah gives a confused half smile, like she isn't sure if James is joking or not. "Well, you're hanging out with us, so . . ."

"I'm not hanging out with you," he says. "I'm hanging out with Hazel, who is hanging out with you."

"Is it because you're waiting on her so you can hook up in the supply closet?" Marisol asks. If she's looking for a reaction, she doesn't get what she wants. Neither bats an eyelash.

There's an uncomfortable pause.

"I thought it was cool to be a nerd," Ezra says, filling in the silence.

"According to nerds, yeah," Hazel tells him.

Marisol shares her cigarette with Ezra. "I notice you didn't actually answer the question," she says to Hazel.

"Because it's none of your business."

It's obvious what's happening: Hazel wants to make Marisol jealous, and it looks like it's working.

"But everyone knows that you're hooking up in the supply closet," Marisol says.

"Then why even ask about it?"

I can't help but scrunch my face. "Can't you go somewhere else?" I say without thinking. Eyes meet mine again, and I hesitate, but it's too late to backtrack now. "I mean . . . that's where we keep the canvases and paintbrushes and everything."

"You don't judge me; I don't judge you," James says.

There's another awkward pause.

Ezra frowns. "What does that mean? Why would you judge him?"

James shrugs, still with his phone out, scrolling through Instagram.

There's a tension building in my chest. James has always been a jackass. I mean, he deadnamed me the first chance he got. It wouldn't be crazy to think that he could be homophobic or transphobic or any other sort of phobic. The silence stretches.

"Why would you judge Felix?" Ezra asks again, his expression carefully blank. Ezra's always been protective of me, but especially now after the gallery, and when he knows I've been getting those Instagram messages, I'm worried about what might happen if the conversation escalates.

James shrugs again. "He's just weird, is all."

"I'm weird?" I repeat.

"You're all proud of being weird nerds, right?"

"Depends on the kind of weird you mean," Leah says. "Are you saying he's weird because he thinks aliens are real and he likes anime and stuff like that? Or are you saying he's weird because he's . . ." She pauses, glancing at me awkwardly, but it's obvious which words are stuck in her mouth: *Black, queer,* and *trans.*

"That isn't what I meant," James says, rolling his eyes.

"That's what it sounded like," Ezra tells him.

"Why does it always have to come back to that crap?" he asks. "It always comes back to that shit for you guys."

"It really only comes up when dumbasses *say* ignorant shit," Ezra says smoothly.

"I just think the dude is weird. That's all."

"Yeah. We've heard."

"So, what, now I'm racist and all that shit because I think Felix is weird?"

"You know what?" Leah says. "Maybe. Yeah. It's a possibility."

James is turning red in the face. He was annoyed before, but he's really getting angry now. "How the fuck does that make me racist?"

Leah doesn't back down. "Would you think Felix is weird if he were also white and straight and cis? Or would you think he's cool? You don't even consider *why* you think Felix is weird, or anyone else who isn't just like you—you just decide you don't like them, and then get defensive when someone calls you out on it."

"It goes both ways, right?" he says. "You decided you don't like me because I'm white, straight, and whatever-the-fuck-the-last-word-was."

"Cis," Ezra says, staring at him blankly. "Cisgender."

"And I didn't decide I dislike you because you're a white, straight, cis guy," Leah says. "I decided I don't like you because you told me lesbians aren't real—we just haven't met you yet."

"It was a fucking joke," James says under his breath. "It's like no one's allowed to joke about anything anymore. Jesus Christ."

"It's a joke to you," Marisol says. "You get to make everyone else the butt of your joke. We don't."

James rolls his eyes. "All right. This was fun. I'm going upstairs now," he says, giving Hazel a pointed look.

"*Idiot*," Leah says the second he's out of hearing.

"He's not that bad," Hazel says.

Marisol breathes out a puff of smoke, drops the cigarette to the ground, and puts it out with the twist of her foot. "You can do better," she tells Hazel.

Hazel sneers. "Who?" she says. "You?"

Marisol shrugs, but the obvious answer is *yes*.

"He says, like, the most ignorant shit sometimes, and then pretends that he's joking, but I get the feeling he isn't really joking, you know?" Leah says.

Hazel shrugs. "He's hot."

Leah shakes her head. "I don't know. Somehow, when someone is a jerk, their hotness level drops by at least fifty percent."

"Really? I guess I can look past that to focus on the physical."

"Don't you think their personality kind of affects the physical?" Leah asks. "When a girl is super smart and knows a bunch of random facts and has poetry memorized and stuff, I think she's really attractive, no matter what she looks like."

"Isn't that just, I don't know, too hard to find? Too long to wait for?"

"I'm assuming it'd be worth it," Leah says. "Better than waiting for someone like James, anyway."

James is disgusting, we all know that he is. He's the kind of guy who says inappropriate shit and tells anyone who gets mad that they're being too sensitive. I glance across the parking lot, at Declan standing alone under the tree's shade. How lonely must Declan be, to hang out with someone as fucking horrible as James?

And it hits me. James. I'd been so focused on Declan being the one behind the gallery that I hadn't thought to consider anyone else. The sorts of messages that grandequeen69's been sending—they're exactly the sort of thing James would say.

Even the name *grandequeen69*, whatever the hell that means, sounds like something immature he would come up with.

I feel like I can't look at anyone without thinking that they might be grandequeen69. It could've been Marisol, keeping up with her ignorant, transphobic shit, but what if it was James, making a "joke" only he would think was funny? It could've been anyone, and the longer I go without knowing who it was, the more the pressure grows in my chest.

TWELVE

The bell rings, and Jill ambles in after the rest of the class to give us her usual morning speech (today is on trying something new, continuing to expand and grow). I look around at everyone in the class. I never paid much attention to any of the other students before, not when it came to the gallery and which of them could be a suspect—I'd been so focused on Declan—but now I stare at each and every single one of them. Leah, when she smiles at me. Harper, who sits at the front of the class, taking notes on everything Jill says. Nasira, whispering to Tyler. Elliott, sketching in his notepad. James, who catches me looking and rolls his eyes before staring forward again.

When Jill releases us to our regular workstations, Ezra is

quiet, still pissed about everything James said. He glances at me over and over again, like he's waiting for permission to ask if I'm all right. Neither of us speaks for a few minutes, but the truth is building inside me, and even if I don't want to admit it, I know I have to.

I glance around, even though it's just the two of us in this corner, and lean in to whisper. "It wasn't Declan."

He narrows his eyes in confusion for a second, before the realization makes them widen. "What? How do you know?"

"He told me himself. We were texting. He was going on about how he'd never do something like that, and he feels sorry for me."

Ezra's eyes soften. "Really?"

When I look around the edge of the wall I'm working on, I can see Declan in the far corner, his back to the classroom. "Yes. But then he went on to say that he also hates me, so he's still an asshole."

Ezra sighs. "Oh." We each have our globs of acrylic, paintbrushes poised and ready. "What're you going to do?" he whispers.

"I don't know. Try to find out who actually did it, I guess. I mean, I have no idea how."

"Yeah," he mumbles. "I could ask Marisol if she knows anything. She might've heard a rumor or something."

I don't want Marisol anywhere near this, not when she's done her own damage. "I don't think that's a good idea."

Ezra frowns at me. "What's wrong with asking Marisol?"

I don't want to get into it now, but Ezra's watching me, waiting for an answer. I shrug. "Nothing. I just wonder if . . ." I glance around the corner again, eyes scanning the room. Leah is toward the front, painting a rose on her canvas.

"How likely do you think it is that the person who did the gallery is a photography student?" I ask Ezra.

He thinks about it for a second. "Pretty likely, I guess."

I hesitate. "Maybe we should talk to Leah."

"You think it was *Leah*?"

"*No*—I mean, I guess it's impossible to know for sure, but I don't think it was her. But maybe she has an idea of who it could've been. She might've noticed someone in her class talking shit about me or something."

He nods. "Okay, yeah. Let's grab her after class."

When I ask Leah if I can talk to her, she seems a little surprised. I guess I can't blame her. We're not exactly friends, even though we've hung out before. Leah's always been nice to me, the kind of person who seems to be constantly smiling and eternally optimistic, which doesn't sit well with my dark, Slytherin soul. I know I've been a bit standoffish to her. I kind of regret that now.

"What's wrong?" she asks as Ezra and I follow her into the photography classroom. There're black curtains leading to the darkroom, and there are clotheslines hanging around the walls with black-and-white photography clipped to the string. The room's empty. Everyone's at lunch.

"Nothing's wrong," I say. "Well, I mean, something's wrong, but it's nothing that you did—well, I mean, I hope it's nothing that you did . . ."

Leah raises a single eyebrow. Ezra makes a *Get to the point, Felix* face.

"You know that gallery?" I say. "The one—I mean, the one that was of me."

Leah's face pales. She stands taller and nods.

"Ezra and I . . . well, I guess mostly me . . . I was thinking that it might've been a photography student. I mean, I guess anyone could hack into my phone to get to my Instagram account, but they figured out how to blow up my pictures, and knew how to frame and label everything, and—I don't know, I just thought . . ."

I feel pretty stupid right now, but Leah isn't laughing. "God, it was so horrible," she says. "I know I've said it before, but—I don't know, I'm just really sorry that happened to you."

I bite the corner of my lip. It annoyed me whenever people told me how *sorry* they were, but right now, I can feel that Leah's being genuine. "Thanks."

"Do you think someone in the photography class might've done it?" Ezra asks. "I know you're not in photography this summer, but usually . . ."

Leah takes a breath, blinking, seeming to consider it. "I hope not. Everyone's usually pretty cool. But I guess you never know, right?"

It isn't exactly helpful, but what did I think? That she'd

say, *Actually, yes, there's this one particular transphobe . . .*

"So you think the person hacked your phone?" she says.

"I have no idea how else they would've gotten my pictures."

"They could've just hacked your Instagram," she says. "There're a bunch of apps for that. It's a lot easier than you think."

Ezra and I exchange looks. Leah looks a little embarrassed. "Not that I'd ever hack an Instagram account. I'm more of a cracker." She notices our confusion. "Cracking is another form of what people know as hacking. But hacking is illegal. That's what people do when they want to steal money, or spread viruses, that sort of thing. Cracking is just for fun. It's like a giant puzzle. It's actually pretty easy." She pauses and makes an expression like she's thinking of telling us something I probably don't want to know. She lowers her voice. "I like to crack into computers and cell phones to leave positive affirmations where people can easily find them."

I'm not totally sure how to respond. Ezra stares at her blankly.

"That's—uh—cool," I say.

She shrugs and looks like she's trying to bite back a smile. "It's not a big deal. A lot more people crack into phones than you'd think."

There isn't really anything else to say after a classmate says that they crack into other people's phones for fun. Ezra asks Leah where she's going for lunch, and she says she'll probably go to White Castle, like usual. As we're walking to the door, the idea strikes me. It's a ridiculous idea, really fucking stupid, but I also don't really have any other way to figure out who could be behind the gallery, who is sending me those Instagram messages. . . .

"Hey, Leah," I say, slowing to a stop. She and Ezra turn around to look at me. "Do you think it'd be possible to—I don't know, crack into other student's phones to see who might've put up the gallery?"

She doesn't hesitate. "Hack."

"What?"

"If I'm hacking into phones for personal information, then it isn't cracking. It's hacking."

"Oh. Okay."

"And yes," she adds. "It's possible. There're a bunch of programs these days."

Ezra looks hesitant. This is *definitely* in get-kicked-out-of-school territory, not to mention pretty illegal. But Leah seems to consider it.

"It's kind of a good idea, actually," she says. "It'd be easy to see traces of hacking cookies on someone else's phone— if they'd downloaded hacking programs, or if they even still have those pictures saved in their gallery. . . ."

I hesitate. "The person's also been sending me Instagram messages."

"That's even better," she says. "I can definitely look at their Instagram message history."

166

I scratch my head. "I can't—I mean, I don't really have any money. . . ."

"Oh, no," Leah says, and looks almost offended, "I wouldn't take your money. I'm happy to do what I can to help and take this fucking asshole down." She smirks. "I've always wanted to be a badass vigilante."

Ezra's eyebrows shoot up, and he glances at me like he's impressed.

Leah grins. "I'd accept a White Castle slider for lunch, though."

"Sold," Ez says.

They continue toward the door, already talking possible suspects—Ezra catches Leah up on how we'd suspected Declan, but we now know it wasn't him, and he wonders if we should check out James and Marc, since they're his best friends, and since James can be such an ignorant jackass—but I pause. The two seem excited, but I know it's a long shot, and the chances of figuring out who was behind the gallery are pretty low. Ezra must see the hopelessness on my face, because he walks back to me and slings an arm over my shoulder, messing with my hair. "We'll find out who did it. I promise."

I know he's trying to make me feel better, but he also doesn't know the whole story—doesn't even know what's really bugging me.

When we get outside and into the parking lot, I see Declan hanging out on one of the benches with James and Marc. And

I can't stop looking at him. Not through lunch while we sit across the parking lot from each other, not in the hallway and back to class, not through our entire thesis session. Declan checked his phone maybe a million times that morning, but after lunch, he must've given up, because he keeps his bleary gaze on the work in front of him, a pinch in between his eyebrows.

He said that he thinks he might be falling for Lucky. And while I'm confused, and even a little incredulous, I have to admit that there's a spark of excitement in me, too. No one's ever fallen for me before, even if they're actually only falling for some fake online version of me. It's scary, this excitement—like if I let myself be happy for even one moment, Declan's going to send a message to Lucky, saying that he's changed his mind, he's realized that he doesn't have feelings for Lucky after all.

I should be trying to focus on my artwork also, but the blank canvas in front of me is as empty as it's always been. I have my phone out, staring at the message Declan sent me.

Should I respond?

What would I even say?

I'm staring at the text from Declan when a new Instagram alert pops up at the top of my screen. I stop breathing. It's a new message from grandequeen69.

Why're you pretending to be a boy?

Who are you? Why're you trolling me?

I'm not pretending to be a boy. Just because you haven't evolved

to realize gender identity doesn't equal biology, doesn't mean you get to say who I am and who I'm not. You don't have that power. Only I have the power to say who I am.

I'm not trolling you. I'm just telling you the truth. You were born a girl. You'll always be a girl.

I'm not a girl. You don't get to tell me who I am. You don't have that power. What do you get out of messaging me like this?

It feels good to tell you the truth.

My heart is in my throat. I stare at the words, trying to dissect them, to see if I can figure out who might've written them. I look around the room. The piece of shit could be here, right now, messaging me this crap.

I stand up and tell Ezra I'm going to take a walk. I wander the halls, not really paying attention to where I'm going or where I'm walking—just lost in my thoughts, in the numbness that's starting to crawl over me. When I look up, I'm back in the deserted acrylics classroom, as if my feet automatically took me down the familiar path and in through the doors. The room feels odd with no one else around: empty tables, empty stools, empty pink corduroy couch. I head for the supply closet. I need to relax, and I know it's strange, but I've always found prepping canvases calming. I push my phone into my back pocket and get to work, grabbing a roll of canvas and cutting off a piece, finding boards a couple of feet long for the backing and hammering them together, stapling and stretching the canvas across the wood. I do that, over and over again, canvas after canvas. I take up the center of the room, pushing and scraping stools out of my way, steady in my work, until I have seven canvases prepped and spread across the floor.

There's the squeak of a shoe behind me. I leap to my feet, spinning around, guilt thrumming through me. Jill stands there with a to-go coffee cup in her hand.

"Felix," she says, surprised.

"Sorry," I say fast, though I'm not even sure what I'm sorry for.

"I forgot my keys," Jill says slowly, ignoring my apology as she begins to inspect the canvases that take up about half of her classroom floor. She raises her eyebrows as she looks my way again. "Plan on actually using those supplies?" she asks.

I hesitate. I hadn't even thought of the enormous waste these canvases would be if I don't actually paint anything on them. "Uh," I say, then nod. "Yeah."

She smiles like she's in on the joke that, no, I hadn't really been planning on it, but I sure as hell am now. She heads to her desk beside the pink sofa, opens up drawers, and clunks through whatever's in there as she rummages for her keys. "You know, Felix," she says, "you're clearly talented, but your paintings are always . . . Well, they're fine."

I wince. The critique is like a stab to the chest. No artist wants their work to be thought of as just *fine*. From the jingle in her hand, I guess Jill's found the keys. She closes her drawer.

"You're probably one of the best artists in the school, to be honest," she says. "It's obvious that you have the eye, the

170

imagination, the creativity . . . But you don't apply yourself like you should."

"I *apply* myself."

She peers down at me. "Have you figured out your thesis project yet?"

Jill already knows the answer to that. I cross my arms, then realize how defensive that looks and force myself to put them at my sides, then realize how awkward that looks, so end up crossing them again. "No," I finally admit, "not really."

"Why not?" she asks. Her tone is soft. I know that she's just trying to help.

I shrug, but she's waiting for a real response. "It's just— hard. It's like there's all this pressure, I guess, to make the portfolio perfect so that I can get into Brown and get the scholarship, and then I keep having these blocks, and I have no idea what to do, and it's just . . . hard," I say again.

"Well, no one chooses to be an artist because it's easy," Jill tells me. "If they do, they're in for a rude awakening." She smiles at her own joke before she pauses for a moment. I can tell there's something else she wants to say, but she wants to be careful about how she says it. "I'm always struck by your portraits, Felix. You manage to capture the spirit, the essence of your subject. But I'm usually left with the sense that you could be pushing yourself in some way." She plays with her keys in her hand, twirling the ring around a finger. "You end up doing the same thing. Painting portraits of Ezra and your classmates."

"And that's bad?" I ask, only a little defensively now.

"No, it's not *bad*. It's just that I've wondered what else you might have in you, if you pushed yourself to try something new. I noticed that you never paint yourself. Why is that?"

I'm surprised by the question—not so much because Jill asked it, but more because I never thought about it before. It'd never really crossed my mind, I guess, to think about doing self-portraits. They've always felt a little narcissistic to me, and I'm not exactly the kind of guy who wants to, or is even able to, stare at myself all day. I never take selfies, and I barely like glancing at myself in mirrors. Dysphoria's played a huge part in that. It's what Dr. Rodriguez first called the feeling I have when I see myself and I know that I don't look the way I'm supposed to—the discomfort I used to have, in seeing my hair long and a chest that wasn't flat. I've been lucky enough to see most of the changes I want to see, but I'm still the shortest guy of all my classmates, and sometimes, I can feel strangers' stares as they watch me, questioning my gender.

"Self-portraits are empowering," Jill says. "They force you to see yourself in a way that's different than just looking in a mirror, or snapping a picture on your phone. Painting a self-portrait makes you recognize and accept yourself, both on the outside and within—your beauty, your intricacies, even your flaws. It isn't easy, by any means," she tells me, then shrugs. "But, anything that reveals you—the real you—isn't easy."

She holds up her keys. "It's just a thought. I'll leave you to it. And make sure you put all of the supplies away when you're done."

She leaves the room, clicking the door shut behind her.

The real me?

I pull out acrylics, a palette covered with dried and peeling paint, brushes of different sizes, some bristles frayed or hardened, and stare at one of the blank canvases. The critique of *fine* still stings, but being at St. Cat's for the past few years has taught me to breathe in critique and breathe it back out again. Maybe a part of me also knows that Jill is right.

The real me.

I take a deep breath, pull out my phone, and snap a picture. I look at the photo, and I feel a flare of embarrassment in my stomach. I have dots of acne, my nose and eyes and mouth are too big, my jaw not square, not as square as I'd like—and in my eyes, I can see the fear. The dread in doing this, in confronting myself—in searching for the beauty, in admitting to the flaws. I lean the phone against the leg of a table, kneel down, dip a brush, and begin some simple strokes of red in the corner of the canvas. I grab the yellow, streaks blending into orange, almost like a sunrise, coloring my skin. The green is next, then the blue around my mouth. A bright burst, like a firework, in my eyes blues and purples swirling together like smoke that shadows my nose, a streak of green on my cheek—

My phone buzzes, a message appearing for a moment

before it vanishes. The colors, the mixtures, the textures—I sink into the canvas, letting myself fall into the image of me. White, almost like a cloud, twisting around a drop of red where my heart—

My phone buzzes again. I sigh and stand up, dropping the brush into a mason jar of brown water and wiping my hand off on my jeans so that I can grab my phone from the floor. I'm afraid that it could be grandequeen69 again, but it's just Ezra wanting to know where the hell I am, if I'm okay. I look at the time in the corner of the phone. Four. It's four o' fucking clock. I've been in here for three hours?

I take a step back from the canvas. I haven't even filled half of it, but what I have filled . . .

It's beautiful. I hate how arrogant that sounds, but it's true. Not me—I don't think that I'm beautiful—but the painting itself. My skin is flecks of red and gold, as though I'm on fire. The colors almost look like a piece of a galaxy, twisting together bits of light blooming out of the darkness. My eyes hold the same fear, the same dread, but there's a strength, an intensity, a determination I hadn't really noticed.

I'm not really thinking when I pull out my phone and scroll past my conversation with Ezra, pulling up Declan's last message to me.

I hope you tell me who you are.

Because this is what's weirdest of all. Sorry in advance.

But I think I might be falling for you.

I bite my lip, staring at the messages, and I take a breath—type and release:

I can't tell you who I am.

If I were Declan, I would've purposely waited at least five hours to respond as payback for my all-day silence, but he gives zero fucks—he answers right away:

Okay. I won't push you to tell me.

I try to imagine him answering his messages—maybe he's at home, curled up in front of the TV on the sofa, or maybe he's hanging out with James and Marc, trying to hide his phone as he texts. Is he surprised I answered? Relieved? I hesitate, then type: You say you're falling for me. How can you like me if you don't even know who I am?

Declan takes a little longer to respond to that one. I know it's stupid. You could be literally anyone. I've been driving myself crazy all day, looking at everyone around me, wondering who you might be. And I don't even know if you really go to St. Catherine's or not.

Same thing I've been doing—looking around, wondering who was behind the gallery, who might still be sending me those Instagram messages. I feel a pinch of guilt. I know how he feels. I sit down beside my canvas, cross-legged. Are you mad I won't tell you who I am?

No. A little frustrated. But only because I wish we could talk in person.

I don't respond to that. Another text comes in.

I'm really happy you texted me back. I was afraid I scared you off.

To be honest? You kind of did.

Sorry . . . I know it's weird to have a crush on you without even knowing who you are. But I really like talking to you.

It's embarrassing to admit to this. I have no idea why I'm admitting this. I like talking to you, too.

Can we keep talking? Even if I have a weird crush on you?

I try not to smile. Yeah. I guess that'd be okay.

THIRTEEN

Hey Mom,

You know when life is just about as confusing as it can possibly be, and then you think to yourself, well, at least it can't get any worse than this, but then life is like, ha, really, you think so, huh? And then, just to prove you wrong, it gets even more freaking confusing than it was before, so your entire life is nothing but a whole-ass mystery—always a shit ton of questions, but never any answers?

Okay. Maybe that's an exaggeration.

. . . Except, not?

I feel like I've never had more questions in my life than right now. Declan isn't the person who was behind the gallery, so the first question: Who the hell was? Leah's been helping, doing things I probably shouldn't put down into an email, before the

FBI shows up at St. Cat's . . . but I'm not sure our plan is really going to work.

Declan, it turns out, is actually kind of *nice* and interesting and smart and funny . . . And, on top of that, he says that he's falling for me. So, second question: How do I feel about him? It seems totally impossible, but—well—I think I might be starting to like him, too. I don't know. It's the first time anyone's ever said they like me, and it feels really freaking good. Like I can rub it in everyone's faces. See? *Someone* thinks I deserve to be loved, even if you didn't.

But my third question is: How would Ezra feel about any of this? I'd be really pissed off, if I were him—pissed off and hurt. Is it fucked up of me, to keep talking to Declan? (I guess that's technically two questions. Oh well.)

Fourth question, completely unrelated to all of the above, except not, because it's the most important question of all: What the hell is my identity?

I've been looking up a shit ton of terms, but every definition—every label—makes me feel more frustrated. There're so many ways for a person to identify . . . So why doesn't anything feel right for me? Is it possible to not have an identity? To exist, without any labels to say who I am and who I'm not? Maybe that'd feel good for some people, but for me, I'd feel anchorless—drifting with no one to say if what I'm feeling is real—if this emotion is something that I've made up in my mind, or if it's something that others have felt, too.

There's another question I might as well ask, I guess, since there's no way in hell I'm going to send this email to you:

Why did you leave?

Dad doesn't really like to talk about it. *Sometimes, people just fall out of love.*

I guess that means you didn't love him anymore. You must've told him that, before you decided to leave us. I wonder how things looked from your perspective. Did you really think that you were just going on a trip to clear your head, or had you already decided you weren't coming back? Was it really just a coincidence that you met your new husband there, or had you actually already known him, had already been cheating on my dad? When you kept extending your trip, did you even notice that you were making fewer phone calls as the days went on? That you were becoming too busy to answer the phone whenever I tried to call, because your new kid always had soccer or homework or piano lessons? You said you'd call me back, but you never did, and . . .

I guess that brings me to my last question: Did you stop loving me, too?

Your son/child/still to be determined,

Felix

I sit cross-legged on the sofa, Captain curled up next to me. My dad's taking his usual afternoon nap, and Ezra's texting me about a Pride party Marisol invited him to, but I put my phone on silent. I bite my lip, then bring up Google. I don't even know what to type—not at first. *Am I transgender?* feels like a stupid question to ask, when I know for a fact that I am, even if being labeled a *guy* doesn't feel completely right, either. I know that I'm not a girl. That's the only thing I know for certain.

I'm transgender, but I don't feel like I'm a guy or a girl.

The results are overwhelming. There are medical articles on transitioning, entertainment sites about Laverne Cox and Janet Mock, Instagram posts showing #transformationtuesday with side-by-side images of people years ago and their photos now, a Tumblr post with a bunch—feels like hundreds—of transgender terms, labels I didn't even know existed.

One of the results takes me to a Facebook event at the LGBT Community Center. The event is for a gender identity discussion group. It's supposed to be tonight at eight o'clock, in about three hours. It's a little too much of a coincidence, right? I click on "Going."

I've only ever been to the Center once before, way back when I was just starting to wonder about my identity. I didn't go to any groups. I didn't even speak to anyone. I just walked up the front steps and into the reception area before I got so nervous that I turned right back around and left.

I walk back into the reception area again now. Not much has changed. White walls, white benches. There're older folk sitting in a café area, speaking with low voices. Two teens closer to my age sit nearby, heads bent together as they share earbuds.

I walk up to the desk and ask the receptionist where I should go for the discussion group, and she sends me up to the second floor and into a broiling room with wooden floors and faded peach-colored walls and large, open windows. Floor fans hum and push the hot air around. Metal folding chairs are set up in a circle. There're already a few other people here. An elderly man with crossed legs, reading a newspaper. A tall woman with brown hair, bright red lipstick. Someone with pink hair waits at the door with a sign-in list and a smile. Their name tag reads Bex, with *they/them* pronouns scrawled beneath.

In my research online, even back from when I was just starting to question if I was trans or not, I remember reading about the nonbinary identity. A lot of people who use they/them pronouns don't feel like they're a boy or a girl, which is something that could maybe, possibly, describe that *niggling* feeling—that being seen as a girl definitely isn't right, but being seen as a guy isn't totally right, either. But there're also times when I know, for a fact, that I definitely am a guy, and I feel like I've just imagined the niggling, the questioning, the confusion. I don't know if it's okay for me to say that I'm nonbinary if there're still days when I know that I'm a guy, too. But if I'm not nonbinary, and I'm not a guy, and I'm definitely not a girl, then what am I? I came here for answers, but it just feels like my questions are growing.

I write in my name without writing any pronouns and sit at the chair that feels farthest away. I wrap my arms around myself and cross my legs, knee jiggling. I don't know why I feel so uncomfortable. Like maybe someone will walk into the room, point right at me, shout, "Fraud!" and escort me from the premises.

A few more people filter in, of all different ages, races— but it becomes pretty obvious that I'm the youngest by far. Only Bex looks like they might be in college. Everyone else is an adult. I start to worry that I'm not allowed to be in here if I'm under eighteen. Would someone tell me that I'm too young and ask me to leave?

Time moves agonizingly slowly, before Bex claps their hands and stands in the center of the circle.

"Welcome to the LGBT Center gender-identity discussion group," they say. "Let's go around in a circle and introduce ourselves. Say name, pronouns, and where you're from. I'll start. I'm Bex, I use they/them pronouns, and I'm from the Bronx."

There are four others. The elderly man—Tom—folds his newspaper in half and rests it on the empty chair beside his own. The woman with the bright red lipstick, Sarah, sits beside a woman with pockmarked skin, Zelda. A man with a Final Fantasy shirt and a patchy beard says his name is Wally. When it gets to my turn, my heart's hammering so hard that my voice shakes.

"Felix. Um. I'm not sure about pronouns right now." I pause, waiting for someone to say that I should leave, but everyone just stares at me without blinking. "I live in

Brooklyn—no, ah—I moved. I'm in Harlem now."

Bex gives me a reassuring smile.

I already know that I have exactly zero plans to speak up. I came here deciding I'd do nothing but listen—listen and learn, try to find an answer to my questions.

"There are too many expectations on gender roles, even within the transgender community. To prove that you're a man, you must act aggressively. To prove that you're a woman, you must be passive." Sarah holds her head high. "I'm an aggressive woman. I won't apologize for that."

"You can't blame people for defining their identity by traditional gender roles," Zelda says.

"I can if those traditional gender roles are harmful," Sarah says.

"I guess we have to decide what's most important," Wally tells us. "Validation through traditional gender roles, or the destruction of those roles."

"Well, those roles are what got us into this mess of a patriarchy in the first place," Sarah says.

"But, then, why have any gender at all?" Zelda asks.

Tom speaks for the first time, and I can tell by the way the room quiets that he holds a lot of respect here. "Some of us don't have any gender at all," he says. Bex smiles.

"Is that the answer, then?" Zelda asks. "To destroying the patriarchy and misogyny? Eliminate gender altogether?"

"I don't think anyone's suggesting that," Tom says. "Though that's the answer for some, it doesn't have to be the answer for everyone. We can't help who we are. There isn't much point to passing judgment on our community. We already get enough judgment from others."

Everyone else nods.

I have so many questions, so many swirling thoughts flooding my mind. My heart's almost out of my throat and in my mouth. My knee won't stop jiggling, and I'm sweating so much in the heat and from nerves that my shirt's sticking to my back. Bex meets my eye, and even though I look away from them, they say my name.

"Do you have anything you want to add?" they ask, and when I only swallow, blinking, they say, "Or is there anything else you'd like to talk about?"

The others watch me expectantly, almost bored. Zelda checks her nails. Wally scratches his beard. There are so many things I want to talk about—so many questions I want to ask—but they're all a tangled twist of words and feelings in my mind, impossible to translate. The silence, as it grows, echoes in my head, and the longer I don't speak with my mouth hanging open the more bored everyone is, staring at me and wondering what the hell is wrong with me—

"I'm sorry," I manage to say, my voice breaking. "I have to go."

No one says anything as I scrape my chair back, stand up, and walk out the door. I hurry down the hall, and embarrassment fills my chest and my throat, reaching my eyes. I'm almost crying. I run out of the LGBT Center lobby, but the summer heat doesn't do anything to help the growing pressure in my chest. Turns out no one needed to actually point and scream, "Fraud!" at me—I took care of that myself just fine.

I'm barely down the block when I hear my name. I spin around. Bex has followed me.

"Jesus, you run fast," Bex says as they slow down, slightly out of breath.

Shit. I can't even look at them.

"Are you okay?" they ask.

I swallow and nod, staring at the sidewalk. There's a crack with a weed pushing through.

"I'm sorry. I didn't mean to put you on the spot. I just wanted to be sure you felt welcome. And you are. Welcome, I mean," they say. They give me a smile. "I remember how hard it was when I was a teen, surrounded by a bunch of know-it-all adults, ignored and . . ."

I'm fidgeting, pulling on the end of my tank.

"I have to get back to the room," Bex says. "But I wanted you to know that you're always welcome to join us. The group meets every Wednesday at eight o'clock. If you have any questions, or if you just want to come in and listen—anything's fine. All right?"

I glance up, meeting their eye for a second, and I can see that they really mean what they're saying. They want me to come back, to try again. And even though I'm still dying a little inside, I don't know—a part of me really appreciates that, too.

I nod. "All right."

It's going on nine o'clock and getting darker, the sun starting to make its way down. I'm already on my way home, walking toward the A and being bumped into by every single person on the street, when my phone buzzes in my hand. I have a new Instagram message. I'd never responded to grandequeen69's last message—but it looks like they decided to send another one anyway.

You think it's so cool and trendy to be transgender. It isn't real. You'll always be a girl.

It's too much. The discussion group, and now this. I can't even stop the tears that sting my eyes. "Fuck!" I yell. A few people startle, turning to look at me. I wipe my eyes, my nose.

What do you get out of being a transphobic piece of trash? Does it feel good, to try and belittle someone because of who they are? I guess it must be a rush of power for you, attacking someone and making them feel like they don't belong. But I know who I am. I know that I'm trans. Transgender people have always existed. Trans people are everywhere through history, even if society tries to erase us. We're not a trend, even if it makes you feel good to pretend that we are. I know that I'm not a girl. You don't get to say who I am and who I'm not. Now leave me the fuck alone.

I press *send*, breathing heavy, tears still building and threatening to fall from my lashes. When my phone buzzes in my hand again, I almost jump—dread fills me, and I think it's grandequeen69 again, but this time, it's a text from Ezra.

WHERE THE FUCK ARE YOU??? Papi Juice is hosting for Pride at warehouse. Come thruuuuuuuuuuu.

I forgot about the Pride party. I'm so, so fucking tired—emotionally exhausted from the train wreck that was the LGBT Center discussion group, the never-ending swirling tide of questions filling my head, and now from this latest message from grandequeen69, too. But before I can even respond, Ezra starts calling literally three seconds later.

"Felix!" he yells. There's background noise and music. I hear Marisol and Leah laughing. "Felix, come through!"

God, he's already drunk. "I don't know. I'm a little tired."

He groans. "Oh, come on. Don't be such a boring fuck. You're seventeen. How many more times do you get to be seventeen, Felix? Huh? How many fucking times?"

I sigh. I'm not in the mood for a party—not at all—but there's no way I can just go home with nothing but my thoughts and questions and grandequeen69's trolling messages and Declan with his texts.

"Where should I meet you?"

187

FOURTEEN

THE ADDRESS EZRA TEXTS ME TAKES ME TO GREENPOINT, past all the closed groceries and bakeries, into the streets with flickering streetlights and the kind of dark alleys I've always been warned not to go down alone. Brick factories that are 100 percent haunted start to pop up. The blue dot on my GPS keeps jumping back and forth, and I can't find the street where the party is supposed to be. I kind of want to *kill* Ezra right now. This is exactly the sort of shady part of town that's just a little more dangerous for someone like me.

I turn the corner, and there's a line wrapped around the sidewalk. People in short skirts, netting, and tanks filter into one of the warehouses. I run across the street, checking both ways even though there aren't any cars around. I join the end of the line, the bouncer checks my fake ID, and I slide in through the heavy metal doors.

A staircase leads up into darkness, music thumping. I hold on to the railing to steady myself as I climb the steep stairs.

There's another pair of doors on the landing—and when I open them, the music blasts so loudly that it almost knocks me off my feet. There're no lights except for red streaks, illuminating faces and hands thrown into the air. Music with a heavy beat vibrates through the floor, up my shins, and the crowd—I didn't even know so many people could be stuffed into a single room—moves as one. I might be the only person standing still. People are dancing against each other, against the walls, against the bar, against the speakers, as if everyone's been cursed to dance until they die.

I don't see Ezra anywhere. I make it through the crowd, across the dance floor, to another set of doors. I burst through them, taking one long breath. I'm on a rooftop. There's enough space for dozens of people to stand around, talking and smoking. The wall is only waist-high. It'd be too easy to trip and fall over the side. A cool breeze wafts in over the skyline of warehouses and factories, glowing yellow lights against the black night.

I text Ez to let him know that I'm here. I'm always a little nervous around huge crowds of people I don't know. I walk through the groups slowly, checking to see if I recognize anyone, glancing at my phone over and over again to see if Ezra has responded. Arms grab me from behind, yanking me into a tight hug, and Ezra laughs in my ear.

"You're so late," he whines.

"Sorry," I say. "Got distracted."

Austin appears at Ezra's side. I feel a twinge of disappointment. Even if I'm tired, I was kind of looking forward to hanging out with just Ezra. I don't really feel like dealing with his maybe-and-looking-more-likely-boyfriend.

"Hey!" Austin says, head bopping to the beat.

I nod and force a smile. We all stand there for a solid five seconds, looking at one another. It's awkward as fuck. When it was me, Ezra, and Declan—I don't know, the three of us just *worked*. We always had something to talk about, to laugh about. I never felt jealous or like I wasn't being included. Before Declan broke up with Ez, we were all friends with each other. And now, Ezra and Austin are both looking at me like they expect the same thing to happen again—for me to just befriend Austin, welcome him into the group.

A new song starts to play, I don't know by who, I've never heard it before, and Marisol screams and runs up, grabbing Ezra's hands and dragging him back inside, Ezra grinning over his shoulder at us as he leaves me and Austin behind. I cringe. Austin lets out an awkward laugh.

"Marisol's cool, isn't she?"

"Yeah," I lie.

"You know, before I started hanging out with Ezra, I'd seen you and him and Marisol around St. Cat's a bunch, and I always thought you guys are really cool and had smart stuff

190

to say in class, and you're all really talented, but the school is so cliquey, so I never felt like I could say hello or anything."

I feel a flinch of confusion, and maybe some guilt. "You were scared to say hello?"

"Well, yeah," he says. "I guess I was just a little intimidated. I mean, your paintings are like—whew, seriously, really freaking good, and I knew that I could never be that good, and you're kind of a badass, you know? Like, you're just yourself so unapologetically. And, I mean, I've had a crush on Ezra for, like, a whole year now. He's really funny and . . . well, really attractive, like he could be a model or something. I've liked him for a while, but I didn't know how to just walk up to him and start talking. And for a long time, I thought that he was going out with you."

I raise an eyebrow. "*Me?*"

"I mean, that's not such a stretch, right? You hang out all the time."

"Yeah. Because we're best friends."

Austin shrugs. "I just assumed you were going out, and then I found out that you *weren't* going out, and I decided, you know what? I should just go for it. What do I have to lose, right? Besides my dignity." He laughs. "So yeah, I went up to him and told him I liked him, and, well . . ." He trails off, face turning a bright red.

Austin's annoying as fuck, but my chest still gets a little warm. I can tell he really likes Ezra. And after all the bullshit with Declan—well, Ezra could use someone who wants to be with him. It makes me feel a little bad for immediately deciding I don't like Austin.

The song changes again. There's a heavy bass that vibrates through the floors. "I'm happy for you," I shout to him over the music. "For both of you." And this time, I notice that there's only a drop of envy when usually I'd be flooded by jealousy. I think that I can be really, truly happy for Ezra and Austin—because for the first time, I might know how good it feels to like someone and know they feel the same way.

"Thanks," he says. "God, I'm so nervous talking to you. I can tell your opinion really matters to Ezra, so I just really want you to like me. And, I mean, I hope you like me just because I think you're cool and talented, too."

I smile a little, despite myself. "Don't worry," I tell him. "I'll put in a good word."

This earns me a radiant grin. "I should find the others," he says. "I owe Leah a drink. Coming?"

I shake my head and watch as he heads back to the doors, disappearing into the crowd. I pull my phone out, leaning against the wall.

Do you ever feel like you're only ever watching? I ask Declan. **Never really participating. Never really doing. Just always watching.**

But he doesn't respond. I slide to the ground, looking through his Instagram, curious if he's busy—maybe he's hanging out with James and Marc, taking pictures of a bar they've managed to sneak into—but he hasn't updated since yesterday. A shadow passes over me, and when I look up, Ezra is sliding down to sit beside me. He puts his head on my shoulder.

"Why're you over here by yourself?" he asks.

"I don't feel like dancing."

He glances up at me, his head still on my shoulder. "So? What do you think?"

"About Austin?" I shrug. "He seems nice. He really, really likes you."

Ezra looks away. "You think so?"

"Don't you?"

"Yeah, of course."

My phone buzzes. Declan's texted me back. **Always watching? Like in that photo you posted?**

Yeah. I don't know, I always feel like I can't figure out how to just stop watching and actually join.

Ezra groans, eyes closed. "I think I drank too much."

I glance at him. "You going to be okay?"

Why do you think that is? Declan asks me.

Ez shrugs. "I think so. I always have a desperate need to drink whenever I see my parents."

I don't know. Maybe I'm just . . . too scared.

Ezra rests his head back against the wall. "I was thinking more about what you said that night. You're right, you know? They give me everything. I know I'm lucky. Beyond lucky. I'm privileged as fuck."

I bite the corner of my lip and look away. I still can't help but be jealous of Ezra's parents, his family's wealth. Does that make me a bad person? A shitty friend?

"You're right," Ezra says again. "It's stupid to complain."

A part of me—the ugly, jealous side—wants to agree. But . . . "Just because they give you material shit, doesn't mean they . . . you know . . ."

"Are good parents?"

"I didn't want to say it that way."

I understand being scared, Declan tells me. **I'm scared all of the time.**

"They're not," Ezra says. "Good parents, I mean."

I frown a little. **What're you afraid of?**

Everything. I'm scared I'm not living my life to my full potential. I'm scared I'm wasting my life when I'm meant to be doing something else, something more . . .

Ez sighs, putting a hand through his hair as he leans against me. "I always felt like they left me in a castle and then abandoned me. Or like I was a toy Pomeranian that they didn't actually want to take care of but were happy to take pictures of and show off. Well, that's what they used to do, anyway, when I was a cute little kid. Now, moody teenager isn't exactly gala-worthy. Sometimes I don't think they even want me there, but they're afraid it'd look bad if I didn't show up."

"I think I get what you mean." The situation isn't exactly the same, but I know what it feels like to be abandoned by a parent.

"But there comes a point when it's up to me to just stop complaining and take control, right? So that's what I'm going to do. I'm not sure *what* I want to do yet, but—you know, you were right. I'm going to try to figure out a plan, a goal, so that I can do what I want with my life and get the hell away from them."

I feel the surprise light up my eyes. I can't help but smile. "That's really great, Ez. That's—I mean, seriously, that's really freaking great."

He laughs a little, so low it's more of a rumble vibrating from his skin into mine. "Thanks to you."

"Not just me. You figured it out for yourself, too."

My phone buzzes, and I read Declan's message. I think that if I let myself get too afraid, I just won't do anything, and I won't be living anyway.

I swallow. That's true. I just don't know how to break out of that fear.

Maybe it's not something you should think about. Maybe you should just do it, whatever it is you're too afraid to try. Just do it. Just say yes.

Ezra frowns at my phone. "Who're you texting?"

I hesitate. I don't want him to know I'm still talking with Declan. I have no reason to mess with him, and I'd have to come up with some explanation—make up a lie—so I wouldn't have to admit that I think I might actually be starting to like him . . . and that he said he's falling for me. "It's no one."

Ezra scratches his cheek, not looking at me. "If you don't

want to tell me, that's fine, you know? But you don't have to lie about it."

"I'm not lying," I say. He doesn't answer. "All right. Fine. I don't want to tell you."

Even though he said it was fine not to tell him, he bites down on his jaw now, straightening up a bit. There aren't many things I don't tell Ezra, and I can tell that he's hurt.

"Is it someone you like?" he asks.

"Why would you ask that?"

"Why else wouldn't you want to tell me who you're texting?"

I hesitate, playing with my phone, twirling it around in my hand. "It's Declan."

His head whips to me. "What? You're still texting Declan?"

"Yeah."

"Are you still planning to—?"

"No, no, I'm not going to do that anymore."

"Then why're you still speaking to him?"

I shrug a little. "I don't know. I just got used to talking to him, I guess."

"But he's—*Declan*. Fucking Declan Keane."

"I know. It's just . . ." I bite my lip a little. "You said it yourself. We don't know the whole story. And Declan—I don't know, he can still be an asshole, but he can be cool sometimes, too."

Ezra's mouth, which had been hanging open, snaps shut.

Fuck. It was a crappy thing to say, I know—telling Ezra that his ex-boyfriend, who's treated us like shit, is *cool sometimes, too.*

"I mean—not *cool*, just . . ."

"All right," he says. "Okay. I get it."

I rub the back of my neck. "I'm sorry. I shouldn't have said that."

Before Ezra can respond, Marisol rushes at us out of nowhere, grin on her face, Austin and Leah trailing behind. Leah's all kinds of drunk. She immediately sits down beside me and puts her head on my shoulder. "Hello, my wonderful friend."

"We're going to Coney Island to watch the sunrise," Marisol yells at us. "Do you want to come?"

I glance at Ezra. He ignores me, forcing on a smile for Mari. "Fuck yeah. When're you leaving?"

"Like, right now," she says.

Austin grins at me. "Felix? Are you coming?"

I let out a sigh and hold my phone up again. Declan's message glows at me from my phone's screen.

Just do it. Just say yes.

FIFTEEN

It's a long-ass trip to Coney Island. There are five of us: me, Ezra, Marisol, Austin, and Leah, who I learn actually turns out to be Austin's second cousin. We occupy a corner of the icy train, Ezra, Marisol, and Austin singing a song from *Rent* at the top of their lungs, Ezra pirouetting around and around, Leah and I laughing. When we get off at our stop, Coney Island is more crowded than I'd expect for five in the morning. The boardwalk, wood swollen with salt and sand, has a group of drunken men laughing and stumbling, a couple standing by the railing and kissing so softly it makes my heart ache, an older woman walking her dog. We jump the railing and land in the cold sand, sneakers off and in our hands. Ezra, Mari, and Austin go screaming, running for the water. Leah shakes her head at them.

"It kind of feels like they were all made for each other," she says.

My stomach twists a little. I was never jealous when I was the third wheel with Declan and Ezra—that's just the way our friendship worked out, before Declan broke up with Ez. But if Ezra becomes Austin's boyfriend, would our friendship change and evolve the way friendships always seem to? What if Ezra and I aren't as close anymore?

We all sit down on the cold sand together, near the edge of the gray water. Leah leans into me. "By the way," she whispers, "I checked out James's phone. The only messages he's been sending on Instagram have been to Kendall Jenner." She looks like she's fighting off a laugh. "I think he's hoping she'll fall in love with him over DMs."

There's a twinge of disappointment. I shouldn't be surprised. It isn't going to be easy to find the bastard behind the gallery, the troll sending me their messages, I already know that.

"Don't worry," Leah tells me. "I'm checking out Marc's phone now. But if it isn't him," she says, "do you have any other idea of who it could be?"

I hesitate. "No. I'm not sure."

She must see the disappointment on my face. "That's okay," she says. "That's all right. We'll find the piece of shit who did it. Okay?"

I nod a little. God, why was I always so dismissive of Leah? "Okay. Thanks. Really. This means a lot."

She snuggles into my side, head resting on my shoulder. Austin and Ezra start to kiss. Ezra wouldn't look at me for the entire train ride, even while everyone was laughing and singing—I really underestimated how pissed he would be to find out that I'm still talking with Declan—but he glances up now as Austin kisses him, and he doesn't look away. My face gets hot and I stare down at my hands.

"Yessssss," Mari says, lying back in the sand, sunglasses on even though the sky is a dark blue, the sun still a ways off from actually rising. "Yes, this is exactly what I fucking needed."

Austin laughs against Ezra's neck. Leah turns her face away against the icy wind coming off the sea to light a blunt, red curls flying everywhere. She takes in a deep breath and hands it to me, her cheeks pink in the cold. "Aren't they so cute?" she asks me.

"Yeah," I say, taking the weed and sucking on it so hard that my throat burns and I start to cough. Leah smacks my back and takes the blunt from me, passing it on to Marisol.

"God, I need to get laid," Marisol says.

"I volunteer as tribute," Leah says without missing a beat.

Marisol passes the weed to Ezra, releases a cloud of smoke. "Been there, done that."

Leah groans and rolls over onto her stomach, playing with the sand. "Have you had sex with everyone here?"

Marisol glances around. "Not everyone," she says. "I haven't had sex with Austin. Or Felix."

Wait, wait. "Hold up. You've had sex with Ezra?"

Ezra's on his back. He scrunches his eyebrows as he passes the weed to Austin. "What's your definition of *sex*?"

"We messed around one drunken night, as one does," Marisol says, waving her hand around. "This was before I decided I'll only be dating girls from now on. Obviously."

"It wasn't a big deal," Ezra says. "We really just made out with some—uh—touching. And I regretted it instantly."

"Same." Marisol has the nerve to smirk at me. "Don't you wish you'd had some fun with me before we broke up?"

Austin leans into Ezra to whisper something, and Ez laughs. Jealousy flourishes in my gut.

Leah won't stop smiling at me. "Hey, Felix," she says, "when did you know you were—you know?"

I know what she means, but I'm in a dicky mood now because of Marisol treating me like trash, like she always does, laughing at the crush I'd had as if I'm just a joke to her.

I stare at the gray, steely water pushing up onto the sand. "When did I know what?"

Leah hesitates, like she isn't sure if it's an okay question to ask—and honestly, I'm not sure if it is. Some people might not mind being asked, I guess, but it's not like Leah and I are so close that she'd know whether it's okay to ask *me*; and sure, I guess Austin probably already knew—but what if he didn't? Leah would've just outed me.

"When did you know that you were—uh—a guy?" Leah asks, trying again—and, shit, I can tell she's at least *trying*.

Even if she's isn't perfect, she isn't the bad guy here.

"I figured it out pretty late," I say, ignoring the tightening in my chest. It's hard to ignore the question if I've actually *figured myself out yet* or not. "Late in comparison to all the stories I hear of people figuring out their gender identity when they were still in the womb, anyway."

That gets a few laughs.

"I think it's really brave of you," Leah says.

"I mean, I guess? I'm just being myself. There's nothing brave about that."

Austin's nodding. "My family friend didn't realize she was a woman until she was an adult. She just came out a couple years ago. She always makes this point of sitting me down and telling me how lucky I am to be a teenager now, without any prejudice to deal with, like she did when she was a teenager."

Marisol responds without turning to look at us. "That's such crap. We've still got so many fucking issues to deal with."

"I mean," Leah says, "I guess in comparison to the way things used to be . . ."

"Where, exactly?" Ezra says. He's still looking anywhere but me. "We're in this bubble in Brooklyn, but go anywhere else and it's a bigotry shitshow."

"Even then, not everything's perfect here, either," Austin says. "There're still people who're afraid to come out to their parents. People being abused, kicked out of their homes."

"We've still got a long way to go," Marisol says, finally sliding her sunglasses up and peering at us, upside down, daring any of us to argue—and, yeah, I get her point, but it's just a little ironic, maybe, that *Marisol* is preaching to us when she broke up with me because I'm quote-unquote *a misogynist.* "This country's fucked, and there're a bunch of changes it needs to make before anyone gets to say that we don't have to deal with prejudice for being queer."

"We should probably start making those changes with ourselves first, don't you think?" I ask. The sarcasm is pretty thick, I have to admit. Marisol scrunches up her face and exchanges a look with Leah.

"What kind of fucking question is that?" She slides her sunglasses back on and gets comfortable in the sand again. "Start with ourselves," Marisol repeats. "Are you trying to say something?"

"I don't know," I say. *Yes.*

Ezra's frowning at me, but he doesn't say anything, not like he normally would. Austin glances between the two of us. Leah leans into me a little. "Felix, you okay?"

"Yeah."

I'm not okay. I'm pissed. I don't know—maybe it was Declan's messages, to just do whatever the fuck I want to do, or maybe arguing with that fucking troll sparked something in me, but now all of the old anger I've had toward Marisol is bubbling to the surface. I told myself I'd just ignore it, but I'm not sure ignoring her bullshit is helping anyone. It's definitely not helping me. I'd wanted to convince her that she was wrong about me—that I was worthy of her respect and love, after she'd rejected me—but I can see that the way she's treated me has been beyond fucked-up. No one deserves that.

"Well?" Marisol says with this annoyed tone, like she couldn't give a crap about what I'm going to say.

I clench my jaw. Ezra, Austin, and Leah are all watching me, waiting. Maybe this is a conversation I should've just had with Marisol first, without this audience. I feel myself deflating.

"It's nothing. Forget it."

Marisol snorts. "Typical Felix. So melodramatic."

I get up, brushing off the grains that're stuck to the backs of my legs, and start walking, feet sinking in the gray sand, sneakers in my hands. I don't even know where I'm going. Back to the train? I climb over the railing, onto the wooden boardwalk, and it's not long before I hear heavy footsteps behind me.

"What the hell was that?" Ezra says beneath his breath, walking next to me.

I'm surprised he even bothered to follow me. "Nothing."

"Obviously not nothing. You've been acting weird as shit lately, Felix." A jab, clearly, at me for still texting with Declan.

I stop walking, rubbing a hand over my curls. "Marisol never told you why we stopped dating, right?"

Ezra shrugs, frowning. "She just said it didn't work."

I open my mouth, fighting to force the words out, and I realize—this is the power Marisol's got over me. She's a fuck-ing bully. "She told me I'm a misogynist for transitioning."

Ezra stares at me blankly for a second, then another. "What?"

"She said I'm misogynistic for *choosing not to be a girl anymore.*"

"Wait—what?"

He doesn't even stay for me to repeat myself. He jumps right back over the railing, heading for Marisol and the others. Fuck—I knew Ez would be pissed if I said something, but that doesn't mean I want him to confront Marisol about it, and definitely not now. I jump over the railing also, calling after him, stumbling in the sand, but Ezra gets back to the others first.

"Marisol, what the fuck?" he yells. The others spin around, eyes wide. Marisol slides her sunglasses off.

She looks between the two of us with an expression of bewilderment.

"You told Felix he's *a misogynist*?"

Marisol glances my way, and I can tell, right then and there—I can tell she'd never expected me to tell Ezra. She knew the kind of control she had over me. Knew that I'd stay quiet, ashamed, embarrassed, afraid that what she'd told me was the truth.

She glances Ezra's way again. "Well—I mean, it's kind of true, right?"

Leah looks surprised. "No one chooses to be transgender," she says slowly.

"I know, but—"

"You've got to be fucking kidding me," Ezra says. This is a whole other level of anger. I can tell, looking at him now, that their friendship is done. There's no coming back from what she said to me. I feel guilty. Like it's my fault, getting Ezra this pissed at Marisol. But no—no, I remind myself, I didn't force Marisol to say the shit that she did.

"I'm not saying anything against Felix, or trans people," Marisol says, "but if someone decides they don't want to be a woman anymore, to me, that just means they inherently don't like women—"

"So trans women don't like men?"

"It doesn't work the other way around," Marisol says, her voice wavering—she knows she's fucked up. Or maybe she sounds this way only because she was caught. "Men—they—there's the patriarchy, and if a man gives up that power to become a woman—"

"You sound like a fucking idiot right now," Ezra says.

"I can still be a feminist and be trans," I say. My voice is pretty small right now, but everyone goes quiet and still, turning to listen to me. My heart's hammering against my chest, and I feel like I'm seconds from crying, but I can't do that—not here, not now, not in front of Marisol. "I love women. I respect women. I was proud to be a girl, before I transitioned—but I realized that just isn't who I am. Being a guy now doesn't mean I don't still love and respect women."

Marisol rolls her eyes a little, but it's to keep herself from crying. "So calling me out in front of everyone and making me look like an ass is your idea of loving and respecting women?"

I stop myself from apologizing. She's probably right—I probably should've made this a one-on-one conversation—but something tells me that if I confronted her privately, Marisol would've figured out a way to make me feel like I'm being *melodramatic*, made me think that I'm wrong. I'm grateful Ezra's by my side right now, even when he has his own reasons to be pissed with me, too.

"You made an ass out of yourself," Ezra says. "You owe Felix an apology."

Marisol presses her lips together. "I'm not apologizing. I didn't do anything wrong."

"You were an ignorant, transphobic fuck," Ezra says, voice sharp. "That's not wrong?"

"I don't think I'm ignorant or transphobic."

"Come on, Mari," Leah whispers. "Just apologize."

"No. Fuck that shit."

The word *transphobic* makes me pause. I've considered the possibility before, but now, it seems more likely than ever that the person behind the gallery could've easily been Marisol, happily going out of her way to humiliate me. If this is how she feels about me, why *wouldn't* she be the one who put up that gallery of me?

I ask her. I say, "Were you behind the gallery?"

Marisol's outright crying now. She knows what I'm talking about. "No. I wasn't behind the gallery."

I don't believe her. "Really?"

She raises her hands. "Everyone already thinks I'm an ignorant dumbass now. I wouldn't have any reason to hide the fact that I did that stupid gallery."

"Do you know who it was?"

"No, I don't fucking know. But you know what? I'm happy whoever it was did it."

Ezra shakes his head, grabbing my hand and pulling me away. "I don't fuck with you anymore, Marisol. Don't look at me, don't talk to me, don't try to pretend to be my friend. We're done."

"Same to you, boo-boo," she calls after us. Ezra just flips her off.

We make it back to the boardwalk, over the railing. I can see Leah arguing with Marisol, Austin's hand on her arm. Shit. All the drama I'd wanted to avoid is now blowing right up in my face. Now that we're far enough away, I let the tears roll. I don't want Ezra to see, but of course he notices. He throws an arm over my shoulder, pulling me close to his side, making it difficult to walk as I keep stumbling into him. He doesn't say anything. Just kisses the top of my head.

"I'm sorry," I mumble, hiding my face in my hands.

"Fuck. I hate when you apologize for shit that isn't your fault. You didn't do anything wrong."

I nod, because I'm not sure what else to say.

"She's such an asshole," Ezra says. "I can't believe she said that to you. Why didn't you tell me?"

I don't know. "I guess I was embarrassed." I hesitate. "Afraid she might be right."

"She's not right. Okay? Seriously, Felix, don't let that shit get into your head. Okay?"

"Yeah. Okay."

"God, she's such an asshole. Christ." He shakes his head, grabbing a fistful of his shirt, uses the end to wipe his face. "And I don't fucking believe her. She definitely put up that fucking gallery."

He's right—Marisol probably did do the gallery, and even if she didn't, she most likely knows who did—but suddenly, I feel exhausted. Exhausted by the drama. Exhausted by the anger. I wanted to know who put up that gallery, for revenge—for closure—but now I'm wondering if I even really need any of that. Maybe it's time to stop fighting, even if it means people like Marisol and grandequeen69 win.

"I'm sorry," I tell him.

"I said to stop apologizing."

"No—I mean," I say, "I'm sorry that I'm still texting Declan."

Ezra blinks, staring down at the boardwalk beneath our feet, shifting his jaw to the side a little. "I can't tell you not to text him anymore. But—Christ, why're you still talking to him?"

"We've just . . . I don't know, connected?" I can't tell Ezra that Declan has a crush on me. If he's upset now, I can't imagine what he'd do or say if he found that out.

"It's not like I can tell you to stop or anything," Ezra says. "Is it shitty of me, to be a little jealous?"

"That's just how you feel, I guess?" I hesitate. "I mean, I was a little jealous back there."

"Huh?"

"With Austin."

"Again: huh?"

God. This conversation's just going around in circles of awkward.

"You're jealous of me?" Ezra asks. "Or of Austin?"

"Not jealous like that," I say. "I mean—just jealous that you two even have each other, you know?"

How easy is it for Ezra? He goes from one guy to the next, one relationship to the next. He falls in and out of love. And I just continue to watch from the sidelines. This *thing*, whatever it is, that I have with Declan is the first time I've experienced a connection like this—the first time I've felt hope that I could be in my first relationship, be kissed for the first time, fall in love for the first time. It feels fragile, this thing—like it could slip through my fingers like water and spill at my feet.

"Are you going to stop texting him?" Ezra asks, glancing at me.

I bite my lip. "Probably not."

He lets out a heavy sigh, rubbing a hand over my curls.

"You still like me more than him, right?"

I roll my eyes. "Of course, Ez. You're my best friend."

But his smile's still strained as we leave the boardwalk and head back to the train.

SIXTEEN

By the time we make it to Ezra's apartment, the sun is high—but it doesn't make any difference, with the dark clouds that roll in, blanketing the air in darkness. The heat simmering over the city breaks, and purple lightning splits through the sky, thunder echoing so loudly that it feels like Ezra's entire apartment shakes. Lightning illuminates the room every time it strikes.

"I love thunderstorms," he tells me.

I hate them. I hate how unpredictable they are, how much it feels like fate is being left up to the whim of a few molecules.

"No wonder all the ancient people thought there were gods living up in the clouds," Ezra says. Another lightning strike, a thunderclap so loud I flinch. He grins at me. "You're not scared, are you?"

"Shut up."

"It's okay if you're scared," he says. "I'll protect you."

I hug my knees to my chest. "Seems like that's all you do recently."

He shrugs, glancing my way. "That's what friends are for, right?"

Ezra decides a thunderstorm is as good of an excuse as any to skip classes today, and I agree, though a part of me wants to go sprinting through the rain to get to St. Cat's. I was actually looking forward to working on my portfolio. I want to see what a new self-portrait would look like, after I've stood up for myself. Would my skin be as purple as the lightning outside, my eyes as dark as the gray sand and sea?

Ezra snuggles next to me, blanket covering him, and even with the thunder and rain lashing against his windows, he falls asleep almost instantly. My eyes are pretty heavy also, but I pull out my phone, tapping on Declan's last message to me.

Maybe it's not something you should think about. Maybe you should just do it, whatever it is you're too afraid to try. Just do it. Just say yes.

I type. **I said yes.**

He responds instantly, like he was waiting all night for me to text. **And what happened?**

I ended up at Coney Island. It was kind of a shitshow.

Fuck. Really? I feel bad now.

Don't feel bad. It was overdue drama.

213

Do you regret going?

No. The fight needed to happen.

He doesn't answer me right away. I glance down at Ezra, asleep against my leg, mouth open, strands of hair covering half of his face. My fingers fly across the keypad—but then I hesitate, delete, rewrite, hit *send*.

Remember you were telling me about your ex-boyfriend? The one who hates you now?

Yeah.

What happened?

He doesn't respond right away to that one either, and for a second, I'm worried that I crossed a line I didn't know had been drawn. Lightning flashes, and a gust of wind rattles the windows. Declan's response buzzes in my hand.

What usually happens, I guess. My heart was broken. Etc., etc.

My chest aches. *Declan's* heart was broken? The way I saw things, Declan was the one who suddenly cut things off and became the asshole we so loved and adored.

How was your heart broken?

You're pretty curious today.

Sorry. You don't have to tell me if you don't want to.

It's okay. It's just not super fun to delve into the details. Long story short, I could tell this guy was going to break up with me.

I frown, tilting my head at that one. Why would Declan think that? Everything had been great between him and Ez. Ezra had been happy.

I decided to end things first. It's kind of pathetic, I guess, but I

couldn't deal with getting hurt, so I pushed him away.

Pushed him away?

I was kind of a dick to him. Still am, I guess.

I'm gripping the phone, staring at the screen. It makes sense now—not that I forgive Declan for treating me and Ezra the way he has, but at least I know the reason for it.

He sends another message. I'm not proud of the way I ended things, and looking back on it I'd probably try to do things differently, but it's too late now. I just wanted to reject him and everything to do with him, before he could reject me.

I shake my head. But why did you think Ezra was going to break up with you?

I realize my mistake approximately three seconds after I hit send. "Shit!"

Ezra rolls away from me in his sleep.

Declan's message comes in. So you do go to St. Cat's?

"Fuck. Ah, God fucking damn it." Why do you think that?

You know Ezra Patel.

"Christ, I'm a fucking idiot."

Ezra peeks open an eye, groans. "What's wrong? What's happening?"

I rub a hand over my face. "Nothing—sorry, go back to sleep."

I don't have to tell him twice. He yanks the blanket up over his head without another word.

I sigh, begin typing. Okay, you're right. I know Ezra.

So, what, are you just trying to get details of our drama to spread gossip or something?

What? NO.

Another second. Then: **Are you Ezra?**

I actually laugh at that one, though I guess that's not too far from the truth. **No, I'm not Ezra. Is that disappointing?**

Not really. I've moved on. A beat. **To you, clearly.**

I raise an eyebrow. **You don't know who I am. You don't trust me. But you still like me?**

The heart wants what the heart wants, right?

I mean, maybe? I wouldn't really know.

What do you mean?

I mean I've never been in love.

You've never had feelings for another person?

I hesitate. I had a crush on Marisol, before it turned out she was a raging transphobe, and I've thought people are cute before, have been interested, but . . . **It depends on your definition of feelings, I guess? I've had crushes before, but I've never been in love.** I don't know what possesses me, I really don't, but I just keep going: **I mean, I WANT to be in love. That's something I've always wanted to feel. What's it like, to be in love and have that other person love you, too? Is it another level of friendship? Another level of trust, vulnerability, always telling that person your thoughts and feelings, sharing every little thing with them so that you're so in sync that it's like you're one person? Is it like every time you see them, your heart goes wild, and you can't think because you're so effing happy? Is it like whenever they're away, you feel like you're missing a piece of yourself? Does knowing someone loves you fill** you with confidence, because you know you're the type of person who deserves love? And what's it like to break up with someone you love? What's it like to decide to try again, and let yourself fall in love with someone else? To decide to take that chance you might get hurt, but still want to try? I don't know. But I want to.

Declan takes a while to respond—a minute passes, and another, and another, and I think with fear and worry and just a smidge of relief, *yes—I've officially done it. I've scared him away.* But finally, my phone buzzes: **What's stopping you?**

I mean, nothing, technically. Except that someone would need to fall in love with me, too.

Can't you love someone without them loving you?

Yeah, of course, but is unrequited love being IN love, or is that admiration, love from afar? And besides, I don't think anyone would fall in love with me.

Again, Declan doesn't answer. My eyes are starting to become so heavy I can barely keep them open. The thunderstorm is finally dying down—there aren't any echoing booms that could potentially be the end of the world, anyway, and the rain isn't coming down as hard—but there are still flashes of lightning. I'm about to lie down when my phone starts to buzz—and doesn't stop.

Declan's calling me.

I freak out. Drop the phone and watch it vibrate on the mattress. I should just let it go to voice mail. He probably called me accidentally, or . . .

Weirdest of all, though? I kind of want to hear his voice.

I snatch it up from the bed and swipe open the answer icon at the very last second. I open my mouth, but then it hits me—what if he recognizes my voice?

Declan speaks on the other end. "Hello?"

He sounds the same as he always does. Once upon a time, hearing Declan's voice would make me want to hand-to-God strangle anyone and anything standing too close to me . . . but now, I only hear his deep voice with an uncertain tone, maybe even a little shy, nervous—but with some anticipation, too.

"Lucky?" he says. "You there?"

I stand up, wobbling on the mattress, and jump onto the wooden floor, slipping a little as I run down the hall and slide into the bathroom, closing the door behind me so that I'm in almost-total darkness, purple shadowed light filtering in through the tiny window. I climb into the tub and huddle against the cold porcelain.

"Yeah," I whisper. My voice squeaks a little, embarrassingly. I clear my throat. "Yeah, I'm here."

"I should've asked if I could call first," he says. "Sorry. I just—without thinking, I just pressed the call button—"

"It's okay. It's all right." My heart's going way too hard, way too fast. I'm nervous as hell. Scared, too. What if he figures out that it's me? Do I have a recognizable voice? Should I try to lower it, so he can't tell?

"I wanted to hear your explanation," he says. "I mean, I can't believe you don't think anyone would fall in love with you."

I laugh a little—I can't help it. "So you had to call me so I could tell you?"

"I also wanted to hear your voice," he admits. "Make sure you aren't Jill."

I laugh harder at that one. I can hear him laughing, too. I'm not sure I've heard Declan laugh, not once since he broke up with Ezra. It's a nice sound—trailing, like he might remember the joke days later and keep on laughing.

He speaks softly. "You really think no one could fall in love with you?"

I bite my lip. "It's a little hard to explain."

"Try anyway."

I rub the back of my neck. "I mean . . . I don't want you to know who I am."

"What does that have to do with it?"

Everything. The fact that I'm Black, the fact that I'm queer, the fact that I'm trans. "It's like every identity I have . . . the more different I am from everyone else . . . the less interested people are. The less . . . lovable I feel, I guess. The love interests in books, or in movies or TV shows, are always white, cis, straight, blond hair, blue eyes. Chris Evans, Jennifer Lawrence. It becomes a little hard, I guess, to convince myself I deserve the kind of love you see on movie screens."

"That's ridiculous," Declan says in regular pretentious-asshole-Declan fashion—except this time, his words make my chest warm.

It's hard to explain. "I guess it just feels like I have one marginalization too many, sometimes. So many differences that I can never fit in with everyone else. I can feel people are uncomfortable with me, so I end up feeling uncomfortable, too, and then I end up standing and watching everyone else make connections, fall in love with each other, and I . . ."

I don't finish. Declan doesn't answer, not for a while. I feel relaxed, sitting there in the tub, phone pressed to my ear, knowing that he's on the other end, even if neither of us is speaking.

"I think I might be falling in love with you," he says. I bury my face in my knees. "Does that help?"

I shake my head, even though he can't see me.

"Tell me who you are," he says when I don't answer him. "Please."

"What if you don't like the answer?"

"You really are Jill, then?"

"No, I'm not Jill."

"You somehow made your voice a lot deeper, Jill."

I laugh into my knees.

"I just want to talk to you in person. I just want to meet you. That's all I want."

I sink into the tub until I'm lying on my back. I take a moment. Try to imagine meeting with Declan. Even if he doesn't freak out that I'm Lucky, and that I'd been trying to hurt him for revenge, I'd also have to explain everything to Ezra. And then, even if Ezra was okay with this—thing, whatever is going on between me and Declan—there'd be other little details to consider. If Declan still, after all that, wanted to date me, would he be interested in me . . . physically? As far as I know, Declan's only ever dated guys. I know that trans guys are guys, and I know that there're plenty of gay guys who're into trans guys, because certain *equipment* doesn't always matter, and shouldn't always matter. But, still, there are parts that I don't have that most guys do, parts that I don't even want, that Declan might end up missing. Even more confusing is that I'm not sure I identify as a trans guy anymore, anyway.

It would suck—really, really effing suck—to go through all of that, just for Declan to reject me.

"Lucky?" Declan says, voice soft. "You still there?"

"Yeah." I sit up, tapping my fingers on the side of the tub. "I'm sorry. I am. I just . . . I can't."

He lets out a breath of impatience that I'm very familiar with and is quiet on the other end for a while. Then, "All right. I'll just have to respect that."

I swallow. "If you don't want to talk to me anymore, I understand." That's what I say, but internally, all of my being is screaming *no*. I've gotten too used to speaking to Declan. To opening up to him about things I'm not sure I can tell anyone else, not even Ezra. To feeling, for once in my life, like I'm the kind of person who gets to be loved, too. I can already feel a hollow loss growing in my chest, at the thought of Declan saying that he doesn't want to speak to me anymore.

"I probably should cut things off," he says, "but I'm not sure I could stop talking to you at this point, even if I wanted to."

I try not to smile. Fuck. This is so weird, and I'm in so deep. "Same," I say.

SEVENTEEN

DECLAN AND I KEEP TALKING FOR HOURS, SPEAKING ABOUT anything and everything, total bullshit about MCU movies and whether Steve and Bucky are a canonical couple, to our theories on love.

"The issue is that we've never really gotten to see our own stories," Declan tells me. "We have to make those stories ourselves. Even if a creator made a character to be straight, they put those characters out into the world, right? So those characters are mine now. And I say that Steve and Bucky are gay as hell."

We play music for each other through the phones. From Khalid to Billie Holiday, until we eventually fall into a pattern of Sigur Rós–like instrumentals. There's a song that Declan tells me played in that Amy Adams alien movie that has me burying my face into my pillow so he won't hear me cry, because there's something about that song, the highs and lows and depth, and hearing Declan's voice asking me if this isn't one of the most beautiful songs I've ever heard, that makes me too fucking emotional.

On Friday morning, I wake up after about only two hours of sleep. I'm back at my Harlem apartment. My dad's already up, making scrambled eggs.

"I'm surprised you're awake," he says to me from across the kitchen counter. "I got up at five to use the bathroom and saw your bedroom light was still on."

"Oh," I say, trying to pretend like it isn't a big deal. "Must've fallen asleep without turning it off again."

He gives me his *I don't believe you* face, and I give him my *I know, and I don't care* face. I sit at the counter while he slides my plate over. My dad takes a bite of toast, watching me carefully. I raise an eyebrow.

"Is there something on my face?"

"You seem really happy," he says.

I raise both eyebrows this time. "Really?"

"It's a good look, kid," he says, reaching out to land a meaty hand on my head. "Smiling does wonders for you."

I swat his hand away, trying not to grin. "Thanks, I guess?"

"So I take it you're staying up until sunrise because you're talking to someone on the phone?"

I scrunch up my face. Guilty.

"You teenagers," he says, "always thinking you've invented the wheel. I'd spend hours talking to your mom when we were kids."

My smile fades. There's always an automatic stab of pain to my chest whenever my dad mentions my mom. When I was younger, I'd hoped they would get back together. It was a few years before I realized it was never going to happen. I could never understand how my dad seemed okay with that. How he decided to move on. She was supposed to be the love of his life, right? I'd asked him if he didn't love my mom anymore once, and he told me that of course he did.

"I probably always will love her," he'd said. "But it was a tough lesson to learn, realizing that I couldn't wait for her to decide she would love me again. It wasn't healthy. If I fall in love again, it'll be with a woman who loves me also—not someone who I have to convince to love me. It's easier, I think, to love someone you know won't love you—to chase them, knowing they won't feel the same way—than to love someone who might love you back. To risk loving each other and losing it all."

He lets out a heavy sigh as he drops the toast on his plate. "Anyway—I'm happy that you're happy. That's all that ever matters, right?"

"Right."

He picks up a glass of orange juice. "Is it Ezra?"

"What? No!"

He narrows his eyes, like he doesn't believe me. "You two

spend every second together, so I just assumed . . ."

"Bad assumption to make. Bad, bad assumption."

He raises his hands defensively. "Okay. All right. Who is it, then?"

It's not like he knows who Declan Keane is, but even so, it feels strange to say his name out loud. "No one you know."

He nods slowly. "And . . . I take it that you're being—ah—safe?"

I stare at him blankly. "Really? You're going to give me *the talk*? Right now? Over *breakfast*?"

He clears his throat. "Well," he says, "you should just be prepared. There are—um—specific things I can't really help you with . . . I don't know a lot about the pill . . ."

I clench my jaw and look away. He's right, I guess, technically. He might not have a lot of information on birth control options, if that's something I wanted to start—testosterone might make Shark Week disappear (thank God), but it wouldn't stop me from getting pregnant, if I were actually having sex—which, obviously, I'm not.

But the way my dad said it . . . Once again, I get the sense that my father categorizes me as his daughter, and not his son. There's always a flare of anger whenever he misgenders me, but at the spark of that anger is hurt, a dull ache in my chest.

My dad chews for a while. "Maybe the Callen-Lorde center could help," he says. "They could give you more information, if you need it. Though I sure as hell hope you don't. You're only seventeen, and fine, I've lost the fight in you not hanging out with Ezra so much, but—"

"I don't," I say loudly, just to get him to shut up. "Need the information."

"You don't?" he repeats.

"Nope." Not yet, anyway.

He mouths, *Thank God.*

It's still pretty early by the time I get to St. Catherine's. The sky is a bright, clear blue, sun shining yellow, birds twittering. Only a few students linger around outside the building. I get through the front sliding glass doors and pass into the lobby. My heart doesn't hammer as hard as it usually does in this space, and my hands don't get as sweaty, so, I guess, progress?

I get to the acrylics classroom about an hour before Jill's supposed to give her usual morning check-in. I have two self-portraits now: one where I look like I'm on fire, and another that I'm still working on from time to time, where it looks like I'm underwater. My latest painting is in the space I occupy with Ezra. I'm excited to get back to it. I haven't worked on the painting in a couple of days now, but the memory of holding the brush, finding peace in the colors, inspiration in the strokes . . .

Paint on the palette, brush in my hand—oranges today, then swaths of red. The red sinks into a darker purple of shadows, which filters in the light of blue, shifting to a color as bright as the sky outside. The bell echoes, but I don't stop. The classroom door opens and closes, voices filter into the room, laughter and chatter, the scraping of stools. The blue meets yellow, then gold.

When I feel someone standing behind me, I assume it's just Jill—she always likes to observe, will offer advice before moving on—but I startle when the person speaks.

"That's good," Declan says.

That's all he tells me. A simple, two-word sentence—but my heart feels like it's about to break out of my chest. He moves on, heading for his regular seat in the back of the classroom. I watch him go as he nods at James, already at the table and talking to Hazel, who lets out a loud laugh. Declan hops up onto his own stool and pulls out his phone, checking the screen with a quick glance—probably looking for a message from me. From Lucky.

That's good.

I turn back to the canvas. Fuck. My heart's going crazy. I try to take deep breaths, air swelling in my chest. I shouldn't be this excited to see Declan, but I am. I have to remind myself: He thinks he's in love with *Lucky*. Not me.

The second bell rings, and I can hear Jill calling for us to quiet down and take our seats. I leave my station and my canvas. Declan sits with James and Marc and Hazel, at the table beside Marisol and Leah. Ezra isn't here yet. There's no way I want to sit beside Marisol now, not after the Great Dumpster Fire of Coney Island, but the two last stools are on either side of her.

Marisol ignores me as I walk up to the table and grab my

stool, pulling it as far away from her as possible, scooching closer to Declan's table. Declan barely glances my way.

"I'm surprised he's willing to be anywhere near me," Marisol tells Leah. "I mean, I'm *such* an ignorant bigot, right?"

Leah shifts uncomfortably in her seat.

Jill begins her daily check-in. "Before we get started, I'd like to remind everyone that we'll be having the end-of-summer gallery again. The administration, myself included, will be choosing one student from all of the applicants. It's a wonderful honor," she tells us with a brilliant smile.

I stare at the table. Just the mention of the gallery makes me feel self-conscious, like everyone's looking at me, thinking of the old pictures they'd seen of me, remembering my dead-name. Jill starts a speech on inspiration and its origins, but I zone out—between Marisol sitting to my right and Declan sitting to my left, there's absolutely no way I can pay attention.

I try not to look at Declan—I really do—but I can't stop myself. He went out of his way to tell me he thinks my painting is good, but he won't spare me a single glance—or even a glare—now. And why would he? To him, I'm just Felix, the prick who hates him.

"If I'm ignorant," Marisol whispers to Leah, "would he really want to be anywhere near me? I find that a little hard to believe, I guess."

"Okay, all right," Leah says beneath her breath, flailing her hands around, like she's trying to wave away the bullshit. "Let's just chill, all right?"

Declan stares straight ahead, listening to Jill. I'm almost too afraid to answer Marisol. If I speak and he hears me, will he suddenly recognize my voice—realize that I'm Lucky?

Marisol rolls her eyes and turns back to the front of the class. James turns his head and mutters something to Declan, and I'm almost jealous. I want to speak to Declan, too—talk to him with the same casual ease. I want to ask him how he is, tell him about what happened at Coney Island and hear what he thinks, ask for his advice on Marisol, if I should just tell her to go fuck herself.

Christ. He said he's in love with me.

I can't look away. Declan has a pinch in between his eyebrows as he listens to Jill. He has this habit, I never really noticed it before, of leaning his head a little to the side as if he can hear better out of one ear. His eyelashes are redder than his brown hair in the yellow sunlight that floods the classroom—but even in the light, his eyes are a dark, deep brown. His nose is almost too fine for his face, and his sturdy jaw is all sharp angles. His mouth . . . his lips are parted, just a little. I'm embarrassed just noticing. Even the word *lips* feels so . . .

He looks up at me, through his eyelashes, and I realize I've been staring. He gives me a look. Like, *what?* He even says it. A low rumble, impatient. "What?"

Breath catches in my throat. I'm still afraid to speak, but even if I wasn't, I don't think I could anyway. I shake my head, sit up straight, and keep my eyes on Jill for the rest of her lecture, pretending to listen but unable to think about anything else but the heat that seems to be radiating from Declan.

What if I did it? Just turned to him, right now, and told him that I'm Lucky?

Well, he'd probably hate me for all fucking eternity.

But he says he has feelings for me. That means he has feelings for who I am, no matter what he thinks my name is, or if we only speak on the phone or in person. Right?

Maybe there's a way I could talk to him alone—get him to realize that he likes me, maybe even loves me, without ever having to tell him the truth. Without him ever knowing that I was Lucky.

By the time lunch rolls around, Ezra's texted me back to let me know he has a cold, and he's skipping today. I ask if I can bring him anything, and he says no.

Stay away. I don't want you to get sick, too.

I don't usually find myself at St. Cat's without Ezra. It's in these moments that I realize Ez is really my only friend here. I'm embarrassed, almost, without anyone to hang out with, anyone to speak to.

When my phone buzzes, I hope that it might be Ezra, and that he's changed his mind—has asked me to bring him some chicken wings and French fries or something—but the notification is for a message from Instagram. My heart starts to pound.

Alone without your friend to follow around?

There's a reason no one else wants to talk to you.

You're pathetic, pretending to be a boy.

What the fuck?

My hands shake. I fight the desire to chuck my phone. Why can't this piece of shit just leave me the hell alone? And—what the hell, are they *watching* me, right here and now?

I look up and stare around at the groups of people in the parking lot—some standing by the lobby's glass doors, Marisol smoking a cigarette. Some stand under the shade of the trees. Almost every single person has their phones out. It could be any of them, literally anyone here.

I'm thinking of giving up, just walking down to Ezra's apartment, when Leah appears at my side.

"A bunch of us are going to White Castle," she says. "Wanna come?"

Tyler, Nasira, and Hazel walk with us as we leave the parking lot, heading down the cracked sidewalk, dodging a carton of chicken wing bones and a clump of tumbleweave blowing in the breeze—that is, until Tyler grabs it and starts to chase Nasira, who screams and runs, Tyler cackling.

Leah winces. "So gross."

"Ten dollars Tyler takes it with him to add to his collage," Hazel says.

"I'm not betting against that," Leah says. "He's one hundred percent bringing it back."

"How's your portfolio going?" I ask Leah. I know that she wasn't happy to be forced into acrylics, when she could've been using the summer classes to finesse her photography for college applications.

Tyler has stopped chasing Nasira and they wait on the corner and start walking as we reach them, the tumbleweave hanging out of Tyler's pocket.

Leah shrugs. "It's all right. It'll never be perfect. I know I have to get over the desire for anything I create to be perfect. But it still sucks when I know it could be better. I don't know—my portfolio's nothing like *your* work, anyway," she says.

"Wait, what? What do you mean?"

"I mean that your paintings are always freaking amazing."

Hazel rolls her eyes. "You know, no offense," she says, "but I don't think Felix is even that good."

She might as well have slapped me. Nasira raises an eyebrow. "Tell us how you really feel."

Hazel continues. "His portraits are technically good, but I never really feel any emotion whenever I look at them."

Defensiveness rises. "Okay. Good to know, I guess."

"It's just my opinion," she says.

"No one asked for your opinion, but all right."

"It's nothing to get so mad about. We should all be used to critique and criticism by now, if we want to become better artists."

"Yeah, but *not good* isn't a real critique," I say. The others don't say anything. I roll my eyes. "It doesn't matter. I don't really care," I say, even though that's a straight-up lie. Of course I care what people think of my artwork, and Hazel's comment stings, a little like hitting my funny bone, the pain vibrating through me.

"I really didn't mean to offend you," Hazel says. "I just get a little tired of these blanket statements. *Felix is amazing.* Like, what does that even mean? And how is that supposed to actually help you grow as an artist? I don't think we should ever get complacent with our work or our talent. We should always be pushing ourselves to become better."

I know that she's right. I guess I just would've preferred to hear what she's got to say in class, when we're supposed to critique each other and I can see it coming—or even alone, in a one-on-one conversation, so that I wouldn't have to feel as awkward as I do right now. It isn't until the next thing she says that I even pause.

"I don't know. For me, it always feels good to tell the truth," she says.

It feels good to tell you the truth. I guess plenty of people believe that telling the truth is important—but that's also almost exactly what grandequeen69 sent to me in an Instagram message. I squint at Hazel as the echoes of embarrassment give way to numbness. What if it's been Hazel all along? I hadn't really considered or suspected her at all, but maybe she was tired of my art and wanted to knock me down off my pedestal—or maybe she really had just considered the gallery to be valid artwork. It was the kind of gallery that I could see Hazel doing—art for the sake of art, without caring how her work would affect others. . . .

I pause and let everyone else walk ahead, but Leah stays behind with me. She seems uncomfortable, holding an arm to her side, and asks me if I'm all right. "It was kind of mean of Hazel to say that," she tells me.

I agree with a nod, but I can't stop the swirling thoughts that've begun to cloud my head.

"I'm sorry about Coney Island," Leah says. It takes a second for my mind to catch up with the shift in topic. "I don't know what's gotten into Mari recently. I mean, I know she's having trouble with her dad and everything . . ."

I didn't know that. I'm not sure I need to know, either. Does having a hard life give anyone an excuse to treat someone else like shit? I'm not sure I need Leah to humanize Marisol for me—that I need Marisol to become some sort of antihero in Leah's version of everything that's happened. We all make mistakes. We all have a chance to learn and grow from them. But we all also have the right to choose whether we'll forgive someone for the mistakes they've made, and I've chosen not to forgive Marisol.

"I feel like I'm supposed to say it's all right," I tell her, "but it's really not."

She nods. "Yeah. Yeah, you're right. I know you're right."

We cross in front of a bunch of bars with Pride signs hanging up outside. Leah asks me if I plan on going to the march. "Ezra invited me and Austin," she says.

I don't know why, but my heart jolts a little at that. "Oh,"

I say. "No, I don't really like the march."

"What?" Leah says, eyes shining with surprise. "Why not? I freaking *love* the march. I mean, I know there's shitty stuff going on with corporations joining in on the parade and everything, but everyone's so happy and it's the biggest celebration of love and self-love and it's the one time of the year where you can just be queer as hell—well, I guess nothing's really *stopping* any of us from being queer as hell every day of the year, but you know what I mean."

The excitement in her eyes makes me laugh a little. "You sound like Ezra."

Her smile fades as we walk in quiet, watching as the others laugh at something Tyler's said up ahead. "I checked out Marc's phone," she whispers. "I didn't find anything except some pictures that have forever scarred me. He doesn't even have an Instagram account."

I should be used to the frustration, the disappointment, but it still sinks into my stomach. I wonder if I should tell Leah that a part of me suspects Hazel now, but I feel an exhaustion I wasn't really expecting. I don't think we'll ever figure out who was behind the gallery, and now, I'm suddenly tired of trying. Leah could check every single person's phone at St. Catherine's, and I think I already know how it would end. "Thanks anyway."

"I don't know, I wonder if I should check out Marisol's phone," she tells me. "I mean, I know she said she didn't do it, but—well, it wouldn't be the first mistake she's made. And even if it wasn't her, maybe she knows who it was. Maybe she talked about it with someone in a text or something."

I hesitate. "I don't think we'll ever figure out who was behind the gallery."

Leah stops in her tracks. I turn around to look at her.

"You're not giving up, are you?" she says. "You can't give up. We've barely even started. It might take a month, a few months, an entire year—but I *will* find out who did this." She pauses. "Unless that's what scares you."

"What?"

"Maybe you're scared of knowing who did the gallery." She shrugs. "I mean, I'm a little scared myself. I've never been great at confrontation."

"I don't know. I just don't know if it's really worth the drama."

"Ezra is here to support you," she says, "and I am, too. So let's catch the asshole. Okay?"

I can't help but smile a little, and she loops her arm around mine as we walk. The White Castle is next to a gas station. A few other students are hanging out in the parking lot with bags of snacks and sodas. Declan's there, I see with a quick flutter of my heart, with James and Marc, just leaning against the wall of the gas station and talking. Tyler walks up to them, and he and Marc start laughing about something while James turns to follow Hazel into the White Castle. Leah grins at me as she hurries to catch up with them.

I hesitate. This probably isn't a good idea. No—no, this

definitely isn't a good idea, not at all. But even knowing that, I walk across the parking lot, slowing down as I reach Declan. He walks away from Marc and Tyler so that he's standing alone in the shade, phone out, scrolling through Instagram. He looks up with surprise when I stop in front of him.

He stares at me.

I stare at him.

He raises an eyebrow. "Yes . . . ?"

I don't know what to say. Shit. God fucking damnit, I have no idea what to say.

He full-on frowns now. "What do you want?"

And it hits me—of course, only now does it hit me—that if I speak, he might just recognize my voice. Over the phone was one thing, but to have heard that voice, and see it actually coming from my mouth—something might click, and Declan could realize I'm Lucky.

But I can't just walk away now. I open my mouth, hoping words will come out, but none do.

He's making the *okaaaaaaay* expression now. He pushes away from the wall, like he's going to leave me standing there, maybe join the others and go into the White Castle—

"Thanks," I manage to blurt out.

He pauses. "For what?"

"For what you said earlier." I swallow. "For saying my painting is good."

He smirks now. "I didn't realize you needed my validation that badly."

"I don't need your fucking validation," I snap.

Declan lets out a laugh. The same laugh, I realize, that I've started to love hearing over the phone. "Sure you don't, Felix."

I take in a breath. "It was just nice of you," I mutter.

"Right. Well, I can be nice sometimes, believe it or not."

I scratch at my arm. "I believe it."

He narrows his eyes a little, like he's waiting for the insult to follow. And I get it. I really do. Usually, I'd jump at the chance to start an argument with Declan. It feels odd, now—so fucking strange—to look Declan in the face and attempt to have an ordinary conversation, without trying to figure out a way to attack him.

"Well," he says slowly, watching me. "I'm going to join the others."

I feel a wave of disappointment, but I shouldn't be surprised. He only knows me as Felix, not Lucky—and this Felix is acting weird as fuck right now. I nod, stepping aside, as Declan heads back over to Marc and Tyler. He glances over his shoulder at me with a lingering frown.

When Declan calls me later that night, he doesn't mention the strange way that guy who hates him was acting today. A part of me hoped that he would—hoped there'd be some sort of acknowledgment that he thinks about me. *Me,* me. Felix. Not just Lucky.

But he doesn't mention me as Felix at all. I'm back in my

dad's apartment, in my bedroom—I'd tried stopping off at Ezra's and buzzed his apartment, but he didn't answer his door, and he wouldn't respond to my texts. I have no idea if he's actually more pissed off at me than he's letting on, or if it really is just a bad cold. When I'd asked Austin about it earlier, he told me that Ezra might just need a little time alone—which isn't, you know, ominous at all.

"What is one thing about you," Declan asks me, "that no one else knows?"

I think about it for a second, but only for a second. "I have 476 emails in my drafts box."

There's silence on the phone.

"Hello?" I say.

"I'm sorry," Declan says. "Did you say 476 emails?"

I hesitate, smirk growing. "Yeah. Is that crazy?"

"Um—you know, I don't know, we all have our quirks . . ."

"It's okay if you think it's crazy."

He laughs. "I don't want to sound judgmental."

"I know it's a lot."

"Why do you have so many emails drafted?"

"Well," I say, taking a breath. "They're all emails I've written to my mom, but have never sent."

I can practically feel Declan's smile fading away. "Why haven't you sent them?"

I take a second, trying to form the right words in my head. "She left my dad when I was ten and started this new life in Florida. She's happier now—loves her new life more than she loves her old one, and she never answers my calls or my emails . . . I'm pretty sure she doesn't love me anymore. But—I don't know, I guess I miss her, so I've always written these emails about everything I'm going through. Maybe one day I'll just send all of them at once and fuck up her in-box." I force a laugh.

Declan's voice is soft. "It's hard to believe that she wouldn't love you."

Warmth spreads over my skin. I smile into my hand. "What about you?"

"My biggest secret?"

"Yes."

He takes longer to speak than I did. In the beats of silence, the irony strikes me: just a couple weeks ago, I'd been desperate to learn Declan's biggest secret. Eager to use it against him, so that I could hurt him in the same way I thought he'd hurt me. Now I only want to know his secret because I want to know more about him. Because I think I might be falling for him, too.

"My father," he says. I play with my bedsheet in between my fingers. "My father disowned me."

I stop breathing. I sit up.

"Lucky?" Declan says. "You there?"

I shake my head. "What?"

"When I told him I had a boyfriend—when I told him

about Ezra," Declan says, "my father disowned me."

Pain swells in my chest. I can feel myself starting to cry.

"We were never really close," he tells me. "He's always been horrible. He was pretty abusive. Not physically, but emotionally. He always made me feel like I was worthless, you know? He does the same shit to my mom, and she doesn't fight back. She just does whatever he says. She didn't fight for me when he kicked me out. It took a while to heal from that. I'm still kind of healing, I guess. And it's stupid, but—even though he hurt me so much, and even though I know he isn't healthy for me, I still want him to love me. It's fucked-up, I know it is. I'm living with my grandfather now, up in Beacon—just takes a long-ass time to get in and out of the city, so I try to stay with someone for part of the week, when I can."

"I'm sorry," I say. That's all I can think to tell him. "I'm so, so sorry."

I get pissed at my dad. So fucking frustrated with him when he refuses to say my name, or when he messes up my pronouns. But I've never considered that he might disown me for being trans. I've been lucky enough that the thought never crossed my mind.

"It's all right," Declan says. "I've been doing better, living with my grandpa. Now the main issue is that my dad was going to pay for my college tuition and everything, and I have to figure out how to take care of that on my own, since my grandpa can't afford it—he's just barely surviving on retirement savings. He's offered to sell the house for me, and it'd admittedly be a huge help, but I can't let him do that. I know that house means a lot to him. I'll just have to figure something out on my own. A privileged-as-fuck problem to have, believe me, I know."

I had no idea. Ezra had no idea, or he would've mentioned it. Declan rarely talked about what he was thinking and feeling, when we were all friends—but this? I hold my phone away from my mouth so that he won't hear me crying. I even cover my mouth with my hand. He hears me anyway.

"Are you crying?"

I don't say anything. I'm crying so hard I can barely breathe.

"Don't cry for me. Seriously, don't. My dad's horrible, and yeah, it hurt—but it was for the best. I hate the commute, but my granddad's great. Really. I'm not just saying that. I'm happy. All right?"

I nod. Force myself to choke out the words. "All right."

We're silent for a while. Maybe Declan's just waiting for me to pull myself together, I don't know. A few minutes pass before I stop crying, before I can breathe again. My voice is stuffed up. "Is that why you broke up with Ezra?" I ask.

Declan must be shuffling through something on the other end. I hear papers. "I mean—yeah, it really fucked me up, and I guess it made me—you know, need some space to figure myself out in my new life, but it wasn't the whole reason." He sighs. "I wasn't lying before. I could tell Ezra wasn't as into me as I was into him."

I frown, shaking my head. This isn't the first time Declan's said Ezra wasn't into him. "What made you think that?"

"Because I'm pretty sure he's in love with his best friend," Declan tells me. "That guy, Felix."

EIGHTEEN

SATURDAY NIGHT, EZRA TEXTS ME, BEGGING ME TO HANG out.

I'm finally over this effing cold and I want to celebrate.

As soon as his name pops up in my phone, all I can hear is Declan's voice. *I'm pretty sure he's in love with his best friend. That guy, Felix.*

At first, I'd thought Declan was joking. That's what I said to him. "You're joking, right?"

"No," he said. "No, I'm not joking. You ever watch the way Ezra looks at him? Or the way he follows Felix around like a lost puppy?"

I'd wanted to correct him. Ezra doesn't follow me like a lost puppy—it's the other way around. Ezra's the only friend I really have at St. Cat's, while everyone flocks around him like he's the sun itself. I caught myself before I started arguing, though. I'm pretty sure Declan would've been able to immediately guess who I am if I did.

Declan kept going. "We all started hanging out at the same time, and the longer we hung out, the more Ezra fell for Felix. Simple as that."

I stare at the text Ezra sent. There's no way Declan's right. Ezra isn't exactly shy about who he wants or who he likes. Case study number two: Austin. Ezra's been all over the guy since his party. Why would he be with Austin if he's in love with me? He would've said something. Declan just misread things, or wasn't feeling the relationship anymore and wanted a reason to break up with Ez.

These are all the things I tell myself, anyway. But there's a voice in the back of my head: *What if Declan's right? What if Ezra's in love with me?*

I type on my phone, asking Ezra if I should meet him at his apartment, but he tells me no—he wants me to meet him at Stonewall.

I hold in a groan. Stonewall Inn? Really? It's ten days into Pride month, so it's going to be packed. A few years ago, I was totally obsessed with the place. It's where the riots began with trans women of color like Marsha P. Johnson and Sylvia Rivera—where the marches started. But after visiting the Inn a few times, I quickly learned I'm not exactly the *partying* type. The crowds, the blasting music, the sticky floors, the white straight tourist girls "accidentally" elbowing me because they think I'm in their way for, you know, existing, the sketchier older guys offering to buy me drinks (which, okay, I've definitely taken, who would turn down a free beer?) . . . It's not exactly my idea of fun.

But Ezra loves anything and everything to do with Pride month, and Stonewall is a part of that. By the time I leave my dad's place and get to Christopher Street, there's a line outside with a group of girls in front of me, laughing and talking excitedly. The line moves quickly, and the brawny, bald bouncer in a tutu and Mardi Gras beads takes my fake ID and stamps my wrist without even looking at my face. Inside, the disco spotlights swirl, and a drag queen sings Mariah Carey on a small stage, shirtless boys covered in glitter screaming along to the words. The floor is so packed I have to squeeze in between bodies to push my way through, past the bar and up the stairs.

On the second floor, the lights are low and music blasts. The crowd jumps up and down to a Journey song. A spotlight shines, and I see him—Ezra is right in the middle of it all, shouting the words, hair everywhere, shirt gone, grin split across his face. He may or may not be a little intoxicated.

He's in love with his best friend. That guy, Felix.

I hope to see Austin, just to prove Declan wrong, but he's nowhere to be found. I push through the crowd of jumping bodies and pull on Ezra's elbow. He spins to me, eyes wide, pupils filling his irises. He yells my name, though I can barely hear it over the music, and grabs my hands to dance with me, but I hate dancing—hate the feeling of everyone watching, of feeling so awkward, unable to just let go. Ez wobbles and almost falls, leaning on me—he smells like mint and wine. It's only eleven. How is he already so drunk?

"Do you want water?" I yell to him.

Ezra nods, so I start pushing my way to the bar. I'm surprised when a hand grabs mine, and I see he's decided to follow.

We go to the corner farthest away from the DJ and the speakers. We can at least hear each other when we shout. Ezra pulls his shirt from his back pocket and yanks it on, but not before I get a glimpse at his abs. Ezra catches me looking and grins at me, but he doesn't say anything about it. "I didn't think you'd come."

"I almost didn't. You know how I feel about Stonewall."

We get one glass of water and two straws to share.

"Where's Austin?" I shout to him.

"Huh?"

"Austin—where is he?"

"Oh," Ezra says. "We broke up."

He's in love with his best friend. That guy, Felix.

"What? Why?"

Ezra shrugs. "I don't know. Can we talk about it later?"

"Sure—yeah." That's what I say, even though this is the only thing I want to talk about now.

We lean in, both sipping. Ezra stares at me as we drink.

"What is it?" I ask when I take a breath, pulling away. He's not in love with me. There's no way he's in love with me.

Ezra shakes his head without looking away. "Nothing. Just thinking about how lucky I am that you're my friend."

God, he's so drunk. "What's your alcohol intoxication level right now?"

"Not that high," he says, defensive. When I give him a look, he rolls his eyes. "I grabbed a bottle of champagne from my parents' place before I left."

I squint at him. "I thought you were at your apartment. I thought you were sick."

He shrugs. "I got a little tired of Brooklyn. I needed a break, so I ended up at my parents' penthouse."

I frown. Somehow, by *Brooklyn*, I think he means *me*. Was he really that upset with me, that I'm still speaking with Declan? Why didn't he tell me that he'd broken up with Austin?

He's in love with his best friend.

The music changes to BTS. Lights of all colors start flashing. Everyone screams.

"Shit, I love this song." Ezra spins around. "Dance with me?"

"I don't know—"

"I want you to dance with me!"

"I'm not good at dancing."

"You're just being self-conscious," Ezra says, tapping my forehead.

He extends a hand, waiting. I know that he's right. I'm tired of doing nothing but sitting to the side, watching and wishing I could join in, but too afraid to actually try. And maybe dancing in Stonewall doesn't feel like much, but it's still something. I grab Ezra's hand, and he pulls me back into the crowd and jumps around to the beat, laughing all the while, spinning me in a circle. He puts his hands on my waist, moving us closer. The song changes again. It's slower, has a deeper bass. The lights get darker. Ezra leans down and puts his head on my shoulder.

"This okay?" he asks against my ear.

Shit. He's in love with me. Declan's right. I think Ezra really might be in love with me.

I just nod, nervous that my voice might crack. Ezra presses closer, and it's not like we haven't touched before—we've hugged a thousand times, cuddled in our sleep, snuggled practically every single day—but his closeness feels different this time. It makes my heart beat a little harder. He pulls his head back from my shoulder and stares at me carefully, like this is totally normal for him, like it isn't uncomfortable for him to hold my eye contact the way that he does now. He watches me like he's noticed something, but he isn't sure what.

The song changes. I let go of Ez and pull away, making my way back to the bar. Ezra follows. His eyes are glazed over.

"You should probably drink some more water," I tell him, sliding the glass over.

"Yeah," he mumbles. "You're right."

We don't dance again for the rest of the night. We sit on our stools, watching everyone else go crazy over songs, laughing and making out and drifting around the dance floor. When Ezra asks me if I'm coming over to his place tonight, I hesitate, a little embarrassed. I liked the way my heart started beating harder, liked Ezra's fingers on my waist . . . Now, suddenly, everything feels different.

I tell him yes, and we're out the door, into the summer heat. The entire street in front of Stonewall is closed off, vendors selling rainbow-colored everything in preparation for the march, tourists wandering and taking selfies. We're quiet as we walk. Quiet as we sit next to each other on the train. Kids shout, "It's showtime!" They start pumping music, doing flips and spinning around poles.

When we get off the train in Brooklyn and start walking back to Ezra's place, past the cars lining the street and piles of black garbage bags fluttering in the breeze, I dare myself to speak. "What happened with Austin?"

He still doesn't want to talk about it—I can tell from the way he runs a hand through his hair, trying to untangle his curls. "I don't know. I'm just not that into him, and I figured it's better to break it off now."

"Why didn't you tell me?" I ask him. "I mean—are you really that angry at me?"

His eyes widen. "Angry?"

"Yeah. You know." I pause. "About Declan?"

He shrugs one shoulder. "I wasn't really angry. Hurt, maybe. But not angry."

We're quiet again.

"I mean," he says, "I drove myself crazy for a little while, you know? Wondering what you two could be talking about. Wondering if you like him more than you like me. Feeling all . . . betrayed, I guess." He takes a deep breath and stretches his arms behind his head. "But I realized that was all immature bullshit. I don't own you. It's stupid that I felt like I did."

We get to his apartment and stomp up the stairs. I haven't been here in a few days, when just a couple of weeks ago, this was practically my home. When Ezra opens the door, I step inside, sinking into the familiarity and the comfort of his space—but once I kick off my shoes at the door and look up, I do a double take. The white Christmas lights are still hanging on the walls, blinking and putting the apartment in a soft glow, but the mattress is gone. There's a giant sofa up against the wall, facing the TV. There's even an end table with a lamp on it.

He sees my face and grins. "I went to IKEA."

The door closes behind me. I cautiously head over to the couch and sit on it, testing it out. I sink about two inches. It's soft as fuck.

Ezra grins at me. "Nice, right?"

"Where's the mattress?"

"In my room. I still need to get a bed frame."

I run my hand over the couch's gray fabric. It's like velvet. Shit. I feel like I didn't get to witness a major milestone in Ezra's life. "I've missed you," I tell him.

He watches me from the kitchen, leaning on the counter.

"Yeah. I've missed you, too."

"Me and Declan—we don't really talk about anything," I tell him. "Just bullshit most of the time. And . . ." I hesitate. Declan's story about his father—about being disowned—feels like Declan's story to tell. I'm not sure I should tell Ezra what'd happened. "And I just tell him stuff about my mom sometimes. That's all." I try to ignore the pinch of guilt that I'm lying.

Ezra walks over, white lights glowing against his brown skin, shining against his black hair. He sits on the couch beside me. "Austin was really pissed at me when I broke up with him."

"Oh." I don't really know what to say. "What happened?"

Ezra groans. "It was so fucking bad. We went to Olive Garden yesterday, because I thought it might be better to break up with him if I took him out for dinner or something, and I tried to be nice about it. I told him he's cute, and I like him a lot, but I just—I don't know, he isn't the one for me. And he started crying and telling me that I led him on and all this shit, and he threw the breadsticks at me."

I almost laugh. I bite my lip to stop myself. "He threw the breadsticks?"

Ez glares at me. "It's not funny."

I nod, forcing a frown. "You're right. Sorry. Not funny."

Ezra and I are quiet for a second before a snort escapes me. Ezra clears his throat, fighting off his own smile, before we look at each other and crumple into laughter. Once we start, it's hard to stop.

"But the breadsticks are the best part," I tell him.

"Right? It was like adding insult to injury."

He wipes his eyes and hides his face in his hands, and I really hope the tears are from laughing too hard. "I don't know," he says, his voice muffled. "I felt like I was forcing myself to go out with him, when I didn't really want to, and I feel horrible, because I think he might really like me, and . . ."

He unhides his face, watching me, not looking away. He's in love with me. He really might actually be in love with me. I almost ask him if it's true. But the heat builds from my chest, up my neck and to my mouth, and suddenly I can't speak. I swallow and look away.

A beat passes. I take a deep breath.

"I'm jealous," I tell him, glancing back at him with a small smile.

His eyebrows shoot up. "Jealous? Why?"

I shrug a little, embarrassed. "I've never had a boyfriend before. I've never been kissed before. I want that, but the fact that it hasn't happened yet—I don't know, it makes me feel like those are things that are meant for everyone else but me."

Ezra already knows. I've told him this before. But now— now, when I think he might be in love with me—it feels like everything I say has a different meaning.

He clenches his jaw as he watches me. We sit in quiet for a long time. So long it starts to feel uncomfortable. I rack my brain for something stupid to say, to get him to laugh, to get us back to the friendship we once had, chilling in the park, high as fuck, talking about anything and everything and nothing at all. God, that feels like years ago now.

Silence. A car passes by outside, lights cast on the wall until it's gone.

Ezra whispers. "Can I kiss you?"

My gaze snaps up to his. "What?"

He doesn't repeat himself.

"Are you drunk?"

"No, I'm not drunk."

He won't look away. He's still waiting for my answer. I can't breathe as I nod. He doesn't hesitate—he leans in, and I flinch, bump my mouth against his, but he only pauses before leaning in again, more slowly this time. His lips touch mine, my heart thrumming, beating against my chest like it's trying to jump into his. I inhale against his lips, and he pulls away. My first kiss.

He still won't speak. His eyes flicker, looking at my own, waiting for an answer.

I lean in this time, and he puts a hand to my face, the other to the back of my neck, and I push my mouth against his, so hard my tooth grazes against his bottom lip. He pulls back an inch. "Softer," he murmurs. I nod, mumbling an apology, pulling him back to me again. All I can feel are his lips, his hands under my shirt, on my legs, up and down my back. Somehow, I end up on his lap, legs on either side of him, and I can feel him, feel his hard-on, which both scares the shit out of me and sends a thrill through me as I press against him, tugging at his shirt—

He pulls back. I try to follow his mouth with my own, but he pulls back again.

"You okay?" I say, breathless.

Ezra nods. He can't look at me. "Yeah. Yeah, I just—"

He shifts uncomfortably. I get off his lap, legs crossed on the couch. Embarrassment races through me. "I—sorry, I got too—"

"No," he says quickly. "No, don't be sorry. God, don't be sorry. It's just—I was getting a little too excited—"

If I was embarrassed before, that's nothing in comparison to now. My eyes automatically glance back down to Ezra's lap, where I was just seconds ago, and where a bulge still very obviously presses up against his jeans. He's embarrassed, too—I can tell by the way he won't look at me as he tries to tug his shirt down.

"I'll be right back." He stands up, leaving the living room. The bathroom door clicks shut. Water starts to run.

I press my face into my hands.

Oh my fucking God.

I can already tell how awkward it'd be if I stayed here tonight—I mean, I can't even look Ezra in the eye—so without saying a word, I'm out the door. It shuts behind me, and I race down the steps and out the glass front door of the apartment building—but I stop before I leave the stoop. I sit down where I've sat so many times before, resting my head against the railing, the insanity of whatever the hell just happened thrumming through me.

I'm not surprised when the door opens and shuts behind me again. Ezra sits down beside me.

"You okay?" he asks, his voice low.

"I have no idea."

"That was a little weird, right?"

"Totally fucking weird."

He laughs for a second, hiding his face in his arms, folded on top of his knees. He glances at me. "I've been wanting to do that for a long time, though."

"Really?"

"Yeah. Is that weird, too?"

I shrug. "I don't know. Maybe a little?" It's hard to look at him. "We're best friends."

He doesn't say anything. He sits up straight again, stretching his knees out, looking at the sky, a sliver of the moon highlighting strings of clouds. "I have something to tell you."

My heart sinks. I already know what he's going to say.

"Don't," I say. His head turns to me. "Just—don't."

I see a flicker of hurt on his face as he looks down to the ground again. "Why not?"

"We're friends," I tell him. "I don't want to lose what we have."

"What do you mean?"

"What if we break up, the way Declan broke up with you?

What if we get pissed at each other and stop talking? I don't want to ruin this. We've got a pretty fucking amazing friendship, Ez."

"I know that," he says, so quietly I can barely hear him. "I can't help having feelings for you."

"Why would you have feelings for me?" I ask. I don't know why I'm suddenly so pissed—why I almost feel betrayed by him, like he's been lying to me about our relationship all along. Underneath that anger is fear. Ezra and I—we'd make so much sense. We support each other, love each other, have always been there for one another. It'd make so much sense, if we fell in love and started going out, if we stayed together through college and then got married and had a cute story about how we were high school sweethearts. It's so perfect that the fear of it all ending, of him realizing that he doesn't love me anymore, of him leaving me the same way my mother left, fills the hollow in my chest.

His eyebrows are tight together. "It's almost like you don't want me to love you."

"I don't," I tell him.

He takes in a sharp breath and stands up so fast I barely register that he's opening the front door—

"Ezra," I call after him.

He stops and turns back around to me. "You're always talking about how you want to be in love. How you think it's impossible for anyone to love you. Here I am. Telling you I fucking love you." He raises his hands up, lets them fall to his sides again as he lets out a breath. "I love you, Felix. But—what, am I the only person in the world you don't want loving you?"

Someone yells out of a window above us. "Shut the fuck up!"

Ezra rubs an eye, his cheek. "Fuck it. You're right. I shouldn't have said anything."

He's back inside, door snapping shut behind him.

NINETEEN

EZRA WON'T RETURN MY TEXTS.

He won't pick up the phone.

No answer when I buzz his apartment door.

He doesn't even bother showing up to class on Monday.

The realization hits me, over and over again. Ezra is in love with me. He has been for a while now. Declan was right.

God, I've been so effing oblivious.

The memories spin in my head on rerun. The way I told Ezra I didn't want to hear how he feels about me—the way I told him not to love me. It was pretty shitty of me, but I was freaking the fuck out. That's what I text Ez, what I tell him in a voice mail: I'm sorry. I was freaking the fuck out.

I regret it now. I should've spoken to him about it more

calmly, figured out where things are between us. Are we still friends? Does he hate me now? Does he never want to see my face again? I was afraid we'd fuck up our relationship, but I still somehow managed to do that anyway.

It doesn't help that I kind of feel like I cheated on Declan.

"What are we?" I ask him. I'm on the phone, locked away in my bedroom. I have the lights off tonight, so my dad won't judge me for still being awake at two in the morning.

"What do you mean?" Declan asks.

I tell him, "I kissed someone."

He's silent on the other end for a few seconds too long. My nerves start to spike.

"Well," he says, "it's not like we're going out or anything, or like we decided to only date each other. You can kiss whoever you want."

"You're not upset?"

"I am a little," he admits. "But mainly because I don't understand why you won't let me have a chance to . . ."

"To kiss me?"

"I was going to say *to meet you*, but yeah—I'd like a chance at that, too. If that's something you want, anyway."

"You don't even know what I look like."

"I'm not sure I need to know."

I open my mouth, almost tell him that he doesn't know if I'm a guy or a girl or both or don't have a gender at all, like Bex—but I hesitate. Even I don't know my own gender identity.

261

"What if you're not interested in me . . . physically?" I ask him.

"Why wouldn't I be?"

"You can't be attracted to everyone in the entire world."

"No, maybe not."

Captain is asleep beside me. When I touch her ear, it twitches back and forth. "What would you say if I told you I'm questioning my identity?"

"I would say okay."

"Okay?"

"*Are* you questioning your identity?"

I scratch Captain's ear, and she opens one eye lazily. "It's weird," I tell him, "because I thought I'd already had it all figured out, you know?"

"But that's normal, right?" he says. "When I started questioning whether I was into guys or not, I drove myself crazy for a while, going back and forth and trying to figure out if I'm into guys or girls or both or neither, and it felt like the answer kept changing every week. I was going insane."

"Did you?" I say. "Figure it out, I mean?"

"Not really. But I looked at a bunch of stuff online. Read posts with other people's questions. Realized a lot of us have the same questions, wonder the same things, and I guess that just took the pressure off to figure it all out, you know?"

There're so many things I wish I didn't feel the pressure to figure out. Now that Ezra has told me he's in love with me, I feel like I have no choice but to ask myself how I feel about him. I love him—of course I love Ezra. But do I love him the same way I would love a boyfriend? The question is so big, so huge, that I'm trying to avoid it. Every time it appears in my mind, I push it aside. I ignore the real reason I don't want to think about it: I'm too afraid of what my answer would be.

"Is there anything that you feel pressure to figure out?" I ask Declan.

"Yeah, all the time. I guess the main thing is my future. If I get into college, how will I pay for tuition? Sometimes I wonder if it's even worth it. Why be in debt for the rest of my life?"

"I know what you mean," I tell him. "I've been so focused on this one goal of getting into college, because—I don't know, I felt like I had something to prove . . . but I don't really think I'm going to get in, and I don't know if there's any point in trying."

"Something to prove?"

The irony of the conversation hits me. This is Brown that I'm talking about—the school that both of us have wanted to get into, the school that we've fought over. "Yeah. I don't think a whole lot of people would think I deserve to get in. I guess I want to prove them wrong."

I can practically hear him shrug over the phone. "Maybe there isn't any point," he says, "but I don't think it's a bad thing to show others that you can get in, just for the sake of proving that you can. There isn't anything wrong with that, is there?"

After we've said good night—it's only three in the morning

this time, as opposed to five when we usually hang up—I pull out my laptop. I haven't been sleeping much anyway, not since everything that happened with Ezra. I bring up Google and type in *I don't know if I want to go to college. What should I do instead?*

The possibilities are endless. Internships, travel with volunteer organizations, vocational work—but instead of excitement at the thought of doing anything that I want, I'm filled with anxiety. There're too many options, too many opportunities. I suddenly know how Ezra felt, unsure of his future. I feel bad for giving him a hard time about it. I was so judgmental, clouded by my own jealousy. I wish I could text him. Apologize. Ask what he thinks about me just giving up on Brown altogether. What would Ezra say?

When my phone buzzes with a notification, surprise and excitement thrum through me. Maybe Ezra could feel me thinking about him—has decided to forgive me. It's been a couple of days now. Maybe he's ready to move on.

But when I check my phone, it isn't Ez.

Are you trying to ignore me?

You can't ignore me.

I heard that your mom abandoned you.

I would, too, if I had a daughter that was pretending to be a boy.

Tears start to sting my eyes. Pain fills my lungs and makes it hard to breathe. I shouldn't let this troll get to me, but they really figured out exactly where to hit me the hardest, what to say to hurt me more than anything else. My finger hovers over the *block* button. I should've blocked grandequeen69 a long time ago. But I don't press it. I feel this need to respond, to stand up for myself, to make grandequeen69 realize I deserve to be treated better than this—that there's an actual human being on the other end of the phone.

I type. **What do you get out of this? Why're you attacking me? Just because you don't understand my identity, doesn't mean I'm not real. That I don't exist.**

They must've been waiting for me to respond.

That's what you don't get. You don't exist.

You're nothing.

Do you really think you matter to anyone?

You don't matter. You don't even matter to your own mom.

I can feel the pain like it's a physical thing, filling my heart and spreading through me beneath my skin. I don't even know what to say to that. What do you say, when a person basically tells you that you're not a human being? *Treats* you like you're not human? The pain sparks into anger, and I fling my phone across the room. It hits the wall with a thud and falls to the ground. Captain hisses, leaping from the bed.

"Shit." I jump out of my bed, snatching up my phone. There's a tiny crack in the corner of the screen. "Fucking shit." I wipe a hand over my face, rubbing away the tears. I shouldn't let this troll get to me like this. I know I shouldn't. But I can feel their words sinking into me, making it harder to breathe.

* * *

When I get to St. Cat's on Wednesday, I'm not expecting to see Ezra—not really, not after he'd skipped class the past couple of days and wouldn't respond to any of my messages—so when I see him cross through the parking lot, I'm completely unprepared. My heart pounds with nerves, and the memory of our *kiss*—of him trying to tell me he's in love with me—makes me feel like I'm about to freak out all over again.

Ezra passes by without a glance. Right alongside the nerves is a flare of hurt. He probably just didn't see me, but the words from grandequeen69 flash in my mind. I don't matter. I don't exist. I call out after him. "Ez!"

He doesn't stop as he walks in through the lobby's sliding glass doors. Ezra's never ignored me before, so I assume he didn't hear me, is way too wrapped up in his own thoughts. I follow him inside. "Hey—Ezra!"

He glances at me now, but the look he gives me is blistering. The sort of look I'd expect him to send Marisol's way—not mine. He doesn't say a word. He just keeps walking.

The hurt's an open wound now, gushing blood all over the pavement. I hesitate, then start following again—slowly at first, before I start running after him, down the hall, my footsteps echoing, until I'm walking right alongside him, struggling to keep up with his long strides.

"Ezra—hey," I say, stopping in front of him. He gives this impatient sigh, looking down at my shoes before looking up at me again. "Listen, I'm sorry. I shouldn't have said the shit I did."

He shrugs, doesn't answer.

I don't really know what else to say. I don't think Ezra's ever been this angry with me before. "Can we—can we talk about it?"

He shrugs again. Even his shrugs are with the least minimal effort required. "What is there to talk about?"

A few seconds pass. "I mean, are you really that pissed because of everything I said?"

"I guess not."

"Then what're you so angry about?"

"I'm not angry," he says. His eyes are glazed, like he also hasn't been getting enough sleep, but behind that glaze is— emptiness? Coldness? Boredom, maybe. Indifference.

I force myself to keep Ezra's gaze, no matter how much I want to look away—no matter how much I feel like I'm seconds from crying. He said that he has feelings for me—tried to tell me that he loves me—but it looks like it only took a few days for him to figure out that he doesn't give a shit about me after all. "Then what's wrong?"

Another shrug. These fucking shrugs. "I guess I just need a second. To wrap my head around everything." As much as I'm forcing myself to look at him, he's looking anywhere but at me. "I just need some space."

"Space?"

He doesn't repeat himself. He stares at the wall, swallowing, his throat moving up and down.

"Okay," I say. "I'll give you space."

He leaves before I even finish my sentence, walking down the hallway. By the time I get to the acrylics classroom, he's moved to an entirely different table altogether, sitting where Tyler usually sits, and Tyler is fast asleep in the stool beside mine.

For the first time in days, I find it hard to focus on my project. As much as I want to sink into my self-portraits, to just let my mind go, I can't think of anything else but that kiss. Ezra. Over and over again, even when I tell myself I won't think about him anymore. Ezra. Even when I close my eyes and take a breath and clear my thoughts. Ezra. My mind immediately jumps to him, again and again. Ezra, Ezra, Ezra.

He doesn't love me anymore. He couldn't, the way that he looked at me downstairs. It took only one argument for him to fall out of love with me and to decide that he hates me instead. In a way, grandequeen69 is right. I don't matter—not to Ezra, not anymore, and Declan thinks that he's in love with Lucky, not me. My self-portrait smirks up at me. I'd gotten a little full of myself, thinking that anyone could fall in love with someone like me.

I'm not thinking when the paintbrush in my hand dips into purple and begins to swathe strokes across my painting's smile, my eyes, my entire face. I push so hard against the canvas that a hole tears, right in the center.

"Felix?"

I look behind me. Jill is watching, concerned. When I glance around, I see that half of the class is looking at me, too. Ezra moved to the opposite corner of the room, his back to me. He's standing still, not moving, like his focus is across the room and on me, though he still refuses to look my way.

"Are you all right?" Jill asks.

"Yeah," I say. "I guess I just got too into it."

She nods slowly, eyeing my destroyed painting. She walks closer, lowering her voice, as the rest of class returns to their art. "Decided this one wasn't working?"

"It was too—I don't know, arrogant."

She puts a hand to her chin. "I thought that it had merit, but in the end, it doesn't really matter what I think." She looks like she's about to move on, before she pauses again. "You know, Felix—there's been a call for the end-of-summer gallery."

"Yeah, I heard the announcement."

"You should consider applying," she says. "Your self-portraits—if you can finish enough in time—well, they're powerful, Felix. Maybe more than you even realize."

She must be just saying that because I'm obviously struggling with something. I know it doesn't make any sense to apply for the end-of-summer gallery. The gallery is pretty competitive. Basically everyone in the summer program applies, and if accepted, their art gets featured in the school's newsletter, which goes out to alumni, which can mean a lot of great opportunities. Several people have gotten internships for winning the gallery selection—and I know it isn't going to be me. What's the point of applying, just to fail?

I tell her that I'll think about it, and she gives me a satisfied smile.

TWENTY

When classes are done for the day, I feel strange, disoriented. Normally, I would walk back with Ezra to his apartment, but he ignores me as he leaves the parking lot. I could go home and talk to Declan as Lucky, but I'm not feeling like myself, and—I don't know, I guess I'm a little afraid that he'll realize he doesn't love me anymore, either. It's only as I'm walking out of the parking lot that I realize it's Wednesday. The LGBT Center will have its gender-identity discussion group in a few hours at eight. I should be too terrified to show my face there again, but I remember Bex and their reassuring smile, their suggestion that I come back whenever I like.

It doesn't take too long for me to get to the LGBT Center, only about thirty minutes. I'm early for the discussion group, so I sit at the café of white walls and sleek tables and chairs, the smell of caramel and croissants filling the air, a sketch pad out as I draw the people around me. I realize, suddenly, that since Bex is nonbinary, any of the people in this café could be, too. Maybe I shouldn't assume anyone's gender as I draw them. There's someone with wrinkles, a blazer, an infectious laugh; someone closer to my age with green hair and a nose ring, showing their braces when they give their friend a wide smile. The longer I sit here and sketch, the better my art becomes—and it helps to look at the people around me, *really* look at them, instead of seeing who I assume them to be.

I almost wish I could just stay in the café and sketch for hours, but I came here for a reason. A few minutes before eight, I pack away my sketch pad and head up the stairs, so focused on my feet that I feel like I'm about to trip. My heart hammers in my chest with nerves, as though I'm about to get up onto a stage in front of one hundred people. *This time*, I think to myself. *This time, I'll be brave enough to speak—to ask my questions and find the answers I've been looking for.*

Bex waits at the door, just like last time, and they seem genuinely happy to see me when I walk up to the table to sign in. "Felix!" they say. "I'm really glad you could make it."

I smile back, even though I'm too nervous to say anything as I sign my name. I take the same seat I did before, as far away from everyone else as possible. The same people are here, too: Tom, newspaper folded in his lap as he talks to Sarah, still with her bright red lipstick. Zelda checks her hair in her phone. Wally wears a Miles Morales T-shirt. He grins and waves at me, and as I wave back, I feel so awkward I think my hand's about to fall off my wrist.

When it's time to begin, Bex has us do introductions again, even though we already know each other—just protocol, I guess—and then begins the discussion. "It's the fourteenth. The Pride march is in a couple of weeks," they say. "But sometimes, it can be difficult to find pride for ourselves. There's very little visibility for people of all genders, and many cisgender people don't believe transgender and nonbinary people deserve the same rights. It's even more difficult for transgender and nonbinary people of color, and especially transgender women of color. Though we have transgender women of color to thank for the Stonewall Riots and the Pride march, they're often erased and ignored, even by other queer people within the LGBTQIA+ community. How do we find and cultivate pride for each other and ourselves when we're in a world that seems like it doesn't want us to exist?"

I wasn't really expecting a discussion topic that would hit so close to home. The words of grandequeen69 cut through me. *You don't matter. You don't exist.* I realize with a flinch of shame that I'd started to believe those words, too. It's hard to feel pride for who I am when it feels like the rest of the world doesn't want me to.

The topic clearly resonates with others in the room also. Sarah already looks like she's near tears. "Gay cis men, especially white men—it's like they're one identity away from being what they'd consider *normal*, so they hold that identity over us, enjoy their privilege and power in their little elitist group, try to push the rest of us away. Treat us like dogs. Just last week, a group of them laughed at me the second I walked into a bar. I wanted to ask them if they'd ever heard of Sylvia Rivera. If they realized they sounded just like those white gay boys who'd laughed at her, too."

"Well, let me ask you a question," Zelda says. "Why're you even looking for their approval? Fuck them," she says. "Who needs to deal with snotty little shits?"

"I'm not looking for their approval," Sarah says, obviously pissed by the question. "It hurts. That's all I'm saying. It hurts to not be included, to be rejected—especially when it's by people you thought would understand and accept you. You have to admit that it hurts."

"Sometimes I wonder if it's better to just—I don't know, only be around people like me," Wally says. "Not deal with the transphobia, the racism, the anti-queerness. Just surround myself with a hundred other Wallys and be done with it. Create my own world, my own bubble, so I don't have to be rejected by anyone else."

"The only issue with that idea," Tom says, "is that not everyone has the privilege, or the ability, to create that bubble we all crave."

"So what do we do?" Sarah asks. "Force the bastards to see that we deserve their time of day? Make them understand that if it weren't for women like me, they wouldn't have any of their damn rights in the first place?"

Tom gives a nonjudgmental shrug. "Is that really what you want to spend your energy on?" he asks.

"What should I be spending my energy on instead?"

"Yourself," he suggests. "Loving and accepting and celebrating yourself, and loving and celebrating and supporting the young women like you who will come next. Changing this world, yes—we need people who will fight for our rights, fight for justice in the courts so that it will be better for the next generation. But creating our own world, not just for ourselves in our bubble, but one that can spread to those who need it most—one filled with our stories, our history, our love and pride—that's just as beautiful. That's just as necessary. Without that, we forget ourselves. Crumple under the pain of feeling isolated, unaccepted by others, without realizing that, above all else, we need to love and accept ourselves first."

I came here with the plan of speaking, of joining in the discussion, of asking my questions. I have so many thoughts, and my heart's almost out of my throat. I force myself to speak. "Excuse me," I say.

Everyone's heads swing toward me.

My voice cracks. "How—uh—do you even know your gender identity in the first place?"

Sarah shifts in her seat impatiently—and I don't know, maybe it's a stupid question to ask; maybe they're already leagues ahead of me, and this is a boring point to discuss. I feel like I should apologize for interrupting, for wasting their time, but Bex gives me another smile.

"It's just," I say, clearing my throat. "It feels like there are so many options, so many genders. How do you know which one is right?"

Zelda speaks. "Too many options," she says. "Too many labels. There's such an obsession with putting everything into a box now."

"I don't know," Wally says with a shrug. "If this was a perfect world, and there wasn't any transphobia or treating other people like shit for who they are, then maybe there wouldn't be a need for labels. But the world isn't perfect, and when I have to deal with ignorant bullshit, it helps me to know there're other trans guys out there."

"Okay, fine," Zelda says. "But why so many labels? Why not just boy or girl? Transgender men, transgender women?"

Bex tilts their head. "If I'd been able to, I would have chosen one or the other. It'd be so much easier than having to explain myself every time I walk through a body scanner at the airport, or not knowing which public bathroom to use when there aren't any gender-neutral options. But one or the other doesn't feel right for me."

"How do you know which one does feel right?" I ask.

There're a few smiles, and I wonder if I said something stupid again.

"It's different for some," Bex offers. "For me, it was just that feeling. The feeling that my identity—nonbinary—explains so much of who I am, who I've always been, in a way that other labels never did."

I grip my hands together. "What if I never get that feeling?"

"It's possible that you never will," Bex says. "There are some who go on questioning forever. That's okay, too. But when it's right, you'll know. There's a confidence that spreads through you, and you know you've found the answer."

Zelda shakes her head. "These younger generations," she says. "Always questioning. Always shaking things up, just for the sake of it."

"These younger generations," Tom echoes. "I envy them. There's so much more space to explore who they are now. To explore and celebrate themselves. I could never have imagined seeing a transgender man on TV or in the movies when I was younger. And now?" He looks at me. "I look at you and wish I could be a teenager again. I know that things aren't perfect," he says, nodding, "and there are still hardships, but don't forget to enjoy these years. Live. Live them for the people who didn't get to enjoy being a teenager. For the people who never lived past being a teenager."

The conversation continues. What it was like to be a teenager back in the days of everyone here—what they wish had been different, what's different now. I'm too shy to say anything else, but Tom's words echo through me.

In my bedroom, time flashing 12:06 a.m., I have my laptop open and on a Tumblr post that lists the hundreds of different transgender identities. Nonbinary. Agender. Bigender. Transmasculine. Transfeminine. Genderqueer. Gender nonconforming. So many terms, so many identities, and I start to feel myself getting overwhelmed again. None of these definitions feel right.

I keep reading, scrolling, eyes becoming glazed, when one word catches my eye. *Demiboy.* A person who identifies as mostly or partly male—I sit up, moving my computer to my lap—but may also identify as nonbinary some of the time, or even as a girl. The niggling in me spreads from the back of my head, down my neck, and into my chest. Most of the time, there's no question—I'm a guy, I have no doubt about that. But other times . . . being called a boy doesn't feel right, almost in the same way that being called a girl feels so completely wrong.

I try saying it out loud. "Demiboy." Demiboy, demiboy, demiboy.

I smile a little. I smile, and then outright laugh, and I might even begin to cry a little, because I know what Bex was talking about now. The confidence that spreads through me. I know that this is right. It's kind of amazing, that there's a word that explains exactly how I feel, that takes away all of my confusion and questioning and hesitation—a word that lets me know there are others out there who feel exactly the same way that I do.

It feels a little anticlimactic, getting the answer to a question I've been struggling with for months now. I feel the need to scream it and—I think with a flinch—to text Ezra, to tell him everything, to tell him about the meeting I went to earlier and the research I did and how perfect *demiboy* feels, and that I miss him, too. There's another question I've been avoiding, ever since the night Ezra tried to tell me that he's in love with me. *How do I feel about Ezra? Am I in love with him also?* Just the thought of Ezra sends a spark through me, the memory of the kiss setting me on fire.

I grab my phone and open up Instagram. I sit up with a grin and snap a selfie. Caption: **Guess who's a demiboy?**

I add a bunch of hashtags and smile as I post it. It sucks that Ezra and I aren't talking, but maybe he'll see it anyway. Maybe he'll be curious and text me, and we can get over whatever the hell is happening between us. I start scrolling through other posts. The images look odd, though, not who I usually follow. . . .

I look up at the corner of my account, and my heart starts to thunder, same way it does if I've just woken up from a nightmare. I'm still logged in as luckyliquid95.

I leap out of bed, almost tripping over my sheets. "Shit, shit, oh fucking shit—"

My fingers are suddenly too big, too clumsy, to get back to the post. I delete it with trembling hands.

I stand there, staring at my phone. How possible is it that Declan was awake and on Instagram at that exact moment? How possible is it that he saw my selfie?

I don't get a phone call or any text messages about it. I sit back down on my bed, staring at the screen. Please, please, please don't let him have seen the post. . . .

That's my mantra. All through my sleepless night and into the next morning, as I travel down from Harlem and walk the few blocks to St. Cat's, I think it over and over again. *Please don't let Declan have seen the post. Please don't let Declan have seen the post.*

I get into the classroom and scroll through Instagram on my phone, as if I somehow have the power to rewind time if I stare at Insta posts long enough. It's still early enough that Jill isn't here yet, but Tyler's sitting up front, Hazel chatting with Leah. The door opens and closes, and before I've even had a chance to look up, Declan's in front of me.

He's staring at me, red-eyed. My heart sinks. He saw the post.

He pulls out his phone. He doesn't look at me as he presses a few buttons. From his screen, upside down, I can see he's in his contacts. Then on his contact for me—for Lucky. He takes a breath, presses dial.

I close my eyes. My phone starts buzzing in my hand.

I don't open them, even after I've heard the footsteps walking away and the door slamming shut. I take a shaky breath and try to let it out slowly. When I open my eyes again, everyone else is looking from me to the door Declan just went through, eyebrows raised.

I jump from the stool and rush across the room, open the door—look down the hall one way, then see Declan disappearing around the corner of the other. I run after him. "Declan!"

He's racing down the stairs. I try to jump a few at a time to catch up. "Declan, please—"

Declan suddenly stops so unexpectedly I almost run right into him. He spins around. His eyes are wet. He's fucking crying.

I don't know what to say. I open my mouth, shaking my head, waiting for the right words to come out.

"Why?" he says.

"I'm sorry," I say, but my voice is so soft I'm not sure he's heard.

"Tell me why."

I realize I'm gripping my hands together so hard they're shaking. I wipe them off on my jeans.

"*Tell my fucking why!*" he yells. His voice echoes in the staircase.

I can barely look at him. "It was supposed to be a prank at first."

"A prank?" All emotion's gone from his voice now.

"For revenge. I thought you were the one who put up that gallery of me, and—"

"I didn't do the fucking gallery."

"I know. I know that now, since you told me you'd never . . ."

He closes his eyes like it hurts, this reminder that the

person he'd been speaking to all along, the person he said he was in love with, was me.

"But even when I realized it wasn't you, I couldn't stop talking to you," I tell him, words coming out fast, desperate to make him understand. "I loved our conversations. It was like you were a different person, and—"

"I'm not a different person."

"You said you were falling for me," I say, lowering my voice. "You said you're in love with me."

He watches me, not looking away, his brown eyes burning.

"I think I might love you, too," I tell him.

He swallows, breathing harder. I think he's trying to stop himself from crying. Trying to get enough of a breath to speak. "Don't talk to me," he says. "Don't even look at me. I don't want anything to do with you."

He brushes past me, and I hear his footsteps echoing on the staircase before the door out into the lobby slams.

TWENTY-ONE

Dear Mom,

It's been a while since we've spoken, but I wanted to let you know that my life is shit right now. I've lost two people I really care about. They both hate me now. There's a troll that won't stop messaging me—no idea who the piece of shit is, but they want me to know that my life is worthless, using you and the fact that you've abandoned me as proof. I don't know. Maybe they're right. I have 477 emails drafted to you. In every email, I act like we're having some kind of fun conversation, where I've forgiven you and moved on. . . but the truth is, you really fucked me up. You know that, right? You fucked me up by deciding you don't love me anymore, by leaving me and my dad behind while you went off to start your new life. There're so many things I've wanted the courage to ask you all these years. Why'd you leave? Do you miss me? Do you still love me? I have 477 emails drafted—and this time, I'm going to send this one to you. I don't know if you'll answer, but I hope you do.

Your demiboy son,

Felix

I stare at the email for a minute, five minutes, ten minutes—reading and rereading, stopping myself from deleting the whole thing—until, finally, I hit *send*. My heart tightens in my chest, and I stare at the screen. I can't believe I did that. I can't believe I just fucking did that. She's had to see the email by now. Everyone's always glued to their phones, their laptops. She's had to see the name Felix Love pop up in her in-box, has made the decision to read my email or send it straight into the trash folder. It's killing me, not knowing which she's chosen to do.

When half a day has passed, I think it's pretty obvious that my mom isn't going to answer my email. I don't want to leave my apartment. I don't even want to leave my room. I curl up in a ball with Captain, lights off and leaving me in the dark, laptop on and playing some reality TV show—but I'm barely paying attention. I have Instagram up and open, shine of the phone's screen reflecting in Captain's eyes, looking through both Ezra's and Declan's pages to see if they've updated, but neither of them has. I gave up on texting Ezra a few days ago now, and when I try calling Declan, I'm immediately sent to voice mail. I get a text a few seconds later.

Don't call me ever again.

God, how did things get so fucked?

My dad knocks on my door, and he peeks his head in as he creaks it open. "You okay, kid?" he says.

I'd told him I wasn't feeling well so that he'd let me come home early—the idea of sitting anywhere near Declan felt impossible—but now it's six in the evening and I haven't eaten anything all day except for a bowl of soup my dad brought me around noon.

I mumble something, even I don't know exactly what.

He flips on the bulb. I feel like a vampire, blinded by the light. I groan and throw my sheets up over my head. Captain must get tangled, because she squirms for a split second before leaping down to the floor.

"What's going on?" he asks.

"Nothing."

"For a sick kid, I'm not hearing a whole lot of sneezing."

I give a fake cough. He laughs. From beneath the bedsheets, I can hear him crossing over and feel the edge of the bed sink as he takes a seat. He puts a hand on my back and rubs.

"Did something happen?"

I sigh and uncover my head. "Ezra and I are fighting."

Realization spreads across his face. "Ah. Okay."

"And," I say, but pause—how do I even begin to explain any of this mess? "The person I like is pissed at me, too."

"So the person you like *isn't* Ezra?"

A few days ago, I would've yelled at my dad for continuing to suggest I have a crush on Ezra, but now? "Well," I say slowly, "it's not like I *don't* like Ezra."

He gives me a smug *I knew it* look. I roll my eyes and grab my pillow, putting it over my face. "Everything's wrong," I say, muffling my voice. "Neither of them will speak to me now. I really messed up."

I feel a gentle tug on the pillow, and my dad pulls it off, placing it to the side. "Well," he says. "I know it might feel like nothing's right at the moment, but things have a way of working themselves out."

I hesitate. "Is that what you thought when Mom left?"

The question takes him by surprise. He inhales a sharp breath. "To be honest, I wasn't thinking much of anything when she left. I was pretty numb. Just trying to keep it together for you."

I frown at him. "Really?" I mean, I knew things were messed up, but I didn't realize he'd struggled that much. When he doesn't say anything else, I tell him I sent an email to her.

His eyebrows pull together. "Okay. Do you want to talk about why you did that?"

"I mean—she's my mom," I say. "It's normal to want to reach out to her and talk to her. Right?"

He's nodding, slowly, but I'm not so sure he agrees. "After Lorraine left, I called her at least once a day, begging her to come back. She said she'd fallen out of love with me and needed some space away. I couldn't understand how she could so easily dismiss everything that we had. It hurt—more than anything else I've ever experienced, I'll tell you that much. I loved her. Still do. Probably always will. But it took me a little longer to figure out that just because I love her, doesn't mean it's a good kind of love. It can be easier, sometimes, to choose to love someone you know won't return your feelings. At least you know how that will end. It's easier to accept hurt and pain, sometimes, than love and acceptance. It's the real, loving relationships that can be the scariest."

Is he trying to tell me that it's wrong for me to love my mom? I can't help that I love her, and that I want her to love me, too. I nod anyway, staring at my hands as I play with the bedsheet. He runs a hand over my curls. "Maybe this is just a good chance to focus on other things," my dad tells me. "Nothing wrong with focusing on yourself every once in a while."

That's what I tell myself as I walk into St. Cat's the next morning (I tried to skip another day, but my dad wasn't having it). When I see Ezra talking to Leah, and he refuses to look my way? Focus on myself. When Declan sits beside me in class, but acts as if I don't exist? Focus on myself. That's what I tell myself when I get an Instagram notification, too. I'm not surprised to see that it's another message from grandequeen69. I automatically hit the notification to read the message—but I pause. Why do I keep reading these messages, knowing that grandequeen69 is only going to hurt me? I remember what my dad had said—that it's easier to accept hurt and pain, sometimes, than love and acceptance. I delete the app from my phone. No more notifications. No more grandequeen69. Focus on my fucking self.

I work on my acrylics self-portrait project. I hadn't taken Jill seriously, but now I'm beginning to wonder if I should apply to the end-of-summer art gallery after all. It's something to pour myself into, and—I don't know, the idea of reclaiming the lobby, the very space that hurt me, feels better than I thought it would. I'm grateful to have something to concentrate on, and maybe it's the raging trash fire that's currently my life, but I find it easier than ever to sink into the colors, to think about nothing as I let my hand and my brush move across the canvas. I do more work than I have in days, flying from one self-portrait to the next, using each and every one of the canvases I'd prepped.

When I'm finished, I step back to take the portraits in. There I am, on fire, underwater, skin like the swirling universe, flying through the sky, lying in the grass, sitting in the dark while a blur of colors rushes around me, smirking with a crown of flowers on my head . . . It's not hard to realize that this, these self-portraits, are what I have to submit to Brown for my portfolio. I wasn't sure if I was going to apply, and I still question why I've wanted to go to Brown so badly—but it doesn't hurt to send an application and see what happens, right? Maybe I don't need to apply just to prove to myself and others that I can get in. Maybe I can apply just because it offers amazing opportunities. There're the other schools I'm applying to, too, and I can also look into gap year options. At some point I'll have to choose what I want to do—but until then, it's all right to keep my options open.

Either way, I know I'll need to do several more self-portraits for my applications and for the end-of-summer gallery. The thought of the portfolio used to give me anxiety, stress—but now, I'm just excited.

Focus on myself.

Midway through acrylics class, I'm washing some brushes by the paint-splattered sink when Leah appears next to me. "Hey, Felix," she says with a smile. I know that smile. It's the sort of smile you give someone when you have bad news. She leans against the counter and bites her lip, glancing all around to make sure no one's close enough to overhear. "So, I checked out Marisol's phone."

I don't meet her eye. I already know what she's going to say. "Let me guess. Nothing, right?"

She lets out a sigh. "I'm sorry. I really thought there'd be something in the text messages, at least—"

"It's okay, Leah," I say, turning the faucet off. "Finding out whoever was behind the gallery was a long shot anyway. I really appreciate you trying to help me."

"Wait," she says, "wait, hold on. There're still more people I can check out."

I shake my head. "I don't know. I've been trying to focus

on myself more, and—I kind of feel like it's time to just move on."

"Just move on?" she repeats.

I shrug. "Yeah. I'm really grateful for the help. Seriously, thank you. But—I don't know if it's worth it anymore."

She's shaking her head. "Okay. I mean, it's your choice." I start to leave the sink, but Leah opens her mouth, like she has something else to say. When I pause, she has trouble meeting my eye. "I'm just wondering . . . Can we still—I don't know—talk and hang out and stuff?"

Leah looks so sincere right now that I can't help but grin. "Yeah. Yeah, I'd really like that."

I've spent all of acrylics class pointedly not looking at either Ezra or Declan, barely speaking to anyone, only working on my paintings—so I'm shocked when Declan marches right up to me a few minutes before the lunch bell.

"Can we talk?"

We end up out in the hall. My hands are covered with streaks of color, and some got onto my shorts also. I don't know why this embarrasses me. I hide my hands behind my back, staring at the wood-paneled floor. Declan crosses his arms and leans against the wall.

My nerves are on fire. I glance up at Declan a couple of times, but he still doesn't speak—just stares right at me. Maybe this is his punishment for me, knowing that it'll drive me insane, just standing there without saying a word.

"I'm sorry," I say, my voice cracking. I clear my throat and try again. "I'm so, so sorry, Declan."

He finally blinks. He pushes away from the wall, but keeps his arms crossed. "I'm so fucking pissed at you."

"I know."

"You lied to me."

"I know. I'm sorry."

"Did you just want me to look stupid?" he asks. "Is that what you wanted?"

"No. Christ."

"Why did you do it?" he asks. "Not that bullshit with the gallery," he cuts in, before I can say anything. "Even after you knew I had nothing to do with that. Talking about—all the personal shit we talked about. Letting me tell you that I . . ." He closes his eyes for a split second, lowers his voice. "Letting me tell you that I love you. What was the point of any of that?"

I bite my lip. "I liked talking to you," I tell him. "I still do. I miss you. I miss hearing your voice. . . ."

"I don't know if I can believe you. What if you're still fucking with me now?"

"I'm not."

He's frowning, watching me closely. "And Ezra?"

His name puts a shock through me. "Ezra?" I echo.

"He's in love with you," he tells me. "I told you that. The person you kissed—was it him?"

I force myself to nod. "Yeah, it was him."

He takes longer to speak this time. "Do you have feelings for him, too?"

I hesitate. I can't lie to Declan again. I don't know how I feel about Ezra for sure, but as much as I've missed Declan, I've missed Ezra even more. There's so much I've wanted to tell him, and even now, the memory of that kiss rages through me. "It doesn't matter," I tell him, "Ezra wants nothing to do with me, so . . ."

Declan takes in a deep breath. "Do you want to get lunch with me?"

I glance up, and he's watching me again—but there's a glint of something I'd never really expected to see on his face. Something other than hatred and condescension. There's warmth. Maybe even some longing.

"Yeah," I say, nodding. "Yeah, I'd love that."

I feel self-conscious when the lunch bell rings and everyone ambles outside. Declan and I walk together, out of the building and across the parking lot. I don't know if it's in my head, but I feel like we're getting a lot of double takes—yeah, definitely a double take when James and Marc look at us from their spot against the brick wall—and really, I couldn't blame anyone for staring. Everyone knows that Declan and I hate each other . . . or that we're supposed to, anyway. We fight every chance we get. So why're we now walking side by side as though we're friends, even if it's in total and complete awkward silence? It's only when I catch Ezra's eye as he stands under the shade of a tree, talking to Leah, that I really fucking wish we'd thought this through.

"Not regretting hanging out with me already, are you?"

I look at Declan. He has an eyebrow raised, glancing away from where Ezra stands.

I shake my head fast. "No. No, no regrets at all."

White Castle is packed like always, filled with kids from St. Cat's and Brooklyn hipsters who wear bike helmets and overalls and Crocs. Declan and I stand in line without speaking, and I stop myself from fidgeting as I try to think of a casual conversation that could possibly make this experience at least 10 percent less awkward . . . but nothing comes to me, and Declan just stands and waits patiently with his arms crossed, like he doesn't feel uncomfortable at all, like he doesn't give a single shit that he's standing here beside me— me as *me* for the first time, and not as Lucky.

We both grab a few cheese sliders and take them out to sit on the curb, eating in silence for a few minutes. Declan's brown curls blow around in the breeze, and he wipes them out of his eyes as he squints at passing St. Cat's students who glance at us, raising hands to say hey with smiles.

"The more I thought about it," he suddenly says—I whip my head around to him so fast it's a wonder my neck doesn't crack—"the more I realized how obvious it was. I mean, the signs were everywhere. You went to St. Cat's. The things you said about art—they're the kind of thing you'd say in acrylics, too. Everything you'd told me, about your identities. And you were acting weird as fuck."

"I wasn't being *that* weird."

"You were weird as fuck, man, always staring at me and suddenly trying to start up conversations out of nowhere. Then there's the fact that you were so curious about me and Ezra. I was even afraid that you might *be* Ezra—but I guess a part of me kind of hoped you'd be Ezra, too."

"You hoped I'd be Ezra?" I don't really know how I feel about that.

"In a way, yeah," he says. "Not like I was desperate for it to be him or anything, but I missed Ezra sometimes—missed you, too."

Warmth spreads over me. I want to ask why he was such a piece of shit to us, then—why not just stay our friend? But I remember what he'd told me. "When we were talking," I start, "and you said that you broke up with Ez because he was in love with me . . ."

"I felt kind of betrayed. Jealous. It was easier to break up with him and not deal with the inevitable heartbreak. Plus I was dealing with all of that bullshit from my dad, him disowning me—my grandpa and I were trying to figure out the legal stuff of him becoming my guardian, so a lot was going on anyway."

"I'm really sorry about that," I tell him, my voice low. "I had no idea that'd happened."

"I know. I didn't tell you guys about it."

"Why didn't you?"

"I didn't want a pity party."

"It can be okay to depend on your friends too, sometimes."

"Thanks for the afternoon special."

I snort and roll my eyes. "Nice to know that you can still be a dick."

"I don't think *you* get to call me a dick right now," he says with more bite than I was expecting. He wipes the curls out of his eyes again, blinking in the sunlight.

"You're right," I say. "I'm sorry. I really am. It was just this mess that'd spiraled out of control, and then I started to—you know, have feelings for you—and I just didn't know what to do, so I kept it going. I should've stopped. I should've told you the truth."

He doesn't say anything for a long time. When he does speak, he leans back on his palms. "The most obvious clue was your voice. I knew you sounded familiar, but I never made the connection. Maybe I didn't want to. I don't know."

"Were you disappointed that it was me?" I ask him. I'm just begging for an insult, for him to hurt me, but I can't help it. I need to know.

Declan watches me for a moment, not speaking, just eyeing me—and as he looks at me, I remember the conversations we'd had. How he said he wanted to meet me—to have the chance to kiss me. Embarrassment flares, but there's fear, too. What if I was right? What if he isn't interested in me?

He finally speaks. "I wasn't disappointed," he says. "I was surprised. I just never thought it would be you. It took a second to get used to the idea, and the more I thought about it, the more it made sense. The more I . . ." He trails off, and his expression becomes heavier. The longing I'd seen earlier is back. It heats me from the inside out.

He clenches his jaw and swallows, looking away. "I'm going back up to my grandfather's for the weekend," he tells me. "In Beacon."

I'm thrown by the sudden shift in topic. "Okay," I say.

"Do you want to come with me?" he asks.

"Come with you?" I say. "To Beacon?"

He waits, still watching me with that same expression—except it's shifted, just a little, back to the expression I'm used to seeing on Declan more. A bit of steel. Protection, armor, I realize, against me hurting him again. I start to hear my dad's voice in my head. It's easier, sometimes, to love when you know it's a love that you can't have. What if this isn't healthy—for either of us?

But still, even though I'm not sure about this, I don't want to risk losing Declan—not again. I nod. "Yeah. Yeah, I'd love to come to Beacon."

TWENTY-TWO

I've lived in New York City my whole life, but I've never—not once—been upstate. I have no idea what to expect.

I meet Declan in Grand Central with a backpack of clothes on Saturday afternoon, under the sea-blue ceiling of golden stars. It's awkward as fuck. We've never really spoken except for on the phone and that one White Castle lunch, so now I can tell we're both trying to figure out how to make this new face-to-face thing work. We talk about nothing at first. How was it getting to Grand Central? Hopefully it doesn't rain, there've been thunderstorms in the area lately.

We get on the train and sit down with our backpacks on the empty seat in between us. When we leave the underground tunnels, I stare out of the window as the brownstones melt away to green—grass, fields, and then finally the river, sparkling blue under the sunlight. It's beautiful. I wish Ezra was here to see it with me.

"And you grew up here?" I ask, glancing at Declan over my shoulder.

"Until I was ten," he says. "That's when my dad got an apartment in the city."

His eyes are glazed over, and suddenly, I just want to grab his hand—know what it feels like to touch him. I let my hand slip over his, and he flinches before he tangles his fingers with mine, staring at our hands intertwined. He smiles a little.

"I kept imagining what it'd be like to hold your hand, if I ever got to know who you are. If I ever got to meet you."

He rubs his thumb over my knuckles. Even though I'd been the one to reach out, having his hand in mine—this closeness—makes me nervous now. "Is it everything you ever wanted?"

He glances up—at my lips first, then my eyes. "Almost."

I start to lean forward a little without even really thinking about it, remembering how good it felt to kiss Ezra, but Declan shakes his head and lets go of my hand. "Not here. Not everyone's as open as in the city."

He goes back to staring out of the window, so I do, too—but the longer we sit there in silence, the more the heat builds in me. I want to touch him. I want to kiss him, the same way I kissed Ezra. The feeling grows in me until it feels like there's a thunderstorm raging inside me. I can't think of anything else.

The train follows the river, until finally we're at the Beacon stop. A light gray cloud moves across the sky, sprinkling us with a drizzle as we hurry to the empty parking lot, and Declan points out an older BMW, the kind that might've been popular in the seventies. A man with white hair and hunched shoulders waits in the rain, smoking a cigarette. He has a wide smile for Declan as we get closer. They hug, and I don't know why, but his face—he's so familiar. I feel like I've met him before.

Declan pulls away, gesturing for a quick introduction—it's obvious he just wants to get out of the rain and into the car—but the man, his grandfather, looks up at me with a smile, then tilts his head. "Ah!" he says. "You!"

I blink. Declan blinks.

"You," Declan's grandpa says again, with even more emphasis. "You're the lad I met on the train. You remember, yeah? You were with your friend, and I told you about my grandson. This," he says, turning his hands to Declan, "is my grandson."

My eyes widen with realization. I'd been with Ezra at the time. I was pissed that this man wouldn't stop staring, but then out of nowhere he told us about his grandson who'd come out to him and his wife. . . .

Declan's grandfather seems to remember that I'd been with another boy then, too, but he doesn't say anything about it—only gives me a sly grin. "You see?" he says. "I told you, you'd like my grandson."

We slide into the back of the car, the inside smelling like leather and cologne, and Declan's grandfather—his name is Tully, he lets me know—reaches to Declan and musses his curly hair with a grin, asking how his week's been, before we're on our way.

It's so strange, being out of the city. There aren't any brownstones, no skyscrapers—just trees and green mountains off in the distance and the never-ending blue sky.

"It's wild, right?" Declan says to me with a grin, like he knows he practically read my thoughts. "I have to readjust every time I leave the city."

We pull into a neighborhood where the houses get bigger and bigger, until finally it's just a mansion every few minutes. Declan's very pointedly not looking at me. His grandpa makes a left, into a paved drive slightly hidden by brush and trees, taking us up a small slope, until the brush clears and a blue two-story house with a gravel drive appears. I remember what Declan had told me. His grandfather had offered to sell the house, to help pay for Declan's future, but Declan refused.

The car stops. Declan and I jump out, gravel crunching beneath our sneakers. The three of us head inside. The door's unlocked. Shoes are neatly stacked by the entrance, next to a coat stand. An antique end table holds a sign declaring the name of this house: The Pig's Head. I've never even been in a house that has a name before.

Tully says he has some reading to do before he winks at

Declan with a smile, and it's a little embarrassing how obvious it is that he just wants to give me and Declan some time to be alone. Declan doesn't seem to mind. He gives me a tour: a gigantic chef's kitchen with white marble and stainless steel with an eating nook, the library with a gigantic oak desk and rows of shelves of books, the parlor and the more casual living room with a giant flat-screen TV, the dining room with its place mats and candles, the guest room where I'll be sleeping, with its own private bathroom and a gigantic claw-foot tub.

This kind of wealth reminds me of Ezra and his parents living in their Park Avenue penthouse. I'd been so upset with Ez—jealous, angry that he was taking his privilege for granted, when he'd only wanted to share his fears and vulnerabilities with me, and when he'd only needed my support. I had no idea how lucky I was to have him in my life. How much I'd miss him, if he decided he didn't want me in his anymore. The question I keep trying to avoid—*how do I feel about Ezra?*—continues to force itself into my mind, even when I try to push it away.

Declan and I pause in the guest bedroom. This house's wealth is a little intimidating, and I'm almost too afraid to walk around or touch anything, but Declan doesn't seem smug about it. I drop my backpack on the floor of the guest bedroom, and Declan lingers, leaning against the doorframe.

"I feel bad getting in the way of you and your grandpa spending time together."

He shrugs. "It's fine. We'll join him for dinner."

I nod, sitting on the edge of the bed. I can't help but have feelings for Declan. It's complicated, and it isn't pretty, and—I don't know, maybe the feelings we have for each other aren't really healthy—but none of that changes the fact that I want to kiss him right now.

Declan smiles a little, and I realize—he's doing this on purpose. The asshole knows I want to kiss him. He's standing there, waiting, challenging me. I stand up, walk up to him, and try to lean in again, just like I did earlier on the train, but he turns his face away.

I ignore the flinch of hurt. "We don't exactly have to worry about other people here," I tell him.

"True," he says, "but I'm not supposed to make out with houseguests. It's a rule."

"Really?"

He smirks at me. "Besides," he tells me, "the payback is kind of fun."

"Payback?" When he just grins at me, I ask, "When will the punishment be over?"

"I'm not sure," he says, gaze falling to my mouth again. He pushes away from the doorframe. "Let's go to the pool."

Of course there's a pool. I close the door and change into shorts before I make my way through the house—get lost around the library and kitchen, double back to get to the dining room and down the hall, to where there's a mudroom and a set of glass doors. I can see Declan swimming in the ice-blue pool. He comes up to the surface, wiping his hair back and out of his face. He looks up at me when I step outside, then does a double take.

Right. My scars. I immediately wish I'd worn a tank, but I've never felt the need to hide my scars before. Why should I feel self-conscious about them around Declan?

"Hey," he says, squinting up at me.

"Hey."

I sit down on the edge of the pool, putting my feet into the water, and he pulls himself up, sitting beside me and splashing water onto the masonry that surrounds the pool.

"When'd you get the surgery?" he asks, voice low, leaning into me so that our shoulders bump into one another. The drops of water on his skin are cold.

"Almost a year ago," I whisper.

"Is it okay if I . . . ?" He reaches, brushing his knuckles against my stomach, my ribs. I nod, and he lets his fingers graze over the scars, following the lines. I tense, and he glances up at me through his lashes. I lean in, close enough that I can feel his breath on my lips, and he shoves me—I let out a squeak before I'm in the water, chlorine up my nose and in my eyes. I splutter, bursting out from the water, and Declan's *dying laughing*. I splash him, and he laughs again, then shouts when I grab his foot and drag him into the water, too.

We spend hours like that, bullshitting around in the pool, until the sun starts to go down and fireflies dot the grass and the garden. When we get tired, we lie down out on the warm concrete. It's in a moment like this that I can't help but think of how much has changed and how quickly—how much I'd hated Declan, and now think I might be in love with him. It's something I've wanted for so long—to have the last name Love, and actually know what it feels like to love and be loved. It's everything I'd wanted . . . So why does it feel like something's still missing?

"This is all kind of wild, right?" Declan says. "Five years ago, I never in a million years would've thought I could have someone like you over, totally open about everything." He shrugs, not looking at me. "My dad is hardcore Catholic. I used to hope that he'd decide to change his mind—that he could accept me, because I was his son. And then I'd laugh at myself. Like, how fucking arrogant is that? Expecting my dad to love me more than he loves God."

I'm not religious. I don't know how Declan feels. "It's possible for him to love both you and God, though, right?"

"I hoped so." He rolls his eyes. "I even tried to write my dad an essay on why it would be okay to accept the fact that I'm into guys. I had this whole thing, explaining that white people once used the Bible as justification for slavery, hoping that'd make him see that—you know, it's more about interpretation, and the ways people choose to use the Bible as an excuse to treat other people like shit. I hoped that'd change his mind, since my mom's Black, but it didn't really do anything. He didn't even tell me if he read the essay or not. And my mom—I love her, but she just does whatever the fuck my dad wants. He's so fucking manipulative and abusive, and he convinced her to kick me out of the house, too. That actually hurt more than anything else. The fact that she didn't even try to fight for me. She just went along with it—let him tell me to leave."

Declan's voice cracks a little, and before I can look at his eyes to see if he's crying, he's rubbing them furiously, not meeting my gaze.

"I'm sorry, Declan," I tell him. "I'm so, so fucking sorry."

He shakes his head and rubs a hand through his wet curls, darker in the water. "Not your fault. And I'm better now anyway, you know? I'm lucky I have my granddad. Not everyone has that."

A chilly breeze sends us back inside, and as soon as we're in the mudroom, Tully's voice calls, letting us know that it's almost time for dinner.

Shit. I suddenly get nervous that I'm about to have dinner in a mansion. I didn't really bring fancy shirts or anything, so I put on my least-wrinkled, floral-patterned T-shirt and some shorts and make my way down the hall and to the dining room, where Declan and his grandpa are already waiting. Tully is super into hugs. He gives both of us one and gestures at us to sit and eat.

We sit. There's baked bread, kale salad with balsamic vinaigrette, pasta with pesto and Parmesan cheese. "I used to cook for fun," Tully explains. "Now that it's mostly me here alone, not as much anymore."

He gives us wine and asks me questions. How'd I meet his

grandson? How is St. Catherine's? Which college do I think I'll apply to? I hesitate, glancing at Declan, who takes a deep breath and looks away. That's one thing we haven't really spoken about. We're still both applying to Brown. Still going after the same scholarship. I know Declan's grandpa is retired, and according to Declan is barely getting by on his savings. He'd offered to sell the house to help pay for Declan's tuition, but Declan wouldn't let him. I understand that. I probably would've done the same thing, too.

Declan clears his throat. "Give Felix a break from the interrogation," he says.

"I have to know if this boy is good enough for you," he says, but he gets the hint and starts telling us instead about his life growing up in Dublin, swimming by the lake, falling in love for the first time. "This was many, many years before your grandmother," he says to Declan. "Her name was Kathleen. I loved her, loved her more than I've ever loved before. Yes, even more than your grandmother. Oh, don't you look at me like that. Kathleen was the love of my life. There's no shame in saying that. There was a fire there that I've never felt again. A fire that I'll never feel again. But, just because we loved each other, doesn't mean we were meant to be together. We would fight just as much as we—"

"Please," Declan interrupts. "Please, don't say it."

"—made love," his grandfather says, as if Declan hadn't spoken at all, and ignores him when Declan hides his face in his hands. "We loved each other so much, but we weren't made to be in a relationship. And just because you love one, doesn't mean you can't love another. Isn't that right?" he asks us, and doesn't demand an answer when neither of us respond.

By the time we're finished eating, we're all pretty drunk and sleepy and ready for bed. Tully gives Declan a kiss and a long hug. He whispers something in Declan's ear, patting his cheek before he comes to me and gives me a hug, too. He's warm and smells like pepper.

"Treat my boy right," he tells me, patting my cheek also with a smile, before he tells us good night, leaving us alone in the dining room.

I notice Declan's eyes are a little wet. He wipes them with his shoulders.

"You okay?"

He nods. "Yeah. He's just being a good granddad, you know?"

Declan walks me to my room, down the mahogany hallway, wood panels cold beneath my bare feet. Instead of leaning against the doorframe of the guest bedroom like he had before, he comes inside, sitting on the bed beside me.

"Thanks for inviting me up here," I tell him. "I think I needed a break from the city without even realizing it. The city, and . . ." I almost say Ezra's name.

Turns out I don't need to. "I noticed you two aren't really talking," Declan says.

"Yeah. Well, things are awkward."

"Because you kissed?" he asks, voice low.

I nod, glancing away, feeling guilty. We might not have said we're dating, and that we're only seeing each other, but I can tell Declan's hurt, can tell he feels betrayed. It's like all I've ever done, even before he told me he loved me, is hurt him. "Things aren't great between us right now."

"I can't say I feel bad about it," Declan tells me. "It's a little hard, I guess, not to feel jealous."

"We're not together," I say. "Me and Ezra, I mean."

"No, but he loves you," Declan says. He watches me, like he's waiting for me to agree with him—to admit that I have feelings for Ezra, too. But I'm not sure if I can—not sure how I feel. I mean, I love Ezra—of course I love Ezra—but do I love him as a friend, or as something else?

"I think what your grandpa said might've been right."

"You really want to talk about my grandfather right now?" Declan asks.

He's watching me again. I've never seen anyone look at me like that—so unabashedly, so unapologetically, so like he doesn't give a fuck that I know he wants me, like he's almost laughing at me, because he knows I want him, too.

"I'm just saying," I whisper. "I think it's possible to be in love with more than one person—and that even if you love someone, maybe they're not really meant for you."

He isn't listening, not really. "Is that what you are?" he asks. "Are you in love with me?"

He's waiting for me. I lean forward, half expecting him to pull away again with another laugh, but the corner of his lip only twitches. I remember what Ezra had said—soft, gentle, not so hard—and I barely breathe against Declan's lips. He grins at me as I kiss him again, and again, until we're leaning back onto the bed. Declan ends up on top of me, pulling our shirts off, mouth on my neck, my collarbone, my scars. I didn't even go this far with Ezra, and my nerves start to pump.

"Slowly," I tell him, embarrassed when it comes out like a gasp. "We should go more slowly."

He nods, kissing my scars and neck and mouth again. "Is this your first time?"

"My first time?"

"Having sex."

I'm surprised. I didn't even realize he'd been planning to go that far tonight. "I mean, yeah, I've never . . ." He nods again, like it isn't a big deal, but I start to worry. "Have you? Had sex, I mean?"

He pulls up, surprised. "Well, yeah. Me and Ezra . . ."

I look away. "Right."

"We don't have to."

"I just don't think I'm ready," I tell him. It's only been a few days since my first kiss.

"Okay."

"I mean, I want to, but—"

"Yeah. I do, too." He sits up, crosses his legs. "Are you nervous because—I mean, I looked up how to have sex with trans guys—"

Jesus Christ. We haven't even talked about the fact that I identify as a demiboy now. "Yeah, that's a part of it, but I mean—I'm just not ready."

"You know, you don't have to be scared."

I go blank. I stare at him, and he watches me, still completely unabashedly, unapologetically. "I feel like you're pressuring me."

He runs a hand through his hair, brows raised. "Okay. Sorry. I didn't mean to pressure you."

Realization burns through me, alongside anger and hot embarrassment. I can barely get the words out. "Did you invite me up here just to have sex with you?"

"No," he says, a little loudly. "I wanted to spend time with you, and I thought that maybe you'd want to have sex, so I looked up how to have sex with trans guys, and now we're here." He takes a big breath, looking away. "We don't have to have sex."

"I know we don't."

He gets off the bed, grabbing his shirt from the floor and yanking it back on. "Would you have sex with me if I was Ezra?"

"What?"

"I'm just thinking you'd probably be more interested if I was Ezra."

I don't even know if that's true—but right now, I kind of hate Declan. "Can you leave?"

He freezes. "Okay. Shit. Sorry." He sits back down on the bed, as far away from me as possible. "I'm really sorry, all right?"

I shake my head. "I don't know if I'd be more interested or not."

"You love him, though, right?"

"I don't know."

But it's a lie, I know that it is. I love Ezra, of course I love him—I always have, even if I've been too afraid to see that. I also know that this, whatever *this* is between me and Declan, isn't going to work. It never was going to work. I remember what my dad had said—that it's easier, sometimes, to run toward the pain and the sort of love that Declan and I have. It isn't as scary. At least I always knew how this relationship was going to end.

"The only reason you're not with Ezra right now is because he isn't talking to you."

Declan might be right. That's what I tell him, and he closes his eyes.

"This is all really fucked," he tells me, leaning forward on his knees. "I really love you. I've never fallen for anyone the same way I fell for Lucky. And I didn't want to believe that I'd lost you, that you'd just disappear from my life when I found out *you* were Lucky, so I decided to just give this a chance, give this a shot, and . . ."

"It's not going to work." I know what he's going to say,

maybe because it's something I realized even before we decided to try this out, before he invited me to his grandfather's house, even the day I decided I'd keep speaking to Declan as Lucky. I knew it wouldn't work.

He shakes his head. "I didn't mean to pressure you. I'm sorry. I just hoped that, maybe, if we had sex, I'd feel like you love me as much as I love you—you as Lucky, I mean, maybe even more than Ezra, and . . . It was fucked-up. I'm sorry."

I flinch. *Love you as Lucky.* This automatically implies he doesn't love me as Felix. But I can't blame him. I can't be angry at him.

"I'm sorry," I tell him, my voice hoarse. "I fucked with you. Manipulated you. Even when you started to have feelings for me, I just kept going. I shouldn't have lied to you like that. I'm sorry, Declan. I'm so, so fucking sorry." I'm starting to cry, which is insanely embarrassing, but there isn't anything about this entire situation that isn't embarrassing at this point.

Declan's nodding, swallowing, like he's trying to stop himself from crying also. "What's crazy is that I think I still love you," he says, "but I also don't know if I'll ever be able to forgive you."

The words are like a stab to my chest.

He smiles a little to himself. "I think I hoped you'd come up here, and I'd be able to move past it and forgive you, and we'd have this magical fairy-tale ending."

I'd hoped we could have that magical fairy-tale ending, too. But no—I realize that's what I've always told myself, but that isn't what I wanted, not really. I wanted to fall in love, but I didn't want to risk the kind of love that'd fill me with excitement and joy. I know that love. It's the kind of love I feel when I think about Ezra—when he laughs one of his loud-as-fuck laughs and when he says stupid shit when he's high and when he holds me to his chest while we sleep. I love Ezra. I love him so much, it scares me.

"Do you think we can still be friends?" I whisper to Declan. Because, despite it all, it's hard to forget the guy that I'd spoken to for hours every day and night. I can't love him in the way I thought I could—but I still care about him.

"God, I have no idea. I love you," he says, nodding, "but I also fucking hate your guts right now."

"Then not much has changed."

He lets out a little laugh. A beat passes, and I know he's thinking about his answer. "Give me some time, all right?"

"Yeah. All right."

"Who knows—maybe Brown will end up giving us both scholarships, and we'll go together."

There's no way that would happen. We both know that. "That'd be pretty great."

He's nodding. "You know, it's so completely messed up," he tells me, "but I also feel a little grateful. I never thought I'd fall in love like that. Now I know it's possible. Even if it's not with you—not with Lucky—I know I'll fall in love again."

Declan leans forward, waiting for me to push him away— then kisses me on the cheek, pulling back with a smile. He leaves, and the next morning, Tully is waiting to take me back to the train station. I can't even look at Declan's grandfather in the eye, and he wears sunglasses so it's hard to see what he thinks of me right now anyway.

"Had a fight, eh?" he says to me as I get into the car, slamming the door shut behind me.

I nod, staring at the palms of my hands. I'm exhausted. After Declan left my bedroom last night, I didn't sleep for a single minute. I kept looking at my phone—opening and closing texts to Ezra. The last time I wrote something heartfelt and vulnerable was that email to my mom, which she still hasn't responded to days later. I'm afraid that Ezra will do the same.

Tully lets out a sigh. "Young love. What else is there to say?"

TWENTY-THREE

THE PRIDE MARCH IS ON THE LAST SUNDAY OF JUNE, IN just a few days. It's amazing just how much can change in a single month. That's what I'm thinking about as I sit in the empty photography classroom with Leah. I took her up on the offer to hang out, and I'm glad I did. It's nice to have someone to talk to, instead of moping around, thinking about the fact that I've lost both Ezra and Declan and have no other friends . . . and besides, even though it took forever for me to figure out, Leah's pretty effing cool.

"Do you think you'll apply for the end-of-summer gallery?" she asks.

"Yeah. I was thinking about it, anyway."

"You definitely should. Your self-portraits are *amazing*. Like, seriously. Really fucking good, Felix. Everyone thinks so."

I can feel my face heating up. "Really?"

The door opens, and we both turn in our seats. Austin is at the entrance, peeking in. A jolt goes through me. The last time I saw Austin, he was still with Ezra. Now I've only seen Austin from across the parking lot, hanging with Tyler and Hazel and the others, our non-relationship back to the way it was before.

Austin sees me, then hesitates. "Oh—sorry, I didn't realize anyone was in here."

"That's okay. Come in," Leah says, taking a bite of her PB&J.

He doesn't move. He looks at me again, then forces a smile. "No. Seriously. I'll just—"

Leah frowns. "Are you still feeling weird because of Ezra? I mean, it's okay if you are, but—"

"I'm not feeling weird."

"Then come in and sit down."

Austin sighs as he walks into the classroom, closing the door behind him. He drags himself over and scrapes out a chair, sitting down at the table and pulling a pizza out of a greasy brown paper bag. "You can be so pushy."

"That's what family's for," Leah says. She adds, "It's okay if you feel weird about Ezra."

"I'm fine. I've decided to move on."

I'm definitely feeling a little more than awkward. I stare at my cup of ramen noodles and the swirling steam. "I'm sorry it didn't work out," I tell him.

"No, you're not," he mutters.

I look up at him, surprised.

"Austin!" Leah gapes at him.

"What? He's not." Austin shrugs. "Now he gets Ezra to himself. They're in love with each other. Everyone knows that. You've said it yourself more than once."

Leah's face pinkens, and she glances at me. It's a question that I myself haven't known the answer to, that I've been confused about—but the more that I think about it, the more obvious the answer becomes. I'm starting to feel like an oblivious idiot. It looks like everyone knew exactly how I felt, even before I did.

"Well, it doesn't matter," I say, leaning back in my seat and crossing my arms, "because he hates me now. He won't even look at me."

No one speaks for a second, until Leah murmurs that she's sorry. "Maybe things will still work out. You never know, right?"

The lunch is awkward—I don't think it could never be *not* awkward, with me and Austin sitting across from each other—but the conversation eventually picks up as we talk about the last TV shows we binged, what movies we're looking forward to, what we'll do during the day once the summer program is over. Once upon a time, it wouldn't have been a difficult choice: I'd spend every second of every day with Ezra. Now I'm not even sure what my life looks like without him. I'll have to do a lot of rebuilding, a lot of reimagining, but

I'm not sure I even want to. I've seen him in hallways, across the parking lot, on opposite ends of the classroom. He always ignores me, and I've been too afraid to reach out to him—to tell him the truth. To say that he was right, about everything. To tell him that I love him.

"Austin," Leah says, "are you still going to that Ariana Grande concert next month?"

I'm swinging my foot beneath the table, but at the word *grande*, I freeze. Austin hesitates. He stares at the cheese pizza he's barely picked at. "Still trying to, yeah."

"Mom's letting me buy tickets, too."

"Okay."

"It should be fun to go together, right?"

"Jesus, you really don't know how to figure out when a person doesn't want to talk about something, do you?"

Leah turns to me with a grin. "He's embarrassed, but he's *obsessed* with Ariana Grande."

"I'm not obsessed." He won't meet my eye.

"You're a little obsessed. It's nothing to be ashamed of—I mean, she's a fucking star. It's okay to be obsessed."

Austin doesn't speak. He glances up at me before looking away again. And even though I'm staring at him, I can barely see him. All that I can see are the text messages from grandequeen69. The anger, the hatred this troll had for me, the fucking gallery of me and my pictures and my deadname, driving myself crazy as I tried to figure out who the piece of

318

shit was, if they were sitting in my class . . .

"It was you," I say.

Leah looks at me, startled—then confused. "Sorry, what?"

Austin still won't look at me. He knows exactly what I'm talking about.

I'm shaking my head. The confusion, the shock, the anger—it spills through me, and I can barely make sense of how I'm feeling, how I should even react. I want to laugh and cry and scream and launch myself across the table to beat the shit out of him all at once. There's only one thing I want to ask him. "Why?" He still won't look at me. "Why did you do it?"

Leah's confusion is turning to fear as she looks back and forth between us, realization dawning on her face, though it looks like she's having a hard time believing it, too.

Austin swallows as he stares at his pizza.

"Why did you fucking do it, Austin?"

"You don't have to shout," he mutters.

I close my eyes and take a deep breath so that I don't freak out on him. If I hit him, I'll be kicked out of St. Catherine's.

"It was a mistake," he tells me. "It was a mistake. That's all."

"It was a *mistake* to hack into my Instagram and take my fucking photos and tell the entire world my deadname? And all those fucking messages—the transphobic bullshit you put me through. That was just a mistake, too?"

He doesn't say anything.

"*Why?*" That's all I want to know, the question repeating itself over and over again in my head.

He takes a second to answer. When he does speak, he says, "I don't know why the gallery was such a big deal. I thought you were proud to be trans."

"Are you fucking serious?"

"You've got to be kidding," Leah says. "*You?* It was *you*, Austin? Please tell me you're fucking kidding."

My hands are balled up so tightly that they're shaking. "I *am* proud to be trans. But that shit was personal. Those photos. My old *name*. It wasn't your place to put it on display." My voice is rising again, but I don't care. "You didn't have my permission to do any of that. It was fucking abusive. It was a fucking attack."

Austin swallows and looks down, hair falling into his face. He swipes some strands back behind his ear.

"Please tell me that you're kidding," Leah says, her voice tinged with desperation.

"You really pissed me off," Austin tells me. "You know?"

"How'd I do that?"

"I wanted to talk to Ezra," he says, "and it was like I could never get a chance to speak to him alone. You were always with him, and he was always fawning all over you, and it was bullshit, because he's into guys, and you—you're not even—"

Leah interrupts him. "Don't," she says. Her eyes are

wet, her cheeks red. She's crying. "Don't you dare say that, Austin."

He has the decency to look a little ashamed. "It felt unfair," he says. "It's not like it's easy to be gay, even if we are in Brooklyn, even if this is New York City, and now we have to deal with people like you taking our identity, taking our space."

"I can't believe this," Leah says.

"Trans people aren't taking anything," I tell him.

"Is that why you wanted me to show you my hacking programs?" Leah's shaking her head, eyes wide.

"And it's annoying, too," he says, "seeing you—I don't know, pushing it in our face that you're transgender. Not everyone can be as open. Not everyone gets to be out. I don't get to be out. My parents wouldn't accept me. But you're just flaunting it every chance that you get."

"I'm not flaunting anything. I'm just existing. This is me. I can't hide myself. I can't disappear. And even if I could, I don't fucking want to. I have the same right to be here. I have the same right to exist."

He's staring at the surface of the table, still refusing to look up. "I just hoped Ezra would see the gallery and remember that you're transgender and not be interested in you anymore. That's all."

"Remember that I'm transgender and not be interested," I repeat. "Like, what, because you think trans people are unlovable? You're wrong, Austin. You know that you're wrong."

"Fucking hell," Leah says, her voice getting louder. "You know, Austin, the real issue isn't that you're jealous of Felix, or that you're pining after Ezra—which, by the way, will never fucking happen, so get the fuck over it. The real issue is that you're used to having everything. You're used to being a white guy in Brooklyn, used to always getting your way—no, fuck, I don't care that you're fucking gay, because people like Felix are queer *and* trans *and* Black, and they have to deal with so much more bullshit than you or me. And, okay, yes, you *are* marginalized for being gay, but instead of being a fucking *ally* to other marginalized people, people even more marginalized than you, you buy into the racist and patriarchal bullshit and act like you're above them because you're a white guy, and you act like they're taking your space, and you think that you're owed this whole fucking world, and when you don't get what you want, you act like a fucking asshole, and God *fucking damnit*, Austin!"

She's screaming now. Her voice echoes through the room, and I'm surprised that people haven't opened the door to see what's going on. Austin is staring at her, wide-eyed, as though she'd reached across the table and slapped him across the face. He's crying. I'm crying. We're all crying.

"I'm sorry," Austin whispers, his voice hoarse.

Leah rolls her eyes, wiping them. "That's not enough. Saying that you're sorry isn't enough."

He can't look at me at all now. "I'm sorry," he says again. "I don't know what else you want me to say. I'm sorry."

God, this is so fucked-up, so fucking wrong in a million fucking ways. But the longer I sit here in the quiet, watching Austin as he stares at the surface of the table, the more the rage I have dissolves, leaving only an echo behind. Yeah, he hurt me, and yeah, the anger is still there—but it's never been more obvious that Austin is just so ignorant. He's created his bubble of privilege, where no one is allowed but people like him, and because of that he doesn't understand the world around him—doesn't *want* to understand the world around him, because it's too scary for him, too challenging. I start to feel a little sorry for Austin. I think of the gender-identity discussion group, with Bex and the others—Callen-Lorde and the LGBT Center and all the different types of people, different genders and ages and races, a quilt of identities that ties all of us together. The people he'll never be able to meet, to learn from and love. Even though he's a white guy, and he has so much more privilege than I do, I realize that he'll never get to experience the world in the way that I can. How can I stay angry at someone like that? I don't want this anger inside me, eating me up from the inside out.

Leah tells him, honestly, that she has no idea if they can get past this—that she never thought her own family would do something like this, and Austin says that he's sorry, again and again. I actually do believe that he's sorry, even if it's only because he was caught. But I also know it's my choice to not accept his apology. To not forgive him. I don't have anything else to say to him. I stand, scraping my chair back, and Leah follows me, holding my hand as I go to Dean Fletcher's office, exactly like I should've from the very beginning.

TWENTY-FOUR

TODAY'S THE PRIDE PARADE. THE LAST TIME I WENT TO THE march, I couldn't even see the parade itself because the streets were so packed with a crushing wall of bodies standing on tiptoe and each other's shoulders, people cheering and clapping and blowing whistles with every float that passed by. It's everything I hate. It's everything Ezra loves.

Leah texts me, asking me if I'm sure I don't want to come. She plans to meet up with Ezra. She says she'd told Ezra about Austin—everyone knows now, I guess, since Austin was kicked out of St. Catherine's. She says Ezra feels responsible, somehow, for Austin's gallery and his trolling; feels guilty for not figuring it out himself when the two of them were dating.

God, of course it isn't his fault.

Maybe you should come to the march and tell him that yourself.

He won't admit it, but I'm pretty sure he misses you.

The idea of seeing Ezra at the march fills me with nerves. No, not just nerves. Outright fear. The last time I saw him was when he said he needed space after our huge fight, and we haven't spoken since. I love Ezra. I know that I do. It's been a slower realization, since Ezra told me he has feelings for me—a realization that just as long as Ezra's been in love with me, I've probably been in love with him. The sort of love I have for Ez—it's the kind of love that fills me so much that I can't stop thinking about him. It's the sort of love that makes me wish that I could touch him, hug him, kiss him again. It's the kind of love where it almost feels like I'm not just Felix, and he's not just Ezra, but we're connected in a way that I've never been connected with anyone else before, like our spirits have somehow mingled together to create one, and . . . Shit, that kind of love is downright terrifying.

I can see myself a little more clearly now. I've been too afraid to let myself love Ezra, but I was willing to put up with Marisol. I told myself I wanted her to realize that I'm worthy of love and respect, but I knew she would never understand that. I was willing to let myself love Declan, knowing that he only loved the idea of me—loved Lucky. I knew our relationship wasn't going to work, but I let myself fall for him anyway. I was willing to reach out to my mom, knowing that she wouldn't reach back to me. She still hasn't responded, and I know that she never will. It's almost like I was looking for the pain and the hurt, because it was easier to live with the idea that, even though I want love, I'm not the kind of person who deserves to be loved.

I'm sitting cross-legged in the living room in my favorite chair, Captain curled up in the corner of the seat. My dad sits on the sofa, crossword puzzle book out, TV on some reality show neither of us is watching. I hold my laptop, skimming through the drafts of hundreds of emails I'd written to my mom. Why do I keep writing these emails to her, knowing that she'll never love me—not in the way that I need her to?

I click on *select all*.

I hesitate, pause—then click on *delete*.

There're so many that it takes a second for my laptop to reload. As it does, and as I see the emails disappearing page by page, I can feel a lightening. Something I'd been holding in my chest, anger and hurt and pain, starts to fade away. It wasn't anger and hurt and pain I'd had for my mom. Though I've got plenty of that, too, this was anger and hurt and pain I'd had for myself, for writing all those fucking emails in the first place—for refusing to let go.

Would it feel this good, to go to Pride like Leah suggested? I imagine walking through the streets—finding Ezra covered in rainbow-colored paint and glitter—telling him that I'm sorry, and that he was right. That I love him, too. Anxiety pricks my chest. What if he doesn't accept my apology? What if he says that he doesn't love me anymore?

God—what the hell should I do?

"What's going on, kid?" my dad asks.

I look up at my dad, who frowns down at his crossword puzzle.

"What do you mean?"

"You're pretty quiet," he says, glancing over at me. I don't answer him—proving his point, I guess. "Things still not going well with Ezra?"

It's a little weird how easily my dad can read my mind sometimes. "Not really," I admit. "He hasn't spoken to me in over a week." We used to speak every day, multiple times a day—we'd eat our chicken, drink our wine, curl up on his mattress, smoke weed out on his fire escape, run through the sprinklers at the park and pass out in the grass. I'm in love with him, but even if he doesn't feel the same way about me anymore, I just miss him so fucking much. The loss is a physical pain, a cramp in my side.

"Have you tried speaking to him?"

"He won't answer my texts." He didn't answer my texts, anyway, for the first few days after our fight. Leah says that he wants to apologize, but he's too afraid and embarrassed to talk to me. Would he answer my texts now?

"Well, fights happen, and people move on eventually," my dad tells me. "Maybe he just needs some time to cool off."

We go back to sitting in silence. I wasn't planning on saying it—wasn't planning on telling him anything about my identity, not when he can't even say my name, can barely remember my right pronouns—but the words are out of my mouth before I've even registered that I'm speaking.

"I went to the LGBT Center the other day," I say.

He doesn't answer. He scribbles something down on his crossword.

"I went to a gender-identity group discussion."

"Okay," he says. Erases, brushes the page with his hand.

"It was a good discussion," I tell him. I'm just stalling now, unsure if I even want to keep going. I suddenly feel like I'm coming out all over again. What if he thinks I'm just confused, or making my identity up? Not a lot of people even know that demiboys exist. The first time I told my dad that I was trans, he didn't exactly react well. Why would this time be any different?

I remember Bex's reassuring smile, and I don't know— maybe it was dealing with Austin's transphobic messages for the past month, but now, more than ever, I feel the need to be real about who I am—to tell my dad the truth. "While I was there, I asked about my gender, because for the past few months, I've been questioning my identity."

My dad's eyes snap up at that one. "Questioning? You're questioning if you're transgender?"

"No—no, I know that I'm trans," I tell him.

He furrows his eyebrows, confused, waiting.

"There've just been a few times—a lot of times, I guess—when I . . . I don't know, feel like I might not totally be a guy. It's a weird feeling to describe, but there've been a few moments when someone calls me a boy, it's not totally right, and I don't feel right being called a girl either, and—I don't know, it's just a feeling."

My dad shakes his head a little. "All right. I'm not sure I understand."

Frustration rises in me. "You don't understand a lot."

He sits up straighter, closing the crossword book. "You're right. I don't."

"You don't try to understand, either."

He flinches at that one. "That hurts."

I focus on Captain's ear, scratching so that it flicks back and forth.

"I'm trying," he tells me. "I'm trying to understand. I want to understand. There's a lot that I don't know, and I've been slow. I know I've been slow to get it, and I know it's been frustrating for you, so I'm sorry. I really am. I'm sorry if I've hurt you. I'm sorry if you think my slowness has something to do with how I feel about you. Because I love you, kid. Don't ever think that I don't love you."

"If you love me, why won't you say my name? My real name?"

He closes his mouth, swallowing. Then, "Felix."

Hearing my name with my dad's voice, coming from my dad's mouth, is like a shock through my chest, my heart, vibrating through me.

"I've had an idea of who you are—who you were supposed to be," my dad tells me. "And your name's been the last piece of you I wasn't ready to let go of—I just wasn't ready." He's nodding. "But I know you're Felix. Your name is Felix."

Tears are building in me. I wipe my eyes fast. "Sorry. That's embarrassing."

"Felix," he says again, with this small smile. "It fits you. It really does. I love you. I don't want you to ever think that I don't. I'll admit, at first, I had a difficult time figuring all of this out. But you know what? I've never seen you happier. I know you're struggling with Ezra and everything, but I've never seen you with this light inside of you. You weren't happy, and now you are, and that's all I could ever want for you. That's all I could ever ask. You're happy. And brave. You've been so courageous, just by being yourself, even knowing that the world won't always accept you for who you are. You refuse to be anything but yourself, no matter what. I look up to that. I admire that."

I hide my face inside my shirt so he can't see it's a mess. It feels like tears are leaking from my pores. I feel a hand on my shoulder, a squeeze.

"If you don't always feel like a boy," my dad says, "are you still my son?"

I pull my shirt down. My dad's watching me with a pinch in between his eyebrows, and I can tell he's nervous about the question, like he's afraid he's getting something wrong.

"Yeah," I say, nodding. "Yeah, I think so."

He sits back with this smile, picking up his book of crossword puzzles again. "And things will work out with Ezra," he says, waving his pencil around. "These things always do."

I pick up Captain and put her down on the floor, get up

from my seat and brush off the cat hair. I snatch up my back-pack, waiting by the door. "I'm going out."

"Okay," my dad says, and from his smug tone, I have a feeling he's managed to read my mind again.

I text Leah as I speed walk to the train. **I'm coming down to the march.**

YES YES YES!! We'll be at 14th and Greenwich. I'm not going to tell Ez you're coming.

Why not?

Let it be a surprise!

I'm afraid she just isn't telling me the whole truth. Maybe if she tells him that I'm coming, he'll leave the second he finds out. I try to push away the fear as I run across the street, against the red light, and rush down the subway stairs just as a train pulls up, jumping through the doors before they have a chance to close in front of me. I'm sweating, breathing hard, ignoring the people who raise their eyebrows at me.

I get off the train at Fourteenth Street. Underground, I can already hear the muffled blasts of music, the shouts and screams and laughter. There're people heading to the parade, eager and laughing with their friends; people coming down-stairs from the parade, covered with sweat and glitter. I emerge from the subway station, out into the bright, summer light and a crowd of screaming bodies, glitter literally raining down from the sky. My eyes can't take in everything quickly enough. People are painted the colors of the rainbow, waving flags and dancing to music that passes by on the floats that move down the center of the street—and the floats, the lace and frills and bands blasting music that thumps through the ground, floats with queer couples getting married and having their first dance, floats with little kids waving with their parents. People watch from their apartment balconies above, cheering and waving their own flags.

There must be hundreds of thousands of people here. I'm just thinking that there's no way—no way in hell—I'd ever find Leah and Ezra in this, when I hear a scream in my ear. I spin around, and Leah leaps into my arms, almost making us fall to the pavement.

"You're here, you're here, you're here!"

She's in a tank top and shorts that show off her curves, and her red curls are flying everywhere. "I'm really happy you came!"

I'm so nervous I can't even speak as I glance around for a sign of Ezra—but I notice Leah's smile fall a little.

"Okay, so," she says, "we were together literally ten minutes ago, and he said he was going to run to the corner store to get some water, and I said I'd be here, but then the police put up this blockade," she says, pointing to an NYPD barricade that lines the sidewalk, "and he shouted to me that he'd find a way around and come back over, but that was a few minutes ago now . . ."

Fuck. A few weeks ago, maybe even a few days ago, I would've been relieved. I would've given up, right here and now, and gone back home, happy to sit with the idea that it wasn't going to work out anyway—I don't deserve the kind of love that I want. But I came here for a reason. I have to see Ezra. I have to tell him everything. I can't give up, not now. I can't imagine just texting him the truth—I have to speak to him, face-to-face. And I can't wait until Monday, the fact that I love him burning me up inside.

"I'm going to try to find him," I yell to Leah.

She grins at me. "I was hoping you'd say that. I'm going to stay here, in case he manages to make his way back around, okay?"

I nod. "Text me if he shows up again!"

"I will!" We hesitate, then Leah throws her arms around me again, just a little emotional—and, I don't know, I guess I'm a little emotional myself. "Good luck!" she shouts.

I start walking, turning the corner and going up a side street. Even here, away from the main parade, the streets are packed with people and vendors. I turn another corner, back up to the march route, and the crowd moves like a river, pushing me along until I see a break—out in the sun, beside the barricade, there's a single spot. I slide into it. It's the perfect place to watch the parade, but I wanted a second to get out of the masses of people and take a moment to look around, scanning the crowd for Ezra. When I don't see him, I try to rejoin the crowd to keep going—but it's become so packed that there's a jam, no one moving. They're like a wall, and in front of me, police officers warn anyone off from jumping over the barricades and into the parade itself. I'm trapped.

Shit. I wanted to find Ezra, but I really don't know if that's going to happen now. I have a pretty good spot for the parade, so I lean against the barricade's railing and try to enjoy the march. A chance like this doesn't come along often, and I know Ezra would ask me what the hell I'm doing, not watching the parade when it's literally right in front of me. Bikers waving flags from their motorcycles rumble along. A float made of balloons and a drag queen singing to the crowd that sings back passes next. There's a marching band that blasts a Sia song, and there's a sports car with a celebrity from a reality TV show who waves and blows kisses. And through it all, everyone screams and screams and screams. I usually hate this parade—hate the noise, the crowds—but when I see the Callen-Lorde float passing by, I feel an urge to scream, too. I *do* scream when the LGBT Center float passes and I catch Bex in the parade, waving with a yellow, white, purple, and black flag tied around their neck like a cape.

Once I start screaming, I can't stop. I scream so hard my throat feels raw and my heart pounds. I'm screaming with joy. I'm screaming with pain. I'm screaming with the awe that I'm here, that we're all here, and that we're here because of the people before us, the people who couldn't be here, and I'm screaming for myself, too. Screaming and cheering and a little bit of crying. I try to wipe my eyes as if it's just dust, but the person beside me catches me with a smile, also wiping their eyes. I don't know this person, don't know their name, probably will never even see them again after this parade, but for that one second, I feel like they're a friend, or a part of my family, and that's pretty fucking amazing. I never really got it before, why Ezra is so obsessed with Pride, but I think I'm starting to get it now.

There's a break in between the floats, the far-off sounds of the marching band and blasting music and the continuous roar of cheers. I glance up, look at the opposite side of the street—and it's like I made him materialize, made him appear with my thoughts alone. Ezra, dressed in all black, shades on, curls flying in the breeze, grin on his face.

I shout his name. "Ezra!"

A few heads turn to me, but he doesn't hear me. Another float is coming. I wave my hands. "Ezra!"

His head turns. Even with his shades on, I can tell he's looking right at me.

I didn't plan for this—didn't think this through. The float is coming, blaring music, everyone on the float dancing. "I'm sorry!"

More people are watching now. Ezra hasn't moved, hasn't spoken, hasn't given any indication that he heard.

"I'm sorry!" I say again. "You were right." He shakes his head, and I don't know if he can hear me. "You were right, I—"

The float's paused. Everyone's watching now, people all around Ezra looking from him to me and back to him again.

"I love you!" I yell.

336

That gets the loudest cheer of all. People start clapping, shouting, blowing their whistles. Ezra pulls his shades off, and for a heart-stopping second, I think he's about to turn away, to disappear into the crowd—but he hops up onto the barricade and leaps over, into the street, ignoring the shouts of the police officers. He jogs up to me, and I stand on the edge of the barricade so that we're the same height just as he gets to me. I haven't seen Ezra this close up in over a week, and just having him right here, right in front of me, makes my heart pump harder and harder, so hard that I can barely breathe, and I just want to throw my arms around him, hold him and kiss him—

"Sorry," he says, breathless, grin on his face. God, I've missed him so fucking much. "What'd you say? I don't think I heard you right."

I bite the corner of my lip, trying to stop myself from smiling. "I said I love you."

He squints at me. "Say that again? Just one more time."

"I love you."

He leans in, hands on my cheeks as he kisses me. I know the screams have gotten louder. I know people are cheering, and that the float behind us has continued moving, music loud—I know all of this, but only distantly, vaguely. Ezra hops over the barricade, taking my hand and pulling me through the crowd—people are literally throwing glitter right at us, clapping and patting us on our shoulders. We burst out from the crowd and onto a side street that's emptier than all the others.

Ezra turns to me, and I can't help it—I almost die laughing. He looks like a glitter bomb exploded on him. From his grin, I know that I don't look much better. He reaches down, wiping glitter from the corners of my eyes and my cheeks. He pulls his hand away, but I wish he wouldn't. I haven't spoken to him, haven't touched him, haven't even stood this close to him in almost two weeks, and—

"You mean it?" he says. Another blast of music, another cheer.

I force myself not to look away from him, even if nervousness and embarrassment make me want to hide my face in my hands. "Yeah. Yeah, I mean it."

He pulls me in for a hug, holding me close, his chin nestled on the top of my head. He holds me so close I can feel his heart through his chest, and I know that he can feel mine, too—pumping hard and fast at first, but becoming steadier the longer we stand there together. Before, when Ezra would hug me, I never thought much about it—but now, there's a pinch of nervousness overshadowed by excitement. Pure joy. Amazement, that I could've been with Ezra like this the entire time, if I hadn't been so oblivious—to both his feelings, and my own. If I hadn't been so afraid of letting myself feel a real love like this.

TWENTY-FIVE

EZRA USUALLY SPENDS THE ENTIRE DAY AT PRIDE, BUT HE takes my hand and walks me to the train so we can head back to his apartment in Brooklyn. I text Leah that I found him, that we've made up and we're going to hang out, and she sends me a bunch of heart and crying emojis.

The silence between me and Ezra on the train is strained, a little awkward—but not necessarily in a bad way. I can tell that we're both just so excited to be next to each other, to have the chance to speak, and that we both have so much that we want to say, but we're waiting for the moment we can finally be alone. He takes my hand, intertwining our fingers and rubbing his thumb over my knuckles.

"Is this okay?" he asks.

I nod, biting back a smile. "Yeah. This is okay."

We get off at the Bedford-Nostrand stop, still holding hands as we climb the stairs and cross the street, walk past the park and toward his apartment. I would've thought it'd feel awkward after a while, still holding his hand—like I wouldn't know if he'd want to let go, or that I'd want to let go and not know how to tell him, but right here and now, I kind of hope that he never lets go again. He squeezes my hand a little, as if he read my mind and wants me to know that he feels the same.

He has to let go to get out his keys and unlock the front door, and we stomp up the stairs until he opens his apartment door. When it closes behind him, we stand in front of each other, staring at one another. Maybe this would've felt awkward or embarrassing once upon a time, but right now, I just want to paint this moment in my mind, something that I can always look back on and remember. I stare at his face as though I'm trying to commit every angle, the darkness of his eyes, the twitch of his smile to memory.

"Can I kiss you?" he asks.

"God, yeah."

He laughs and leans in, kissing me softly. It feels like we've got all of the rest of time to kiss like this, to be together, to love one another. I take his hand and pull him to the couch, and we just sit there together, his head in my lap while I play with his curls.

"I can't believe things turned out this way," he says with

a low voice, eyes closed, his fingers rubbing up and down my arm.

"Me either. I thought you were going to hate me forever."

"I never hated you. I could never hate you."

"Even after everything I said?" I internally flinch, remembering that night on his stoop, telling him that I didn't want him to love me. I'd been too afraid to let myself feel this way. That feels like centuries ago now.

"I was hurt," he admits, "but I could never hate you."

"These past weeks were hell," I tell him. "I missed you so much."

"I missed you, too," he says.

"So much has changed so fast," I whisper.

"What've I missed?" he asks me.

I hesitate, then say, "You know how I was thinking about my gender identity?"

He opens his eyes. "Yeah."

"Well, I went to this discussion group at the Center, and I did some more research, and I found this term—I don't know, it's just a word, but it feels like it captures so much of who I am in a way that nothing else has."

"What's the word?" he asks, and he seems so genuinely curious that it makes my heart ache.

"It's *demiboy*."

"Demiboy," Ezra repeats, like he's trying the word out on his tongue. "I like it. It reminds me of demigod or something."

"I'm not exactly a god."

"Depends on who you ask, I guess."

A laugh escapes me, and Ezra grins as we fall back into a comfortable quiet.

Ezra swallows. "I was—you know, pretty ashamed about the way things ended, and I was such an asshole to you that I didn't think you'd want anything to do with me. I kept trying to work up the nerve to apologize, but then I'd see you and Declan together, and I thought you'd moved on."

I feel a flare of embarrassment at the mention of Declan. "I don't know why I tried to—you know, be with him in that way," I say.

"I can't judge you. I have no idea why I agreed to date Austin." A shadow crosses his face, and I know he's thinking of Austin and his gallery, his fucked-up Instagram messages. "God, if I'd fucking known it was him—shit, looking back on it, it's so obvious. He'd ask me these questions about you, get me to tell him stuff about you, but I thought he was just being curious about my friends."

"It's okay. You can't blame yourself for not knowing. Even Leah didn't know, and she's his cousin."

"I didn't even like him that much," he said. "I knew I was in love with you, but I was—I don't know, I guess a little lonely, so I decided to try being with him. I thought it couldn't hurt to try."

"I thought it couldn't hurt to try with Declan, but I knew that it was never going to work, and—yeah, I like him, and I hope that we can be friends someday . . . But he isn't you, Ez."

He smiles a little. "Damn right he isn't me."

I roll my eyes with a laugh.

"I love you," he says below his breath, almost like he's just talking to himself. "I've loved you for a while now."

I remember, suddenly, what Declan had said—that he realized Ezra was falling for me. This would've been in our first year at St. Catherine's. "How long have you felt this way?" I ask him.

Ezra looks up at me, and I'm surprised by how comfortable I feel, looking right back at him. "Since the day you found the kitten in a box and decided to take it home."

"When I found Captain?" I say, surprised. "Really?" That was within weeks that we'd met.

"I always liked you. You're freaking hilarious in this dry, sarcastic way, but you're really caring, too, in a way that I don't think a lot of people get to see. I'm lucky that you let me in. That you let me see that."

"I don't know when I fell in love with you," I admit. "I think I must've fallen for you slowly. I realized I loved you when I thought I'd lost you."

"I was afraid I'd lost you, too," he murmurs. "I'm really sorry, Felix. I shouldn't have reacted that way. I should've respected your feelings. If you didn't love me, then that was your choice."

"But I *do* love you," I say. "I was just too afraid of—I don't know, letting myself feel this way. This kind of happiness. It can be scary, right? There's this fear that I don't really deserve it, this fear that it might not even last. . . ."

He sits up, resting his forehead against mine. "You deserve to be loved," he tells me, then kisses me. "You deserve all of my love." He kisses me again. When I kiss him back, we lie down on the couch, kissing slowly and softly, as if time is at a standstill, and we'll get to do this for the rest of our lives.

A month can go by pretty quickly. Like, blink and it's already over, and July has come and gone. It's a few days into August. Summer program classes are winding down so that we can have a couple of weeks off before the new semester begins in September. I'm almost finished with my portfolio. I have over a dozen self-portraits now, a few that I scrap and some that I continue to work on details for, starting new paintings when the inspiration strikes. I've been working on my college applications, too—Brown, of course, but a few other schools also, in case I don't get in. The thought of not being accepted to Brown doesn't feel as devastating as it used to. Yeah, I still want to go to Brown and RISD, but no, my life won't be over if it doesn't happen. Declan meets my eye from across the classroom sometimes and nods with a twitch of a smile, but he still isn't talking to me. I accept that. I really fucked up. I know I did. But I also know that everyone makes mistakes. All I can do is try to learn and grow.

When I think about it, not much about my life has actually changed. I still hang out with Ezra every day, just with more—you know—kissing, which was insanely embarrassing to think about at first, but isn't that embarrassing now. I mean, what's actually embarrassing about kissing? Is it because it's an act of loving someone so much that there aren't even any words, so the only thing you can do to express that love is to kiss instead? Maybe it's not the kissing that's embarrassing, but the fact that you love someone so fucking much, which really shouldn't be embarrassing at all. What's so wrong with loving someone, right?

Two weeks before summer classes end, there's an announcement over the loudspeaker reminding students that the end-of-summer gallery submission application deadline is coming up in a few days. There's a fear in my gut that someone might use the gallery to try and hurt me again, but Ezra tells me that there's no way in hell that would happen—not after we've all seen Austin get kicked out of St. Cat's, and especially not when everyone knows Ezra is my boyfriend, and that he'll beat the crap out of anyone who tries to fuck with me again.

"You can't beat the crap out of anyone, Ez."

He raised an eyebrow. "Really? You sure about that?"

So, now, I'm basically just praying that no one fucks with me so that Ezra doesn't get kicked out of St. Cat's. I'd already decided that I would go ahead and apply to the gallery—the idea of not getting chosen is scary, and I know it'd hurt—but I'm also finally realizing that, even if I'm not picked, the gallery isn't a measure of my worth.

A lot of people have straight up stopped coming to class so close to the end of the summer program, but I've been coming in early and staying late, working on my self-portraits for the gallery, adding a dash of color here, smoothing out the background texture there. Working on the paintings reminds me of who I am: the strength inside me, the beauty and determination and power. I'm surprised when Jill walks up to me after the class bell rings. I'm trying to add in a few more strokes of yellow to a background when she smiles at me.

"These are really fantastic, Felix," she tells me.

My face gets warm. "Thanks."

She keeps watching me work, which makes me self-conscious, but I'm just glad she's not hurrying me out of the room and to lunch. Ezra's packed up and waiting for me by one of the tables as he talks to Leah.

"Have you decided to apply for the end-of-summer gallery?" Jill asks me.

I nod. "Yeah, I think I'm going to do it." The thought alone scares the crap out of me. The gallery itself is pretty competitive, and to be judged on my artwork by a panel of Brown professors is one thing . . . to be judged by my peers, who I have to see on a daily basis, is another.

"Good," she says. "St. Catherine's would be lucky to have your work on display."

As the deadline looms closer, it's all I can think about: the possibility of having my artwork in a gallery. To reclaim the lobby and its space with me, the real me—reflections of who

I am, and how I see myself, and how the world should see me, too. The last word against people like Marisol and Austin. The chance to put up one giant middle finger to anyone else in the world who doesn't think I deserve to be here—to exist—right alongside them.

The day before the deadline, I go to the school's website and gallery application, snap a few photos of my self-portraits with my phone and write a 250-word summary on the project, and why I think my artwork should mark the end of the summer program. I click *submit* before I can second-guess myself. I don't tell anyone about it, not my dad or Leah or even Ezra. I don't want to deal with the awkwardness if my art isn't accepted. They'd have to console me and tell me I'm a good artist and all that, and the thing is, I know that I am. I know that I'm talented. I don't need anyone else, or even this gallery, to tell me if I am or not. But if I could have the chance to fill the lobby with images of me—the real me—then I sure as hell will.

I'm surprised when, a few days later, I get an email from Dean Fletcher congratulating me on the fact that my artwork has been chosen for the end-of-summer gallery. There's going to be an opening where the entire school will be invited, and I'll be asked to give a speech based on the 250-word summary I'd submitted. The idea of standing in front of the entire school and explaining my work is, you know, completely fucking terrifying—but there's a reason that I submitted my artwork. I can't stop now.

I grab my best pieces and bring them to the dean, who accepts the canvases as though they're treasures, smiling and appreciating each one. The artwork is hanging on the lobby walls by the end of the day. I walk into the lobby, Ezra beside me, and we stand there and stare at each of the pieces, hanging exactly where my old photos had been hanging months before. Each painting's title has my real name. Emotion builds in me, remembering the day I'd walked into this lobby and seen my old pictures and my deadname, knowing that the entire school had seen, too. The embarrassment, the pain, the anger. Ezra takes my hand and squeezes it.

"I'm really proud of you," he says.

The opening will be during lunch, when all the students usually head off campus—that's what I tell myself, anyway, so I won't be too nervous . . . but today, just as the opening is about to begin, it feels like the entire student population stays and packs the lobby. In the past I might've hid if it was an option, gone to Ezra's place and pretended that my artwork wasn't up in the gallery. But I wanted a chance to speak my truth in front of everyone, even if I feel like I'm in the middle of a nightmare where I walk onto a stage and suddenly realize that I'm naked.

The lobby is crowded with echoing voices and laughter. I stand right outside in a dark hallway with Ezra, who seems to always know exactly what I need. He doesn't fill the silence with "You'll do great" and "Everything will be fine." He smiles whenever I nervously meet his eye, and when I pull him in for a hug, he wraps his arms around me tightly, holding me close so I can breathe into his chest. It blows my mind to think that I could've been hugging Ezra like this all along.

Jill opens the door and pops her head out into the hallway. "It's time. Are you ready?"

I let out a shaky, nervous breath and nod. Ezra kisses my cheek, and I take his hand so that he'll follow me out into the lobby. It's so packed that I can barely see the paintings on the walls, but I catch glimpses of them. The strength in my eyes, even when it looks like I'm lost under water. The power in my stare as I watch the viewer, my skin on fire. The crown of flowers on my head as I smile, knowing for a fact that I'm worthy of love and respect.

Dean Fletcher calls for everyone's attention. "Quiet down," she says, clapping her hands together, and the students fall to whispers until there's silence. "At the end of every summer program, we hold a gallery featuring a chosen student's work. This gallery is particularly special. For the first time in St. Catherine's history, the judges decided unanimously that this was the project they would move forward with. I'm proud of the growth of this young artist, and I know that he has a bright future.

"Felix?" she says.

Ezra squeezes my hand, and I step forward with a deep breath.

"Uh," I say, my voice cracking. Everyone, maybe all one hundred of the St. Cat's students, stares at me blankly.

Leah is in the front, camera in her hands and clicking away as she snaps a picture of me every other second. Marisol stands in the back, arms crossed, muttering something to Hazel. Once upon a time, seeing her might've made me anxious—but now, I only wonder why I'd been so desperate for her attention, for her approval.

I had a speech practiced and ready to go, but for a moment my mind blanks—but when I look at Ezra, he gives me a smile and nods, and the words come back.

"So, a lot of you know that at the beginning of the summer, there was a—uh—gallery of me. It wasn't with my permission. It showed a bunch of my old photos. Pictures I didn't want anyone seeing. It really hurt, and for a while, I was kind of obsessed with figuring out who it was, and . . . I don't know, making them pay for hurting me so much. I wanted to make them pay for what they'd done."

I look across the crowd, and I lose my breath when I see Declan, standing against the far wall and watching. I keep going. "But then I started these paintings. I wasn't really expecting to do them, to be honest. Someone suggested that I try, which I'm really thankful for . . ." Jill nods her head with a small smile. "And it was more helpful than I expected. More . . . empowering, to put up these paintings I created, of who I know I am, instead of what someone else sees me as. I am Felix. No one else gets to define who I am. Only me.

"I was hurt this summer, hurt more than I thought I ever could be. It could've been easy to say I was hurt because I'm trans, because someone singled me out for my identity, but there's something weird about that—something off, about suggesting that my identity is the thing that brought me any sort of pain. It's the opposite. Being trans brings me love. It brings me happiness. It gives me power." Ezra's biting his lip as he grins at me. I shrug a little. "It makes me feel like I'm a god. I wouldn't change myself for anything."

Everyone's still staring. I think Jill might have some tears in her eyes, but I'm not totally sure. I hesitate, awkward in the silence. "That's it, I guess."

Claps explode, a lot louder than I was expecting. I try to walk back to Ezra as calmly as I can, even though my legs are shaking. Before I even reach him, people start rushing up to me, saying I'm brave and that my paintings are amazing and all that, which does feel good, I'm not going to lie—but I didn't do this for anyone but myself. When I finally reach Ezra, he wraps his arms around me and buries his head in my neck.

"You're so fucking cool," he says, laughing a little. And I'm honestly not sure things could ever get any better than this.

Leah joins me and Ezra in the park to have a picnic. Pot brownies may or may not be involved. She snaps photos of us as we lie back in the grass, laughing as we get drunk on Pabst in the heat, reggaeton blasting from a nearby party, smoke from the grill stinging my eyes.

"You guys are so great," Leah says. She's a loving drunk. "I'm so lucky that you're my friends. I really love you guys."

"I love you, too," Ezra says, grabbing her in a tight hug.

I think that this mushy lovefest would've made me want to die with discomfort a few months ago, but now, happiness seeps through me. There isn't anything wrong with love. There isn't anything embarrassing about love. "You're freaking amazing, Leah," I tell her. I think of the day she stood up to Austin, of how she helped me and Ezra during Pride. Ez and I begin an attack, tickling her and wrestling her and me lying on top of her stomach while she screams and laughs. An older couple who sits on a bench close by smiles at us.

I could stay like this for hours, for days, just doing nothing but enjoying the time that I get to have with two really freaking amazing human beings. But then I see the time on my phone.

"Shit, Ez, we're late." My dad's expecting us for dinner tonight. Ezra's started to look forward to coming over to hang out with me and my dad and has even stayed with us some nights—sleeping on the couch, of course; even though I sleep over at Ezra's all of the time, my dad doesn't even let him look at my bedroom.

We hug Leah goodbye, grabbing trash to toss on our way out of the park, and hurry down the sidewalk, running for a train just as it pulls up to the station. Ezra and I sit down with heavy sighs on the orange seats, sweaty and hot, but I can tell that he's happy to be here with me, just as happy as I am to be with him. I glance at the window, then do a double take. R + J = 4EVA.

What're the chances that this is the exact same train, and that we've taken the exact same seats? I think it's more likely that R and J have written graffiti on as many trains as they could. But while I would've rolled my eyes once upon a time, shoving down the jealousy, I smile a little now.

"How likely do you think it is that R and J are still in love, on an anniversary somewhere like Fiji or Bermuda?"

When I nod at the graffiti, Ezra grins. "I'm pretty sure R and J are two government spies and on the run and living secret lives in Cuba."

"Is that right?"

"Yeah," he says with a firm nod. "But it's not fair they get to write this everywhere. They're not the only ones who're in love."

I hesitate. This is stupid, I know it is—but, suddenly, I understand where R and J were coming from, publicly declaring their love with a black Sharpie. I reach into my backpack and grab one of the pens I use to sketch, and I make bubble letters on the wall before filling them in.

F + E = 4EVA

Ezra smirks at me, then kisses the corner of my mouth. "That's so fucking corny."

"I know."

"I love it."

"Me too."

He leans back in his seat. "You know, I was messing around online last night, and I ended up down a rabbit hole, looking up a bunch of random shit . . . and I remember you told me that *Felix* means 'lucky' in Latin—but apparently, it also means 'happy.' "

"Wait—what?"

"Yeah. There was a site that said *Felix* means both 'lucky' and 'happy.' " He shrugs. "Not huge news, I guess. I just thought it was cool."

For years I'd thought *Felix* had only meant 'lucky,' so now there's a whole other definition to my name to wrap my brain around . . . but I can't say that I mind it. These days, I'm pretty freaking happy, too. I glance at Ezra, and the corner of his lips twitches into a smile, before he leans forward and kisses me. He takes my hand, fingers brushing together, like he never wants to let go, and I don't want him to, either.

AUTHOR'S NOTE

It wasn't until my mid-twenties that I discovered my trans identity, but when I look back on my life, the hints and clues were always there. I'd been assigned female at birth, but I often had dreams of being in a different body, similar to the one I have now. I remember being jealous of the boys in my grade at school, desperately wanting to be their friends, though I didn't really know why I was jealous or why I wanted to be accepted by them. I even remember outright telling my mom, once, that I thought I might be a boy. (This was probably the most obvious clue of all.) But the thing is, at that time, I didn't know that being a boy was an option. I thought I was trapped in the body of a girl for the rest of my life—thought that, because of my body, I had no choice but to *be* a girl, too. I hoped, and prayed, that if reincarnation was real, I would be born as a boy in my next life.

Transgender people and characters were sprinkled throughout my life in books and movies and TV, but I never really understood what being transgender was, or what it meant. I hadn't even heard of the term *nonbinary* yet. One day I had the urge to re-watch *Degrassi: The Next Generation*, and as I got sucked into the show and the characters' worlds, I was introduced to Adam. Adam was the first transgender character I'd ever seen who explained what his identity meant to him. He explained that he was uncomfortable with his body. He made me realize, suddenly, that though he'd been assigned female at birth, he'd been able to become who he really was.

That episode changed my life. I began to question my gender identity. In my research, I realized that there was more than the binary of girl and boy and remembered that even as a child I'd always been drawn to the idea of people being unable to assume my gender based on my appearance. With the help of friends and family, I began my social and physical transitions as a nonbinary, transmasculine person who uses they/them and he/him pronouns. I'm so lucky that I discovered Adam—so lucky that he helped me understand myself and helped me realize that I could transition. I'd wanted to be reincarnated as a different gender—and in a way, I do feel like I've experienced a reincarnation into a new body, a new life, a new me.

I hope that readers took away a lot after reading *Felix Ever After*: laughs and tears; a roller coaster ride of a romance, empowerment, and validation; and a story they thoroughly enjoyed. But above all else, I hope Felix can do for even just one reader what Adam did for me: that a reader picks up *Felix Ever After* and learns more about themselves and their identity, and that becoming who they truly are is a possibility.

For support or more information on gender identities, here are some resources:

translifeline.org
thetrevorproject.org
glbthotline.org
http://www.transstudent.org/definitions
genderqueerid.com
teentalk.ca/learn-about/gender-identity/
https://www.refinery29.com/en-us/lgbtq-definitions
-gender-sexuality-terms
https://www.plannedparenthood.org/learn/sexual
-orientation-gender

ACKNOWLEDGMENTS

Felix Ever After is a deeply personal story and one that I put my heart and soul--and a strong dose of vulnerability—into. Felix and his journey mean the world to me, so I want to thank everyone who touched this book and handled it with love and care.

First, Beth Phelan has been the rock of my career and a true friend, and it's difficult to put into words how much I appreciate her for everything that she does, and for her constant support and guidance. Thanks also to the entire Gallt & Zacker team and especially Marietta Zacker.

Thank you to Alessandra Balzer for your patience and amazing insight. You've made Felix's story so much stronger.

Thanks also to the Balzer + Bray/HarperCollins team: Caitlin Johnson, Ebony LaDelle, Mitch Thorpe, Michael D'Angelo, Jane Lee, Liz Byer, Laura Harshberger, Patty Rosati, Mimi Rankin, Katie Dutton, Veronica Ambrose, Chris Kwon, Kathy Faber, Andrea Pappenheimer, Kerry Moynagh, and everyone who has helped put this book into the world. And thank you, Alex Cabal, for the beautiful cover!

Thank you to the early readers and their feedback and notes: Gabe Jae, Elijah Black, and Gaines Blasdel. Thank you to the authors who gave early blurbs for *Felix Ever After*: Mason Deaver, Jackson Bird, Justin A. Reynolds, Becky Albertalli, and Nic Stone.

Thank you to my family for your unending support of my writing and of me: Mom, Dad, Auntie Jaqui, Curtis, Memorie, Lisa, Martha—thank you!

And finally, to all the educators, librarians, and readers of all ages who have shown so much love: thank you, from the bottom of my heart, for accepting my stories and words. You're the reason I keep going.